JINGER AND THE DJINN

KELTIC MULTIVERSE: CHILDREN OF THE TRIAD

BOOK THREE

*LIZZIE STARR

Dokopot Books

Cover and interior design by Cat & Doxie Author Services

Photo Credit: Tolokonov @ Depositphotos, apichartham @ Depositphotos

DEDICATION

For Jinger... finally!

CHAPTER
ONE

J inger curled her toes into the fine, black sand and gazed at the air-brushed colors of a golden sunset. The damp breeze ruffling her hair failed to bring her the usual rise of joy. She'd left the family gathering and come to her favorite place to mourn in private.

Today, her place of solitude held little comfort. Her cousin Chance had died a hero's death in the World Between Worlds seven years ago. She'd thought the memories and coming together with family on this day would become easier. She'd told herself she'd adjusted to the empty gap left in the clan by his passing. Today she missed him deeply.

As did the rest of the family. She certainly had no claim on sorrow. She turned from the sky and wandered along the wide beach. Lavender waves crawled up the damp sand, bringing tiny crustaceans that either scurried back to the water or dug themselves into the coolness the water left behind. In the distance a flock of ravens chased by a larger flying creature she didn't recognize dipped behind a cliff. Their harsh calls were a playlist of her sorrow.

So many new places had been discovered and recorded in Gowthaman's circles of interconnected dimensions and single worlds. Not really caring, she'd never bothered to learn about this one. She shrugged. Coming to this beach usually brought her comfort.

A few hours alone, a few tears, and she'd be ready to face the family again. Days like this she wished she could bury herself in the sand and simply forget. Times such as this, her heritage wasn't a blessing. Half-fairy and descendant of Robin Goodfellow, she found it difficult to dwell in darker emotions. Oh, that really wasn't a bad thing. Being happy was good, and bringing that happiness to others, even better.

Still, on this day of remembrance, she grappled with the sadness, the anger and hurt that remained from Chance's untimely death. She was no different from the rest of the family in her sorrow. Especially his parents and sister Breanna, who hid their deepest feelings behind half-smiles and softly spoken memories.

Jinger toed a small rock then kicked it to the side. A soft clink drew her attention. The stone had rolled a short distance and stopped against a cobalt bottle nestled in a depression. Curiosity danced against her sadness and she shrugged. Might as well take a look. She was a curious fairy, after all.

She knelt beside the bottle.

The wider bottom held a strange glinting sparkle, as though a myriad of colors were contained inside and fought to escape through the dark blue. The neck was long and narrow, ending in a wide lip, stoppered with a plain cork. She hesitated, her hand hovering inches from the bottle.

Curiosity would get her in deep trouble one day. At least that's what her parents continually drummed into her head. No matter their concerns, she was her father's daughter and found wonder in odd places.

Holding her breath, she pressed her palm to the sun-warmed glass. A tingle of electricity skittered up her arm, much like the opening of a portal from one place to another. Interesting. She stroked the glass and the surface warmed further. When she curled her fingers around the neck the awareness intensified to a prickling sting. The bottle was either created of magic or there was magic contained within the glass. She didn't recognize the power as belonging to any of the fey races she knew.

Curious, she angled closer and touched her fingertip to the cork.

The discordant ring of chimes danced around her. She snatched back her hand and frowned, glanced around, then grinned. This puzzle captivated her imagination and she simply had to discover the source of the chimes and the purpose and contents of the bottle.

Catching back a laugh, she ignored the renewed chiming and cupped her palm over the dark cork. Sharp prickles stung her palm, reminding her of how difficult it was for those of Fairy to pass through a Gentry portal unless the proper blend of magics was used.

The murder of ravens returned, circling above her, their harsh, raucous cries an odd harmony to the gentle lap of waves against the beach. She stood to watch the birds disappear over the distant trees and planted her hands against her waist. The bottle knocked her hip. She stared at the bottle, shook it. She didn't remember picking it up.

Casting aside the vague warnings filling her mind, Jinger tugged on the cork. Looser than she expected, she was able to wiggle the stopper until it cleared the wide lip.

Waves of heat rolled over her, coursing up her arm and across her shoulders to envelope her body. A deep, unscratchable itch danced between her shoulder blades and ribcage. She struggled to open her hand, but her fingers remained tight around the bottle.

Sharp pain between her shoulder blades made her gasp and arch her back. Using her free hand, she reached over her shoulder and tugged on the loose cotton of her top, pulling the bottom hem to her shoulders. Another flash of pain, this time in twin lines down her back, inches from her spine, made Jinger bite her lower lip. The magical habit of hiding her wings was failing. That had never—.

Her wings burst free, caught the breeze and staggered her forward. The pain faded. Blowing out a sigh of relief, she allowed the hem of her shirt to fall in an awkward drape over the base of her wings. A quick, whispered phrase altered the fabric to create long slits to allow her wings freedom.

What just happened?

Because she spent so much time in the human world, keeping her wings hidden was as natural as having wings. The breeze smoothed over the top curve of a fully opened wing washing away the pain. Jinger rolled her shoulders and sighed with relief.

Still wrapped around the bottle's heated neck, her fingers tingled. How did the heated glass hold her fingers captive? With a soft curse, she concentrated on forcing her fingers to open. The neck slipped a little. She shook her hand. Her grasp seemed looser.

"Get off," she shouted at the glass and made a sharp throwing motion. The bottle sailed a short distance through the air, landing with a heavy plop, digging a new cradle in the dark sand.

Jinger flexed her fingers and glanced at the bottle. "That was interesting."

This odd occurrence wasn't something she should keep to herself. Even though there hadn't been a threat to her clan for seven years, she knew from family history to remain vigilant. Didn't Nightshade say complacency gave birth to danger and ultimately to failure? Granted, the man seemed overly conscious of such things, but he had survived a long stretch of lifetimes.

Jinger chuckled. She'd tell the Alastriona first, because informing the Defenders of Mankind was the proper course of action. Perhaps she'd make a game of telling Nightshade, see if she could ruffle his feathers a bit. Yes, they both enjoyed guessing games.

Turning her back on the bottle, she lifted her hand to form a portal to her home and paused. She wouldn't be able to keep secrets from anyone if she arrived fully winged. Besides, because of her fairy blood, the gentry portals were prickly and uncomfortable at times. Having her wings exposed might increase that discomfort.

Concentrating on the magic she'd used almost every day since she'd first understood what magic was, Jinger waited for her wings to recede. But the cool breeze off the water stirred the tips rising just above her head and made the narrow, rounded tails curl around her calves.

She closed her eyes. Focus.

Increasingly stronger gusts whipped around her, turning hot as a desert wind, and as wild as a dust devil. But the sand remained smooth at her feet, her wings and clothing didn't flutter the least bit. Then the force centered on her and a magic beyond her experience dragged her backward. Her bare heels cut deep ruts in the sand. She flailed her arms and cried out.

The potent essence of a world-spanning portal wrapped around her. She struggled to speak the short spell to ease her transition from one world to another but the powerful magic whipped the syllables from her lips.

The undeniable force steadily drew her toward the unknown. This was no normal step from one world into another.

She fought to keep her eyes open to recognize and categorize this new magic. There might be some clue in the portal or the transfer process to help her find her way home. She'd need to recall as much as possible to tell the Defenders.

Her heartbeat slowed. Minutes passed between one breath and the next. She felt—stretched, elongated. With a gasp, her breath returned, tightening her chest with fear. She found nothing to focus on, no indication how she could find her way back through this odd portal.

Her family would assume she came to the beach. How might they find her now? Fear threatened to steal her voice, but she managed to call out once again.

There was no one on the beach to answer, no one to grab her outstretched hands and help her to safety. Just the pull. The power. The heat. Overwhelming heat. As though she was being drawn into an oven. She glanced back over her shoulder. A whirl of winds exited the mouth of the bottle to form a funnel—widening until it was large enough to encompass her.

She shouted again then grimaced. She needed to save her strength to free herself from this strange portal. Her struggles brought not even the slightest break from the captive winds, but she was able to whip around to face the bottle.

Terror widened her eyes and stole a scream from her throat.

The lip of the bottle had become a vibrating, spinning portal. She didn't have the strength to counter the pull. She shouted a few phrases of fairy magic, but the portal only seemed to boil at the edges, as though angry with her attempts. She had magic from her gentry mother as well, but not as strong as that from her father. She attempted combining the two.

The pull increased, speeding her approach. Now she saw what lay on the other side, a faint orangish-pink, with a distant grouping of dusty gray clouds. A sky, a sky with nothing below it.

If the portal sucked her through, she'd fall into that nothingness. How far would she fall? She scrabbled against the loose, giving sand but found no purchase. Seconds later she hovered at the edge of the portal, her toes hanging in the clear air. She managed to stretch her arms to the sides and grasp the expanded round glass opening.

The pull disappeared. Stunned by the physical feel of the portal edge, she took a relieved breath. Before she could step from the opening, a wall of intense, fiery heat shoved against her back, pushing, pressing, tearing her fingers from their slippery grip.

Horrified, she stared down at a wide, turquoise sea.

The thin line of a pale beach stretched toward the horizons. Deep woods edged the beach in a blaze of greens and browns.

Tears burned behind her eyes. Too far down. Hitting the water would kill her. Or she'd be hurt so badly, she might as well die. Frantic, she struggled against the undeniable force, her breath coming in harsh pants as she silently called for her family, for the Alastriona, for anyone who could prevent her fall.

For a brief moment, the pressure against her back eased and a tiny spark of hope blossomed in her chest. Until the heat touched her wings, sensually caressed the length then curled the edges to tight, painful rolls. With a moan Jinger gave in to the odd sensations. The wind lifted her, held her erect, and carried her through the portal.

Desperate, she caught the edge with one hand and scraped her fingernails along the shimmering glass. This magic wouldn't have her so easily. Unable to fight the wind to grab hold with her other hand, she glanced down to eye the distant water.

She blinked. Of course. Silly fairy. Her wings. She had wings. She was out of practice but could certainly fly. She wouldn't fall to injury or death. She'd fly herself safely to the ground, then return to this cursed portal and find her way home. As the thoughts eased her mind, the edge of the portal grew fiery hot and sharp as broken glass.

With a gasp she lost her grip and fell into an unknown world.

Taj woke disoriented and remained still until he sensed his location. He hadn't returned to his tiny lodge and had spent the night on a wide stretch of beach. The salty tang of the sea filled his nostrils and he allowed himself the barest stretch of his lips to smile. Being near the water cooled his anger and centered his thoughts. The night ocean had allowed him a few hours of rest.

Taj shoved errant strands of hair back from his face, tightened the muscles across his shoulders and scowled. Magic buzzed in the air, flickering along his skin like tiny biting insects.

He was meant to be in this place, on this beach. But why?

Long ago, before becoming a man, he'd often been compelled to some location, for some reason. More often than he cared to remember, the reason had been a foul, abusive game the sorcerer played for his own entertainment. When Taj grew older the games had turned to dreams that taunted and teased. Wearied of the sorcerer's attempts, he'd learned to fight the dreams.

His sire was a cruel man.

Eventually Ib must have tired of him for even the dreams ended. Taj still remembered how he'd felt upon awakening. Just as bewildered as he felt with today's rising of the sun.

Taj scanned the beach, the line of low, thick foliage protecting the edge of the forest then the sky. The hairs on the back of his neck prickled. He rubbed at the irritation, freezing when he noticed the clear, dark blue circle of a gateway. This was the reason he'd been compelled to this stretch of beach. Soon a female would be drawn into the world.

The gateway seldom opened in the sky, for that meant the death of whatever being had been pulled through. An opening on the land, or even just above the sea was still dangerous, but manageable. Once he had comforted a creature too frail to heal from the fall. The moment life retreated from her he'd made a vow to her spirit.

A rise of sorrow for the beautiful, crystalline creature filled Taj's chest with pain and he glanced toward the rise of a single, stony brown butte topped by a many-towered castle. Ib's sanctuary. Taj's vow remained solid in his mind and in his soul. No matter the cost to him— for his life mattered little—no more would die to bring the sorcerer pleasure.

A warm, colorful wind created by the arrival of the firefox curled around him. Sensing the love radiating from the animal, he added to his silent vow. No other woman would suffer as his mother had.

He knelt and rested his hand on the head of the fire-fox. "You feel it as well, Ommi?"

Bright black eyes studied him before she pointed her dark nose toward the gateway. Taj sensed her thoughts, understood the rush of mental pictures she communicated to him.

"But the gateway opens too far above the sea. Even if the fright of the fall doesn't destroy, the impact against the water—"

A thin stream of light arced from the castle to the gateway, brightening the blue edges to a blinding shimmer. Taj shaded his eyes and straightened. A dark shadow twisted in the gateway before bursting through and tumbling through the clear sky.

"No," he whispered and ran. Despite knowing he might never even discover where the newcomer fell, he would search and honor the life of one who didn't understand their destruction. The firefox kept pace then leapt into the sky, a trail of brightly colored air following her. She yipped once and turned toward the castle.

Desperate to take positive action, Taj focused on the falling figure. Wings of purple and a greenish-blue opened wide and with graceful sweeps slowed the being's fall.

But not enough. She fell too fast. The large wings flapped awkwardly as though unaccustomed to the motions.

You must try.

As if hearing his unspoken command, the woman forced more power into the down sweep of her wings and the speed of her fall lessened. Then he heard the golden, tinkling sound of her laugh as she rose, twirled then directed her flight toward the beach.

A winged woman. Frozen in wonder, he watched her descent.

His fingers curled with the need to touch her.

Blinking, he shook his head. Touch her? No, he would warn her. Inform her of Ib's designs.

Learn the texture of her wings. Stroke his fingers through her hair.

No. He forced himself to turn from the enticing vision. Perhaps she was merely a waking dream or some new magic the sorcerer tested on him. Taj shook his head fiercely then stilled and listened to the silence in his mind. She wasn't a vision projected by his father to torment him.

This woman was real and in danger.

This time, Taj would find the way to defy his sire, prevent the woman's death and deny Ib any increase in his power.

Lost in his thoughts, Taj barely had time to slip into the cover of the trees before the woman hovered over the beach then fell heavily to the sand with a startled curse. She continued to mumble then lifted her head and laughed.

She pushed to her knees, brushed the sand from her arms, and stood. If she'd been hurt, it wasn't badly. He didn't understand her laughter. Perhaps she was addled.

No matter. Should she face any danger, he would intercede. As she stood and stared at the gateway while continuing to brush sand from her body, he studied her appearance. Her wings were a mix of deep purple and the color of the depths of the sun-brightened sea. The colors swirled in patterns demarked by thick veins of shadowy black. Never had he seen anything so magnificent.

Watching and waiting proved more difficult than he imagined. His fingers twitched with the need to feel the texture of her hair, shining with the color of a ripe tanga fruit. Or to gauge the softness of those impressive wings that often seemed to be in the way of her movements.

He held a leaf to one side to watch her pace between the water and the tree line. The oddest notion filled him. She would be a torment, but in a purely delightful manner.

TWO

F rom the second tower of his castle high on a cliff, Ib peered through a narrow slit in the thick stone wall. He smiled and patted the open book resting on the table at his side. At his urging, the gateway had discovered a creature of magic to draw into his world. Believing in his power rather than any aspect of luck, he knew it to be a female. If not, disposal was easy enough.

The time of his release approached. He simply needed to nudge fate in the proper direction, and he would be free of his prison. He sneered at the sun—both the giver of power and his captor. "Soon I will be strong enough to face you again, god though you claim to be. This time stronger, filled with more power, a power of my own. And I shall strike you down. Imprison you in cold darkness, as I desire. It is time for gods to fall. For new powers to arise."

He studied the disc of the sun. Eons had passed since the elemental had responded to his threats, pleas, or taunts. He wondered at the lack, for at first the fire elemental had delighted in his pain. Gods were capricious fools. It mattered not. Once he created a child—.

Returning his gaze to the sky, he willed the female to appear in the glowing blue circle. Ah. His breath stalled in his throat and he rubbed his hands together until his palms heated. There. Hovering at the gateway. Resisting.

"Fall," he commanded with a harsh rasp.

The distant body strained against his insistent power. This one was strong. Good, that would bring more benefit from the child. Ib increased the heat in his hands and lifted his palms toward the gateway. He couldn't control the passage—yet—but he could augment the ferocity of the winds to push the being through. "Come. Now. Fall and find your fate."

At his command, a thin stream of fire shot from one palm to the gateway. The outer edge of the opening brightened with the added heat. He closed his fingers and twisted his fist, adding sharp points to edge the gateway. "Enter. Mine. You are mine. Come."

The body lurched forward and fell. Ib considered, briefly, slowing the being's descent. It would take longer to get a child on a broken body, but such things were still possible. Still, the last time the gateway opened had been ages ago. A bit of companionship might be enjoyable before he fulfilled his destiny.

Perhaps he would woo this one. Such would be a pleasant challenge. He'd continued to learn and exceed in his craft and knew other aspects of the prophecy could be speeded along. In truth, having someone respond with even a modicum of intelligence when he spoke would be a relief to his boredom.

He opened his palm as if to catch the falling body, but before his magic reached across the sky, wide wings spread, flapped and slowed the female's fall to a near stop. Ib squinted then pulled a thin frame from the wall. He held the device holding a pair of polished crystal sheets a few inches apart to his eye and grinned.

A lovely female. A winged creature of beauty and grace, a woman with the gift of flight. Possibilities swirled through his mind as he watched her descend toward the beach. Her hair sparkled in the sun, a golden red glistening with an aura of magic. Ah, fate was kind to him. At last.

He left the observation window and made his way down the narrow stone steps to a modest hall. He'd long since tired of the grand chambers of his prison and shut off many of those rooms. Perhaps with a guest he would reopen the opulent areas.

Curse the prophecy for decreeing the child must be born of a willing female, else he could simply take her and be done with the foolishness. He seldom traveled beyond the castle walls. The dark shadows of the forest stole his power too quickly, leaving him weakened. So she must come to him here. Ib bit back the anger burning at his lips and crossed to a long wall covered by a fringed tapestry.

Within the confines of the thread and weaving lay a representation of the land beyond his castle and the few inhabitants. He gave the tapestry a cursory glance, noting the location of each. Except one. The threads had never shown him the firefox. Bitch.

Nor had he been able to alter the time it took for the weavings to show happenings in the world around him. He'd discovered recently how to slow or speed time within his castle, yet the tapestry continued to weave at the same, methodical pace. He glowered at the small, blue circle of the gateway high in the sky. How long would it be before the female appeared in the tapestry?

One day or many didn't matter. He needed time to prepare for his guest. To prepare himself to woo and seduce. His slow grin felt unusual and he touched a finger to his lower lip. Far too long he had denied himself pleasure of any kind beyond the gaining of power. Far too long since he had tortured the embodiment of failure the firefox had stolen from him. Far too long since he last sent a dream to torment his son.

A blur of bright colors swirled at the edge of his vision. "So, you have come to witness the arrival as well."

Putting his back to the tapestry, Ib crossed his arms, arched his neck and stared down the length of his nose at the dainty firefox crouched on a wide, stone window ledge. Though anger simmered in the back of his mind, this time he would not attempt to destroy the creature. The witnessing of his success would prove more painful for the damnable transfigured djinn.

He wanted her to feel that pain, burned to observe and absorb the energy of her realization and her fear. Then he would force her to be a participant when he sacrificed the new child and destroyed her worthless son. With her last breath captured between his palms—his fingers flexed against his upper arms—he would squeeze until the djinn who thwarted him was no more. Not even a memory.

A soft whine rose from the firefox as though she guessed his thoughts. The fiery red of her fur dulled and the colors faded from the air. Good. The swirling borealis of light and color surrounding her movements drove pinpricks of pain behind his eyes. He could ill afford to lose focus now that his freedom was near.

The whine rumbled to a growl and a ridge of the firefox's fur lifted along her slightly arched spine.

Ib chuckled. "There is nothing you can do. The motion has been set, the tapestry woven. You have no influence. Your pathetic son can do nothing to stop me. Go. Leave me, fox. I should have hunted you when you were newly transformed, weak and confused. I should have killed you then."

The firefox yipped. The edges of her lips curled and she snorted, then yipped again.

"You dare laugh at me? Challenge me?" Ib fisted his hands and angled his body toward her, calling on power to increase his presence. His skin stretched and tingled before adjusting to his new height and bulk. He exposed his teeth and snarled. "Where is your challenge now, fox?"

Defying him, the firefox danced in a tight circle upon the ledge. The colors swirling around her deepened. Ib blinked back the fierce watering of his eyes. She would not dare.

In a burst of brightness, she leapt and ran through the air, circling him twice, cocooning him in agony. His fists flew open and he slapped his palms against his eyes. His body snapped back to his normal size. He groaned and sank to his knees.

The firefox circled him once again, coming closer while dragging an intense rainbow of lights behind her. Ib lifted one hand to grasp at the flowing light, but the trail exploded into sparks that burned his skin. "Triple cursed are you. Triple shall you suffer, fox."

The firefox danced into the darkening sky, her barking laughter echoing through the window. Her trail of light expanded, reaching high above the castle in waving curtains of color.

Ib rose and stumbled to the opening. He pounded his fist against the stone lintel before opening his palm against the cool, gray stone. The remnants of the bright pain faded, but his anger remained steady. He vowed to use the anger to fashion the demise of the djinn and her son.

Tucking the rage away to recall at the proper time, Ib spared a glance at the gateway tapestry. With the time delay, he would see nothing more until the morrow. Night dulled his powers but was beneficial to the preparations for his magic. He had much to do.

CHAPTER
THREE

The dark circle remained open high above Jinger, and she stared into a long, dark tunnel. A pinpoint of light blue centered the distant end and for the oddest reason, the tunnel reminded her of the tall neck of the bottle she'd pulled from the waves. Rolling her eyes at the notion, Jinger returned her focus to the new world around her.

The breeze played with her wings, so she rustled them leisurely. The movement relaxed the tension from her abused muscles, and she longed to allow herself the freedom of unrestrained wings. But she needed to discover where she was, how to reach the tunnel and how to get home. Unless wings were common here she'd stand out too much. She wasn't willing to take that chance, so she closed her eyes, visualized her beautiful purple and teal wings receding into her back and spoke her spell.

Nothing happened.

She tried again. Although magic flowed around her and centered as it should between her shoulder blades, the incantation remained ineffective. She plopped down on the sand and rested her chin on her fist. This had never happened before. Always one to discover the best of a situation, she straightened and grinned. If destiny decreed she'd have wings in this world, she might as well use them while she explored.

Sighing with long denied, barely remembered pleasure, Jinger set her wings into a gentle, yet powerful motion and lifted into the air. How long had it been since she'd allowed herself the joy of flight? She spread her arms and turned her face to the bright, yellow sun.

Laughter died on her lips and she wrapped her arms around herself, letting the casual rippling of her wings keep her aloft. Now was not the time for play. She had to find her way out of this world before her family became worried. Returning with information for the Defenders about the portal's strange characteristics would help ease any concern from her being away too long.

Determined to make her father proud, she glanced around, memorizing the landforms in the distance. Both ends of a range of craggy peaks curved toward the water creating a bowl shape filled with a forest of thick trunked trees and dense foliage. No signs of animal life. The white sand stretched in both directions.

Jinger shrugged. Nothing remarkable. Unless something, or someone, remained hidden among the trees. Now, that was an intriguing possibility. She turned inland.

No. Finding her way back to her world, or at least to one she recognized and could use to get home, was her primary focus.

But it felt so good to fly. So fly she would. Up toward the deep blue circle, her focus on the tiny blue speck she suspected was where she belonged. She tested her wings by flying a tight circle then dropping and rising in rapid succession. Despite the long periods of keeping her wings hidden and denying herself flight, the intrinsic ability flowed through her as effortlessly as she flowed through the air.

Hovering in place, she tilted her head to one side to study the dark circle. The disk had elongated slightly to form an oval, but other than that change, she sensed no movement near or within the portal.

Jinger set her lips in a determined line and angled her flight directly toward her target. She flew higher attempting to gauge the distance between the land and the portal and glanced down. The sandy beach was far below her but her fall from the portal hadn't seemed from so great a distance.

Her gaze jumped between the land and the portal. While she appeared to be rising higher from the land, the dark oval hadn't gotten any closer.

The sense of strange magic weakened. The portal remained the same size, but faded until the edges merged with the pale, summer-blue sky.

"No," she cried and increased her speed, beating her wings in strong, full strokes.

The portal snapped from existence.

Jinger continued her breakneck advance until her lungs burned. Fighting for breath, she hovered and closed her eyes in defeat. The magic tingle dissipated, surrounding her with nothing but the cloudless sky.

Trying to gather her thoughts, Jinger wrung her fingers together. She was trapped in a place unknown to her. She clenched her jaw. She could handle this experience. The Defenders had trained each member of her family in what to do in situations like this. She may not have been the best student, but she knew enough to survive.

Didn't she? She blew out a long, cleansing breath. She'd be fine. She could do this.

Sunlight glittered in her eyes. Streaks of colors announcing the setting sun filled the distant horizon. Jinger shivered and turned her back on the sky to focus instead on the land. Her first night in a strange, new place and despite all her self-talk, she was completely unprepared. However, there wasn't much time to seek out a safe place to spend the night.

Since her magic hadn't worked to keep her wings hidden, she assumed she'd be on her own with only non-magical survival skills. Thankfully, Nightshade had taught them basic survival training as well. She managed a half-grin. His insistence all the children learn Morse Code had provided a means to bring a rescue party back from the World Between Worlds.

Sadness overwhelmed her and she sank swiftly toward the ground. The rescue party and the leader of the Alfar-Sindhu had returned. But not her cousin, Chance.

Jinger sniffed back tears. So what if that portal was gone. No worries. She could make one of her own. She hovered in the clear air, closed her eyes, and visualized where she wanted to go. Home. No, to the chambers of the Alastriona. The Defenders needed to know about this place and the odd portal.

This time her magic would work. With a nod she set her intention and waited for the buzz of magical electricity against her skin.

Only the warm air caressed her. She opened one eye

to peek then both as she turned in a circle. Nothing. Not even the faintest of shimmers to indicate a magical opening. Reviewing her procedure, she determined all the elements were in place, done properly. She crossed her arms then propped her chin in one hand to study the nearly cloudless sky.

Oh. Maybe forming a portal only worked on the ground. She'd never attempted one in mid-air. Magic needed a solid foundation. She'd try again on land.

Angling her flight toward the beach, she descended faster than she wanted. Her back and shoulder muscles burned with the effort of slowing. She grimaced. Still too fast. The beach was too close.

Drawing a deep breath, she beat her wings twice, then curled them around her body, tucked and rolled awkwardly over the sand. Face down, she lay panting and curled her fingers through the loose grains. How was something so giving so hard?

With a groan she rolled to her back, arched in pain and sat, carefully tugging the edge of her wing from under her. She definitely needed to work on her landing skills.

Thank goodness no one had witnessed her second awkward tumble. Releasing a long breath, she finished brushing the sand from her chest and stomach. There was no time for aches and pains, only survival.

She stood and called upon the magic needed to form a portal. No rise of power answered her call. After two attempts she dropped to the beach and slapped the damp sand. Maybe Morse Code would work here, too. There had to be a way to create a message in hopes someone, somewhere, might hear.

Defeated, she wrapped her arms around her legs, and

rested her chin on her knees. Only the soft brush of wave against the sand and an occasional rustle from the forest disturbed the evening air. The bright circle of the sun flattened against the distant horizon. Cotton candy colors streaked the darkening sky.

The sunset was beautiful and Jinger wished she could enjoy the experience without worry—or fear. When she'd been alone on *her* beach, she'd felt safe, still connected to her home, her worlds, and her family. Today she'd wanted to escape from the crowd, the noise, the memories. But all that, and more, were always within her reach.

She carefully rubbed sand from a scrape on her forearm. Now her attempts at creating a portal had gotten nowhere. Every trick she knew, every ancient incantation she and her cousins had been taught as children, had failed. Even simply sending a message had failed. The magic bounced back to her as though reflected off some hard shell surrounding her.

She wasn't really *inside* the bottle, was she? That didn't seem possible, although there was no guarantee the physics and logic of the human earth translated to every world.

Jinger laughed then covered her mouth with her hand. Logic and physics? So not in her make up. Fearing the noise may have attracted unwanted attention, she glanced from side to side and angled her upper body to glance at the dark forest. Blowing out a frustrated breath, she moved her wing to see a wider view of the trees.

What was it with her wings anyway? Why didn't they retract when she wanted? She'd even added a seldom used compulsion to her incantation and although she'd felt the tremors of that compulsion, her wings had remained exposed and awkward.

Once she got home, she'd allow her wings freedom more often to become accustomed to them. She was a fairy. As the daughter of the king, she should honor her heritage. Once she got home.

Sighing, she returned her attention to the sunset.

The last sliver of sun disappeared leaving behind a dark twilight and fingers of light stretching from the horizon. Hoping to fix her position in this world and wishing even more to find a point of reference to connect to home, she lifted her gaze to the bowl of sky above her.

No moon. Not necessarily an issue. There were worlds with no moons. Or the moon could be in a dark phase. She shrugged the unease from her shoulders and searched the sky.

No stars. Not even a glint or glimmer of light. Unless the stars were too far away or too faint to compete with the sunset. She'd check again when it was darker.

She considered the beach. At least with a clear space around her she could see if something came at her. Not that she had much hope in her defensive skills. She'd completed the routine training but had hated the ongoing practice bouts. Nightshade insisted she learn more and despite her disinterest, had continued to drill her on those skills. "Thanks, Shade," she whispered to the darkening sky. "I hope I do you proud."

Hoping and doing were two different things. Skirting the trees, she gathered sticks and created a small pile. Tomorrow she'd figure out some way to build a fire. As long as the night didn't get too cold, she'd be okay. She reached for a stick, sat, and drew a pattern in the sand.

"I'll be okay," she promised herself. "I'll find my way home.

With one last glance around, she arranged her wings and lay on her side. Drawing a longer, thicker stick close, she curled her hand around the smooth wood. Even if she couldn't sleep, she needed rest. Tomorrow...

Oh, if only she hadn't thought she needed to be alone that afternoon. She allowed herself the luxury of a few tears. She'd never really thought about the differences in being alone and being lonely.

Tonight, she was both.

CHAPTER
FOUR

I b instructed his servant to set a small worktable in the hall to enable him to watch the tapestry as he created a dream for the female. Once his servant brought him the required components, he would begin. Despite the damping of his power with the sunset, creating dreams took little effort. He must properly welcome his guest.

The odd time distortion created by the weaving showed the winged woman still falling through the sky but he knew she had touched the land. He'd felt the vibrations, the subtle differences. As the night fell, she would need rest, sleep, and be open to receiving his dream.

He narrowed his eyes at the dull oval indicating the location of his son. Too close to where the woman might be. Perhaps he would direct a dream of warning to the abomination, a warning to lay Ib's claim. He chuckled. Perhaps he would be kind and then send a pleasant dream if the boy did as instructed. He laughed again and shook his head.

Laying the vials in proper order, he dismissed the servant with a wave of his hand.

He waited until the soft, damp pop of his servant's return to the wall faded before palming a small, red metal bowl. As he poured the contents of each vial into the bowl, he muttered the words of power. A fine mist formed above the surface of the eddying liquids.

With a soft breath, he released the dream. The mist hovered, shimmering with dull colors. He directed the vapor toward the tapestry and into the fine weaving of a woman with wings.

Ib touched a finger to the liquid in the bowl and waited for the stinging burn of connection.

There. Ah, her sleep was restless, hovering at the edge of wakefulness. He dipped a second finger into the bowl and sensed her reluctant welcome of deeper relaxation. After a moment, he cast a glamor over himself, softening his countenance and stepped into her dreams.

Welcome to my home, lovely one. Welcome and be at peace. You are safe under my watch.

She shoved at the dream as though she didn't accept his presence. Ib squared his shoulders. A little fight in this one. Good. She would bear him a strong child. A worthy child.

Do not fear. No harm shall come to you. Although I am unable to meet you in the forest, do not fear. The gates are open to you, awaiting your presence. Although the path through the trees may seem frightening, I shall watch over you. Come to me, lovely one. Be welcomed. Be safe.

Though she didn't speak, he sensed her rejection, then deeper, where she attempted to hide from him, a powerful curiosity. And the key.

Come, lovely one. I await your light, your beauty, to relieve my...loneliness.

Drawing his fingers from the bowl, Ib allowed his presence to slowly fade from her dreams. He'd planted the seed. She might not attempt to find him the following day, but soon her curiosity would lead her to him.

Toying with the abomination of his son lost appeal as he formulated plans of seduction and power. Determined to discover other means of exploiting the female's emotions to twist her to his will, he set the bowl on the table and turned toward the stairs leading to his workroom.

After a long and frustrating night searching for the magical words he'd discovered previously, Ib gathered energy from the spots of sunlight dotting the floor. He paced the arched hallway of his palace, moving back and forth in front of the wall-sized tapestry. He paused to study the movements of the tiny threads forming a new picture. Nearly a full day had passed since the gateway had opened and provided a female. The slow weaving of the tapestry showed only hints and teasing glimpses of possibilities. The time delays maddened him.

Charged with magical energy, the air shimmered around him bringing his flat grin. A creature of enchantment and magic had been drawn into his prison, guaranteeing his success. After uncounted eons he would gain access to the worlds beyond the gateway.

He rubbed his palms together. What new power might he discover once he escaped? How strong might he become in his new freedom? Just as power knew no boundaries, his mere presence, his essence would become as boundless. Ah, what glory he would achieve in that moment.

But first, he needed to absorb more power. After the last—donation—he'd been nearly able to reach the gateway.

Ib stepped to one side to watch the oval representing his son. His son? Bah. The mother, a foolish djinn, had thought she could save the child he'd gotten on her from sacrifice. By birthing a child with no magic she'd only delayed the inevitable. Taj would die, even if he had no magic to increase Ib's power. At the moment Ib rid himself of that thorn, of the reminder of how ultimate power had long resisted him, the satisfaction would be enough.

The threads of his son's oval reformed slowly, but in a way Ib understood Taj had witnessed the arrival of the latest acquisition and could be near the female. Without doubt the boy thought he could prevent Ib from simply taking what he wanted.

Ib laughed, tilting his head to listen as the echoes faded against the stone of the immense hall. The pattering footsteps of his servant beat against the echoes. He was in no mood for the company of a sniveling, kowtowing fool. Ib held up one hand to the direction of the creature's advance and spread his fingers. The footsteps ceased. Ib closed his fist, and a soft, damp sucking sound returned the servant to its containment.

Although fools did have their place. Swift strides returned Ib to his pacing.

The frantic weaving slowed so he stopped to lean closer to the tapestry. The threads gathered at a spot indicating a small clearing in the forest. Yes. One of the springs. "Show me," he muttered and held his palm above the weaving. Despite knowing he had no control over the weavings, he commanded again, "Show me."

Drawing a deep breath, he withdrew his hand. This time he would be successful and the worlds beyond his prison would be his.

Impatient, he glared at the tapestry until the weaving slowed, stopped and tucked the tiny, frayed ends of threads under the completed picture. A welling of satisfaction filled his chest. Yes. This was the time of success. His escape. His revenge and glory.

Lower, his body responded unexpectedly to the vision before him. Not only had the gateway provided him a young, healthy female, this winged creature was a delight. He'd sensed her beauty when he'd visited her dreams, but this completed vision of her stirred a long-forgotten lust. He would take time and enjoy filling this one with his child.

At last, he would have a son worthy of sacrifice.

He whirled and strode across the hall, his footsteps echoing in the still, heavy air. Pausing in the vestibule outside his workroom, he drummed his fingertips against a small table with a thickly scarred wooden top. Even with the requisite willing partner, force and dominance had not served him well in his previous attempts to sire the perfect child. Mayhap he should approach this female in a different manner. Gain her confidence and adoration. He blew out a harsh breath. Doing so would take time he didn't wish to waste.

His fingers moved more rapidly. In one of the oldest

volumes of magic he'd collected he recalled a spell. Yes. In the book he'd retrieved from beneath another world's ocean, long before the false god imprisoned him in this single, useless world. Of course. An incantation to speed the time of a child from conception to birth.

Lifting one hand, he spread his fingers then drew the tips together. The damp, sucking sound preceded his servant into the vestibule. Arching one eyebrow, Ib planted a visual into the creature's dull mind. "You know where to find this book?"

A sharp nod tossed the servant's lank hair over its eyes.

"Bring it."

A second nod. Ib spread his fingers then closed his fist. The servant disappeared.

Ib folded his arms, leaned his hip against the table, and grimaced. Taking time to woo this female fought the immediacy of his needs. Yet with so many eons already passed, he could afford the few days necessary to ensure success. Drawing out the anticipation might prove beneficial as well, both to his pleasure in procreating and to the joy of destroying the firefox and her son.

The book appeared on the table. Damp, musty air rose from the thick, fish-leather bound volume. Ib inhaled and allowed the promise of ancient power to fill his lungs. Supremacy throbbed with each beat of his heart. All this, and he hadn't yet laid the book upon his worktable and rested his fingers against the spells. His eyes drifted closed with the bliss of yet unknown power.

Smiling, he hefted the oversized book and entered his shielded workroom. Yes. He had much to do.

CHAPTER
FIVE

W arm water tickled Jinger's toes. She grumbled and shoved at the air. She wasn't ready to wake up. She'd been dreaming the strangest dreams and wanted to see what happened. The warmth returned, crawling a bit higher on her foot.

A muggy breeze swirled over her, lifting stray hairs from her cheek. She must have left the window open. She wiggled. The mattress was hard, and her pillow gone. Something gritty pressed against her cheek. Water washed up her ankle.

She gnawed on her lip. *Please let this be a dream.* Even as she cast her wish, she knew the futility of the hope. She opened her eyes and sat to peer toward her feet. Tiny waves foamed as they rolled in to wet the sand, each reaching higher on the beach, and on her legs.

With a shriek, she scrambled backwards, catching one wing under her hand, and yelping with the sharp pain. Rolling to her hands and knees, she crawled toward the forest, looking back over her shoulder at the water. Did the incoming tide reach as far as the trees?

Finally, she stood, brushed at the sand clinging to her clothing and faced the sea with her hands on her hips. "Fine then. I'm awake. Oh, no, no. Bring that back."

One wave had crested higher than the rest and stole the long stick she'd clutched through the night. Her protection. She high stepped through the water and snatched the damp wood. "I don't have much, but this is mine."

Once back on dry sand she held the stick flat against her palms. What kind of damage did she think she could do with this? If attacked, the best thing would be to fly away. If she could. Her shoulders ached from the previous day's efforts. Simply moving her arms made her wince. She needed to fly to reach the portal when it returned, but at that moment, didn't know if she'd be able to lift herself even a foot from the ground.

So today would be about survival and practice to strengthen her flying muscles. Her stomach rumbled. Survival meant food. She glanced around. Where did she begin?

The soft lapping of the sea against the shore drew her attention. And water. That was even more important than food. She tiptoed to the edge of the sea and cupped a bit of water in her hand. The tip of her tongue burned at the bitter salinity. Great. This world's ocean was even saltier than those in the human world. Oh how she longed for the cool, clear water of Faerie.

She licked her dry lips. A river. If there was a river, and she traveled inland from the beach, she might discover palatable water. She'd need a pot. And a fire to purify the water. Nightshade's lessons crowded her mind and she fought to find order in the confusion. Tears burned her eyes. Fat lot of good crying would do—tears were salty, too.

So, she laughed.

After staring across the wide expanse of the sea for a few minutes, then into the sky where she imagined the portal lay hidden, she turned and started back toward the tree line.

She froze.

A large leaf rested on the ground near where she'd stopped when escaping the advancing waves. The stem end looked like it had been curled up and slipped through a slit toward the opposite end of the leaf to form a bowl.

That hadn't been there before. Had it?

Tentative and with both hands clutching her stick like a baseball bat, she moved closer, trying to watch both the forest and the empty beach. When she stood over the leaf, she discovered it filled with water. Bracing the back of the flimsy leaf bowl, a pair of small, bright yellow fruits rested on a flat strip of bark. She eyed the offering. No, this definitely hadn't been here.

Someone had provided water—and food.

"Come out and show yourself," she whispered then cleared her throat and spoke her command with slightly more authority. "Now."

Not even the breeze rustled the foliage. No rasp of footsteps against sand announced the presence of another living being. Yet she didn't feel alone. Someone, some... thing was nearby. Watching her.

Casual in her movements, she knelt and dipped one fingertip in the water. She brought her finger to her lips and licked at a tiny droplet.

Relief washed over her. Sweet, cool, and so much like

water from a Faerie spring, she could almost imagine she was home. Her parched mouth demanded she drink deeply, but wisdom disguised as one of Nightshade's warnings stayed her hand. The water could still be dangerous to her. If she fell ill, she might never have the strength to discover her way home.

Same with the fruit. Pressing her hand against her empty belly, she shook her head. How had Nightshade told them to test strange foods? After a long moment she thought she remembered to taste only the tiniest of bites then wait for any unpleasant reaction. Right or not, she'd take the chance. She had no other choice.

First she wanted to draw out whatever being watched her. She gestured toward the leaf bowl. "Thank you for the water and food. Who are you? Where are you?"

A distant birdcall answered her, and she grimaced. Great. Her benefactor was shy. "Take your time. I only have to figure out how to survive then find my way home. No hurry."

The bitterness in her tone made her chuckle. She really didn't do sarcasm well. Resting her stick at her side, she sat facing the trees, carefully picked up the leaf, and cupped her hand under the bowl to prevent losing the water. She took a tiny, tentative sip, held the moisture in her mouth for a long moment then swallowed.

She waited and nothing happened. Trusting the water to be safe, she tried a bit of the fruit dug from the small orb with her fingernail. While she waited for tingling, or her throat to tighten, or any possible adverse reactions, the sun rose completely to heat the sand and air. The beginning of a burn tightened the back of her neck.

But she didn't move. Instead, she replayed the strange dream that had settled firmly in her mind. The dream of a man hidden in a haze, with a cultured voice, low and compelling. A man who spoke to her of safety. Who promised—something she couldn't quite remember.

All she needed to do was enter the forest and eventually she'd find her way to the man. He would know what to do, how to help her find her way home. Wouldn't he? He'd promised that—hadn't he?

In the dream, she'd been confident finding him was the right thing to do. Now in the light of day, sitting under a sun growing hotter by the minute, doubts wrestled with the certainty. Nor was she sure she wanted to take the chance to find out. Something about the man, about the dream, didn't ring true in the daylight.

She rolled her eyes and relaxed her shoulders. By heritage and personality, she assumed the best of people. In truth, she'd been hurt by those expectations a few times, and had tried to remember and learn from her mistakes. But she hadn't mastered the lesson all that well either. Reining in her easy trust wasn't something the Alastriona or Nightshade could teach.

Even asleep she'd felt an aura of something unpleasant around the dream man. Despite his soft, calm voice and pretty words, she didn't trust that *something*.

Jinger attempted to ignore the vague misgivings and set the dream aside as simply a dream. Only the wish of her heart in a moment of panic, the desire for someone to take care of her, to show her what to do.

There wasn't anyone here to do that for her.

Except, maybe, whoever left the fruit and water. She

ran her tongue over her teeth. No negative effects from the fruit either. She was so hungry and needed food for energy. Making herself eat slowly, she consumed one piece, drank a bit of the water, and after looking longingly at the second fruit, tied it in the hem of her shirt to save until later. Just in case.

The sunbaked beach grew increasingly uncomfortable, and the deep, cool greens of the forest beckoned to her. She shaded her eyes and stared into the sky. If the portal were to open again, and one of her family discovered this place, she needed a way to let them know she was here. Burning her fair skin to a crisp on the beach wasn't going to do any good.

She chuckled at the thought of using branches or stones to spell out SOS like from some old shipwreck movie. But since the tide continued to eat away at the sand, narrowing the beach to a thin sliver, her hard work could be washed away.

With her hands flat against her thighs, she played a finger game to help her concentrate. What kind of message could she leave?

An idea brought a soft, "Ah." She tugged a ring from her finger and bounced the thick circle in her hand. Her cousins and she had all worn similar rings most of their lives as a magical link to each other. Gifts from Gowthaman, the librarian. Anyone of the Zeroun clan, or one of the Defenders, would sense and recognize the magic. She should have remembered that connection sooner.

But she couldn't just leave her ring on the beach. The tide might carry it away. Or some animal. Or something.

The long tail of her shirt flapped in the breeze bringing her smile. She tugged the cotton to her mouth and bit through the loose weave. Breaking the threads took more gnawing than she expected but before long she was able to carefully tear a thin strip from the hem. She tied the ring to the center of the cloth with a tight knot then studied the area for a suitable place to leave the ring. This treasure needed to be safe, yet still easily visible.

A tree with a thick trunk and exposed roots crawling far out into the sand drew her attention. Low branches with tight bunches of leaves would allow her to fasten the ring high enough to be protected and not hidden by the foliage.

The tree would have to do.

H idden in the undergrowth, Taj had watched the woman through the night. She'd been restless, and he'd been surprised she'd slept at all. He sensed the sorcerer's magic, knew his sire sent her a dream. He understood the power of Ib's dream casting and imagined what false promises may have been made. Concern for her grew and he nearly left the forest to stand over her.

But her arms had moved as though pushing something away and he'd felt Ib's retreat. Taj spent the rest of the night pondering his sire's actions.

Fascinated, Taj had covered his mouth to squelch his laughter first when the warm sea waters woke the woman and again when she chased after a stick being drawn from the beach by the waves. He'd also used her distraction to place his offering of fruit and water close to the trees.

When she demanded he show himself, her soft, low voice nearly made him comply. It was too soon. He didn't wish to frighten her. Although she often seemed at a loss or unsure of herself, he nodded to himself when she was cautious with the water and fruit.

He didn't understand why she tied a piece of cloth to the tree. Perhaps it was a ritual of her kind. Curious, he eyed the fluttering strip of cloth then turned from the tree. He would not disturb her offering.

When the woman moved toward the forest with slow, determined steps, Taj rose to a crouch. She finally understood the trees provided a safe refuge from the heat of the sun. And Ib. The few creatures who shared the forest were for the most part unseen and harmless, but if in her hunger she tasted an unripe fruit or chanced upon the rare flight of the greenspan moth, her safety would be jeopardized.

A deep pain centered in his chest. He rubbed the spot and frowned. Keeping her safe without being seen would be an easy game. If he presented himself to her to soon... Taj scrubbed one hand over his face. The idea was too tempting. Too dangerous.

He huffed out a breath and glanced toward the beach. His heart pounded. He leaped from the forest to the sand and searched in both directions for her red-gold hair and colorful wings.

She was gone.

SIX

After a day spent wandering under the trees, sleep didn't come easily for Jinger that night. Being surrounded by the thick forest was oddly comforting, much like her family's home in the faerie otherworld. During the day she'd wished for more breaks in the heavy tree canopy where the sun could pierce the gloom to bring light and warmth to the ground. She shuddered and stared into the twilight sky. She'd left the intense, bright, and hot sun of this world on the beach. Perhaps the thick tree canopy and closely growing trunks prevented the land from becoming a desert.

She'd followed the winding twists and turns of a clear, shallow creek until she discovered this tiny clearing late that afternoon. Water trickled cold and pure from tiny fissures in a tall rock outcropping to a tiny pool, sparkling in the sunlight. Thankful for the water and a break in the heavy tree canopy, she'd also found a bush bearing fruit similar to that left for her on the beach. She decided to wait to test the fruit in the morning.

Questions with no answers fought for dominance in her mind. Who left her the fruit and water? Twice during the day she'd sensed someone, or something, close by. But when she'd paused to listen or casually glance around, the feeling died. The most reasonable possibility was the man who'd visited her dreams. But if he was able to leave provisions, why didn't he simply wake her? Why the dream visit?

A niggle of doubt settled in the pit of her stomach. She didn't believe such a reasonable possibility could be the truth. There wasn't much reasonable in her current situation.

The silence disturbed her. At home, the open meadows were filled with the furtive rustling of small animals scurrying about, the chirp of insects, the soft and often mournful calls of night birds. When she spent time in the human world, the nights were awash with light, excitement, and the noise of movement and life.

Her family was always close by, there for her even when she didn't want them. She wanted them now. She had no idea being alone, totally alone, could be so lonely. Too many times during the day she'd turned with an expression of delight, or a concern on her lips, to find no one there. She was tired of talking to herself.

Especially since she didn't have any answers.

She didn't know how it could be possible but the silence of the coming night was even more oppressive. Jinger imagined too much; bright, glowing eyes watching her, plans and decisions being made about her, never having another intelligent person to share with. The fairy optimism deep in her soul was hard pressed to remain positive.

She wiggled to find a more comfortable position in

the nest of leaves and grasses she'd piled against the broad trunk of a squat tree. A tiny fire would be nice, but she hadn't figured out how to make that happen. She'd gathered dry wood of various sizes and created stacks of tinder, kindling and larger branches. Nightshade would be proud.

Then shake his head at her inability to create a fire. During those long ago camping trips she'd tolerated with her cousins, she'd learned many simple charms and bits of magic used to create an igniting spark. But tonight, try as she might, over and over, she'd been unable to make any spell work. Just like the incantation used to hide her wings.

She shifted again, then gave up on sleep and sat with her back against the tree. The curl of her wings over her shoulders offered little real warmth, though provided a small comfort. She tugged the tail of one wing to her lap and traced the fine, slightly raised edges of the webbing separating the colors. More than the warmth, she wanted a small fire for light.

Since no stars dotted the sky Jinger couldn't gauge how much time had passed. She might have been glaring at the cold, dry teepee of kindling in her tiny stone encircled fire pit for five minutes. Or for five hours. Had her previous night on the beach been this dark? Maybe without the trees creating shadows within shadows, the open space had seemed less oppressive. She wished for any spark of light to hold back the velvety dark.

She hadn't discovered any evidence of large animals on her trek through the forest. Only birds and a single, pale green moth with wings larger than the length of her arm, crawling along a tree branch. Nothing had appeared dangerous, but even the most beautiful of creatures could be deadly. Unknown forms of wildlife that could see better in the darkness than she could, might certainly roam the night.

Now she was simply making herself frightened. She drew her branch closer and patted the wood. Her trusty protector. Time to shake off the heebie jeebies and make a plan.

A rustle in the treetops drew her gaze to the sky. The tight set of her shoulders relaxed with her sigh of delight. She'd gotten her wish. Sparkling ribbons of light similar to the aurora borealis, waves of yellows and oranges with spots of red undulated across the sky. High above her the colors faded.

She drew in a sharp breath. Great. Fire in the sky, but none in her pile of sticks. She needed a fire that would last.

A new streak of colors circled directly above her then spiraled down as though heading directly to the glade. Snagging the tip of one wing on a low-hanging branch, Jinger shrank into the deeper shadows of her tree root cocoon. She tugged until pain lanced across her wing but couldn't free herself. With her stick shaking in her hands and holding her breath, she waited.

At the leading edge of the spiral a small animal pranced through the air and landed softly on a boulder beside the spring. A faint haze of brightness surrounded the creature. Red-orange fur, subtly streaked with yellow and brown, covered it except for its black face and tiny black feet. White fur tipped the bushy tail. The dainty animal turned an intelligent gaze to Jinger.

Feeling as though she was being judged, Jinger squared her shoulders. The movement freed her wing, so she stood, lifted her chin and returned the animal's inspection. A fox. She was having a stare down with a fire-colored fox. The absurdity made her chuckle.

Jinger caught her lower lip between her teeth. If she started laughing now, she wasn't sure she'd be able to stop. Half-fairy, and a descendant of the original Puck, she dealt with many emotions inappropriately, often with laughter. Riding such an odd emotional roller coaster wasn't conducive to relationships. Not when that meant she was afraid to be herself.

Her family claimed to understand. Her father offered advice and encouragements, but being of pure fairy blood, he didn't see the problem. Or understand her concerns. If only she'd inherited more of her mother's calm, gentry nature. At least she might have a little more control.

A soft huff distracted her thoughts. Hesitant but fearless, the fox moved closer. The haze moved with the animal as though lighting the way. Just as wary, Jinger followed the animal's progress across the clearing. She didn't believe the fox was dangerous, but she'd seen movies where seemingly innocent beings had turned evil and dangerous.

Now she did laugh and clapped her hand over her mouth. Did she expect the slender, petite creature to transform into a muscle bound, hairy daemon? No, but this wasn't her world. Hairy daemons might be the norm here.

The fox paused, shook its head as though dismissing Jinger's thoughts then angled toward the cold campfire. It circled the pile of sticks twice before uttering a series of sharp yaps.

A tiny, bright flame burst to life in the center of the kindling. The fire caught, crackled through the dry sticks, and filled the dark with the promise of light, warmth and safety.

Jinger's stick-weapon fell from her grasp. She clasped her hands and grinned. "Oh, thank you. I couldn't get that lit. Thank you."

The fox sat and swung its black muzzle toward the pile of thicker branches then back to the fire. After it repeated the movement four times, Jinger thumped her forehead with her fingertips. "Of course. I need to add wood to keep the fire going. Thank you again. I'm sure you can tell I'm not experienced at camping. I don't know how I got to this world, and I don't know... how... I'll..."

The sledgehammer of fear and hopelessness she'd barely been able to keep at bay slammed into her chest. She struggled to keep from crumbling under the weight of the unknown. A single sob escaped before she covered her face with her hands.

A low whine drew her attention to the fox. Making soft, soothing noises, the animal twined around Jinger's calves like a cat. Fur soft as down brushed over her bare feet, each tickling movement lessening her fear. Her breathing eased and she lowered her hands.

"How do you do that? Make me feel calmer? Your magic is for more than fire, isn't it, little fox?"

Never pausing in its caress, the fox answered with a quiet yip.

"May I touch you?" Jinger bent and presented her palm like she did when she encountered an unknown dog. The fox pressed its muzzle against her hand, rubbed and silently encouraged Jinger to scratch behind its ears.

"You are a sweet little thing. I hope you'll stay around. I can use the company."

The fox moved out of reach and Jinger caught her lower lip between her teeth, hoping she hadn't chased away her only friend in this world. But the animal winked at her and curled beside the dying fire with its dark nose tucked beneath the twitching tail.

"Oh, the fire." Spurred into action, Jinger gathered larger branches from the pile and fed the fire until there was no danger the blaze would die. "There, that should be good for a while. So, my little fox, I need to give you a name so it's easier to talk. Now, names are important, so I have to think of just the right name for you."

"Her name is Ommi."

CHAPTER
SEVEN

The rasp of a deep male voice filled the glade. A premonition she didn't recognize skittered against the back of Jinger's neck. Nightshade's and Derrik's lessons snapped into place. She snatched up her stick, whirled, and curled into a defensive posture with her weapon raised.

She forgot to compensate for the added weight of her wings and how they altered her center of balance. The branch flew from her fingers and Jinger landed flat on her back with a loud, frustrated cry.

Before she could fight her way out of the tangle of her wings and scramble to her feet, the fox leapt over her and stood before the intruder. A series of yaps, whines and barks halted Jinger's struggles, and she studied the odd pair.

The tiny fox sat before the shadow-draped figure of a man standing just beyond the edge of the tree line. Jinger couldn't see his face in the flickers of light from the fire, but his body was impressive. Not overly tall, nor overly muscular, yet she sensed he held a great deal of physical power in check. He listened intently to the fox before kneeling and bending closer to speak in low tones.

Did the animal belong to him? He'd said it had a name. Jinger managed to sit and allowed her shoulders to droop. There went her one friend. The odd conversation continued while she rose and slowly backed to the far side of the fire.

Keep the minimal protection of the fire between you and your adversary. The admonition in Nightshade's voice made her giggle.

The man's attention jerked to her. He straightened and after a long moment stepped fully from the shadows. Dark hair brushed his wide shoulders. The bottom of an open vest skimmed his waist exposing not quite enough of his bare chest for her perusal. A narrow cloth belt topped wide, flowing trousers and soft suede boots.

Jinger had the insane desire to discover if under that loose material his legs were as toned and defined as his abdominal muscles. With her tongue.

Blinking away the inappropriate thought, she struggled to steady her balance and plant her feet firmly in the dirt. Her own body would not defeat her again. Her stance softened and she lowered her weapon as the man continued speaking in low whispers to the fox. He didn't appear threatening. If he'd wanted to harm her, he could have done so long ago. Before she even knew of his presence.

Though his expression remained calm, the lowering of his brows caused a deep furrow in his forehead. Poor man didn't smile much. He'd be quite handsome if he relaxed and let a grin tug at his full lips. She did so wish to see him smile. At her.

The man fell silent. Jinger canted her head, continuing to study him. What happened next was up to him. This was his world, and she the unwilling interloper. If he told her to go, she would. But where? And how?

She stared into the night sky. The bright borealis left by the fox had faded to the faintest wisps of color, much like her hope for finding a way home.

Unfortunately, her family was accustomed to her short disappearances. She wasn't much different than any of her cousins in that respect. Maybe the tendency was genetic—the fey did love to experience anything new. What was better than discovering a new world?

Except when she couldn't solve the mysteries of why she was here. Or how to find the way back home.

How long before her parents began to wonder at her absence? She desperately needed to be home before their worry set in and they sent the Alastriona to find her. That would be embarrassing. She'd never escape the good-natured ribbing from the Defenders. Or her family.

Still silent and staring at her, the man shifted and crossed his arms. Firelight flickered and highlighted the tight muscles in his chest and shoulders. Jinger caught the corner of her lip between her teeth before she sighed and, defying the way her body responded to him, stretched her spine to appear taller. Despite the flutter in her belly, she could at least appear to be in control.

He took a single step forward and she was lost in his dark, questioning gaze. Forget the Alastriona. Forget finding a way home. All she wanted—needed—was a bit of time with this man.

"Who are you? How did you come to be here?"

Power filled his words then quickly faded on the air. Jinger had the strange feeling he didn't know or under-stand the magic surrounding him. Interesting. But she did. It was one thing she could do well, so the Alastriona had improved her natural skills in identifying magics. A skill of which she was actually rather proud.

Why hadn't her ability kicked in when she first discovered the bottle or felt the prickles of the opening portal? Wasn't there an old saying, something about pride before a fall? She'd certainly fallen into this world. Pressing her lips together to stop another bout of inappropriate laughter, she bounced her stick against her palm.

The man took a step closer and tried to appear threatening, but the confusion in his eyes softened the effect. Jinger could find no harm in answering him. Besides, then she could ask a question or twelve.

That thought lightening her mood, Jinger gave a nod worthy of the royal princess of Fairy she was. "I am Jinger Goodfellow, daughter of Korin, the king of the Fairy realm, and his chosen Nanceen, sister to the ruler of the Faerie Gentry."

His eyebrows arched but he remained silent.

Dropping the regal pose and her weapon, Jinger spread her hands. "I know. It's confusing. Two different worlds. It's easier to figure out when you see the words fairy and faerie written out..."

Great. She was babbling. What else had he asked? Oh, yeah. "As to how I got here—I'm not sure. I found a bottle on a beach and was drawn to this place. Some kind of portal I didn't recognize."

"The gateway."

The man certainly didn't talk much. "I tried to get back to the por—gateway, but it was too high in the sky and the closer I flew, the further away it appeared."

The fox yipped before disappearing into the forest.

The man watched then returned his intense gaze to Jinger. Although the questions remained, his expression had relaxed. "That is the way of the gateway. You are safe here. For a time."

"For a time?" Was he making a threat? She didn't sense any danger from the man. However this was a world unknown to her. Perhaps he was one of those shapeshifting, hairy daemons. Or something worse. Mentally searching for additional weapons beyond her probably useless stick, she took a step back. "What do you mean, for a time?"

He uncrossed his arms and opened his palms to her. "There is no danger from me. Ommi and I believe you were brought here for a purpose."

"Purpose?"

Taj winced. Unaccustomed to speaking to anyone other than his mother, he'd inadvertently said too much. To distract the woman from her question, he drew a deep breath and rested one palm against his chest. "I am Taj."

The distraction didn't work. She planted her hands at her hips and frowned at him. "Tell me. What do you mean 'for a time'? What purpose?"

"It is a long tale." At her sharp inhalation, Taj searched for the words to continue. The need for her to understand the danger was imperative, yet at that moment he wished only to observe her movements, to study the myriad of emotions crossing her expressive face. Her beautiful face. Ib had never cursed him with a dream so lovely, so...perfect.

She stomped one foot. "I don't have anywhere to be, Taj. Get on with your story."

"Sit, then, Jinger, princess of Fairy." By the lords above, the way her name tasted on his lips surprised him. He wanted to say her name again. Many times, until the flavor became a part of him. Hoping to chase away the strange compulsion, Taj shook his head.

She glared at him, then her expression grew soft and wistful. She pressed her hand to her stomach. "Was it you who left the water and fruit on the beach this morning?"

Taj blinked. Her thoughts leapt from one to another with no pattern. He gave a slow nod.

"Thank you. You probably saved my life."

He drew breath to speak but she waved her hand and continued. "I don't mean to sound all dramatic, but without the fruit, and the encouragement to search for water, I'm not sure I would have left the beach."

She stared into the sky. "I'm not as brave as I'm pretending to be."

He knew no words of comfort to offer her.

She waved again. "I'll be okay. But, um...you don't...um, you don't have anything to eat now, do you? I thought about trying the fruit here, but it's a little different than what you left at the beach. I was worried it might not be safe. I do have a clue how to take care of myself, you know."

She glanced to the side and mumbled. Taj strained to hear her words then shrugged. Food he could provide. "Jinger, sit. The fruits are safe, though a bit under ripe yet. I have bread."

With a sigh, she sank to the ground, retrieving then drawing the stick she'd carried from the beach across her lap. "Thank you, Taj. I can't think straight when I'm hungry."

Lords. Hearing his name spoken in her melodious voice created an ache deep in his chest. What magic did she possess? What strange control over him? Firming his determination to provide safety, nothing more, he ignored how she affected him and turned toward the trees laden with sweet fruits.

While he searched for the ripest to offer her, she added wood to the fire then settled again with a soft rustle of her wings. Fingers curled around a plump, orange fruit, he paused. Would Ib force her to carry him in flight to the gateway? Ib controlled great magic but even with flight, Taj didn't believe the sorcerer would be able to pass through the gateway of their prison. Hadn't the gateway retreated from her attempts to reach it?

In a rush of anger, Taj crushed the fruit. Ib would never touch Jinger, nor force her to bear a child for sacrifice. Taj didn't know how he, one empty of magic, could protect the beautiful, winged woman. He closed his eyes and with a deep determined breath, repeated his silent vow. No matter the cost, he would discover the means.

Leaving the destroyed fruit for the birds, he wiped his hands with his belt then quickly gathered a selection of fruits and turned back to the clearing.

Jinger stared into the fire, her elbows resting on her knees. Her wings were folded against her back much the way a new-born insect appeared when emerging from the cocoon. A length of one of the thin, nearly transparent wings curled to the side around her hips like a tail. If he hadn't already witnessed her in flight, he would never believe such flimsy wings could lift and support her.

Mindful of startling her again, he stepped on a twig, allowing the sound to announce his return. Still, she gasped and shrank from him as he approached. He knelt at her side and offered the fruits in silent apology. She glanced at him curiously then reached for the largest orb. Watching him with wide, dark eyes, she took a small bite. He imagined the sweet juice filling her mouth then wondered how her lips might taste.

What thoughts were these? To hide his confusion, he lay the rest of the fruits near her then sat and angled so she couldn't see into the bag hanging at his hip. When still a child, he'd been angered to have been born of two powerful, magical beings, yet only contain within himself insignificant skills allowing him to survive. Now, using his simple abilities, he could bring sustenance and comfort to this woman.

Concentrating, he formed his command then reached into the bag for a small round loaf of his favorite bread. Studded with seeds and sweetened with honey, the bread would fill her empty belly.

Her eyes grew wider when he presented the loaf and her tentative smile made him ache to give her more. To distract his thoughts, he grabbed a fruit and took a large bite. Unfortunately, his choice contained a broken pit that had spoiled the fruit from the inside. He grimaced at the bitterness flooding his mouth then spit the bite into the fire. The remainder of the fruit followed to sizzle in the flames.

Jinger made an odd sound, so he glanced sideways at her. She covered her mouth, but the sound continued. Had another of the fruits been rotten? Concerned, he rose to his knees. She moved her hand, pointed at him, and laughed. He froze in wonder at the clear, joyous tones.

"You got a bad piece of fruit, didn't you? You should have seen your face."

Taj drew his eyebrows together. "Why?"

"Your expression after you took that bite. Oh, I'm sorry. Don't be mad that I laughed. It's been a day."

"Yes, a day. And night has come." He had no idea what meaning to make of her odd words.

"No, I mean I've had a bad day. A couple of days really. First the family gathering to remember my cousin. Then I ended up here. I just..." Her words faded and she cast her gaze to the bread in her lap. "I just want to thank you for your kindness. I shouldn't laugh at you, and I apologize." She graced him with a wide grin. "But your expression was pretty funny."

At her trill of renewed laughter, he sat back on his heels. "The flavor surprised me. The pit of that fruit often breaks and spoils the flesh. It is difficult to tell from the outside."

She nodded and held out the loaf. "Would you like some of this bread?"

"No." He softened his denial. "No. My thanks. It is full dark. You will be safe in the clearing. With your permission, I shall gather grasses for a bed."

She jerked and shrank from him again. What had he said? But, when he looked into her eyes, he sensed only an odd curiosity, and something, some heat, he didn't fully understand.

"The grass will soften the ground."

Her eyebrows arched. "I know. I made myself a little nest earlier."

Firelight played over her features, and he cocked his head to watch the flow of light and shadow. She must still fear for her safety. Understandable. Why should she trust him only because he provided fruit and bread? Under the circumstances, he doubted she'd believe much of what he needed to tell her. He needed to gain her trust before explaining Ib and the dangers the sorcerer presented to her.

"I will keep watch while you sleep." The offer should encourage her trust. But the sparkle in her eyes dimmed and a slight downward tilt to her lips made him sad. As though he'd disappointed her.

He had no idea why.

The odd feelings and emotions this winged woman brought to him disrupted his normal calm and acceptance. Though he promised to watch over her, at this moment he needed distance. Distance to clear his mind and organize his thoughts. He rose and glanced around the small glade. "The water is fresh."

"Yes, I know. I tried some earlier."

"I shall return by the time you finish the bread and fruit." Without waiting for her comment and struggling to tame the wild, wild beating of his heart, he strode into the darkness of the surrounding forest.

EIGHT

J inger stared at the spot where Taj disappeared into the darkness and shivered. She wasn't cold and she refused to be frightened, still she huddled closer to the fire and ripped off a hunk of the crusty loaf. At the first bite, she held the piece closer to the fire to examine the soft, chewy interior. The slightly sweet bread tasted freshly baked, no more than a few minutes from the oven. How did he keep an unwrapped loaf so fresh?

Unless... She took another bite and savored the unique flavor. Unless he knew enough of the magic surrounding him to create food. But why hide that ability?

He had his reasons, she supposed, so she'd allow him the privacy of his secret. Besides, it was much more interesting to contemplate how he made her feel.

That was a magic of a different type. The heated flash of desire was easy enough to understand. Taj was a handsome man. She reached for a small fruit and brushed a bit of dirt from the surface before carefully taking a bite. A good-looking man who didn't realize his effect on a woman. At least he didn't preen and posture like other men who'd attempted to gain and keep her attention.

In fact, he'd acted as though he noticed the heat between them but didn't know what to do with the attraction. He'd almost seemed frightened by the rise of desire.

Sorting through her thoughts, Jinger frowned. That left two possibilities. Either he was gay or had been alone his whole life and was innocent of such things. A chuckle shook her shoulders. Like those stories of Tarzan, only instead of great apes, Taj had been raised by a fox.

Oh, good grief. Now she was being silly. She finished the fruit and only half of the bread—just in case he wouldn't or couldn't provide more—then rose to wash her hands and face in the cool stream. After drinking from her cupped hands, she stood next to the fire and glanced around the tiny clearing. For all she knew, she'd scared him off and Taj wouldn't return, leaving her to fend for herself.

Deciding against banking the fire just yet, she added a few small branches and used her foot to clear more stones from an area close to the fire large enough for her to curl up for sleep. Even laying on the ground, this would be a more comfortable bed than her nest of leaves. The fire made a huge difference.

Her muscles ached. The tight pull across her shoulders and between her wings was evidence of how little she'd flown lately. Not that she'd done much digging for stones and dried wood either. She sat with her toes close to the fire and carefully extended her wings.

Rolling her shoulders then stretching and contracting her muscles eased some of the ache. She'd still be sore tomorrow. If the portal—the gateway—returned, she'd need to attempt to reach it no matter how her body felt. And if the way home remained hidden, she'd still need to fly to strengthen those muscles to be ready whenever the gateway did open.

The stinging in her eyes surprised her. Even more startling—she didn't know if her tears were because she might have to remain here or that she'd be leaving. She rubbed the dampness away with the side of her finger. Silly fairy. Getting emotional over some guy she might never see again.

She needed to focus. Focus on survival and getting home.

She glanced up and across the small fire. He stood there. Her gasp was loud in the silent night, and she scrambled to her feet. "Don't scare me like that."

Taj remained frozen, watching her. He cleared his throat. "How do you fare?"

"How do I fare? Stupid question, Taj. How do I fare?" Jinger slapped her arms to her sides then fisted her hands at her hips. "What do you think? I don't know where I am. I don't know how or even if I can ever get home. I don't know you. I don't know what's out there in the dark, what might want to eat me. Hells bells, I'm great. Just great." She paused and softened her tone. "So, how are you?"

His eyes grew wide but to his credit, he didn't flinch or back away from her outburst. He held out a bulky armload of long grasses wrapped in a dark blanket. "I beg your pardon. I have returned with bedding."

Jinger tilted her head. Where did he get that blanket?

More of his hidden magic? She took a deep breath. "I'm sorry, too. You didn't deserve that tirade. I guess everything that's happened the past couple days finally got to me. So, thank you. For helping me."

Taj took one step to the side and nodded an acknowledgment. He glanced around the tiny glen.

"I cleared the stones from here. Is it too close to the fire?"

He moved to where she pointed, shook his head, and knelt to unroll the blanket. After fluffing the vegetation, he spread out the blanket, and stood. "Do not roll toward the fire."

A man of few words. Finding out more about him, and this world she'd landed in, might be interesting. Jinger believed herself up to the challenge. In fact, she looked forward to it. "Will you tell me more about your world?"

A myriad of possibilities danced through his eyes. Or maybe the flicker of firelight created false emotions. Unsure, Jinger sat on her makeshift bed and glanced up at an expression so bland as to be carved from stone. Intriguing.

He shook his head as if clearing his thoughts. A few long strides carried him to the thick tree trunk where she'd rested earlier. He sat on her pile of leaves with his back against the rough bark. "Daylight will be soon enough for talking. Rest. I will watch from here."

Jinger shifted so when she lay down she'd be able to keep her eyes on him. Nightshade would urge her to use care and to think more than twice before so easily accepting Taj's help. While the dream man had promised safety, this man was here. Just his presence chased away her fears. Perhaps it was only because this was his land, and she was the stranger.

Trusting this man was right and her trust ran deep. She didn't care why. She was simply glad he was there. Watching.

Both the hard ground and the fact she'd only slept with her wings once before made finding a comfortable position a challenge. Through every toss and turn, every grumble and attempt at fluffing the pile of grass, she sensed Taj's gaze on her.

And she didn't mind a bit.

Once the woman, Jinger, finally slept, Taj stretched his cramped muscles then whistled softly. His mother had remained nearby and he had questions only the firefox could answer. The small animal approached and rested one paw on his thigh, glancing from him to the woman and back. He sensed her smile.

To not disturb the sleeper, he kept his voice soft. "Ib knows she is here." Not a question, a fact.

Ommi gave a single nod.

"He called her here?"

A vision formed behind his eyes. The sorcerer had been surprised at her appearance. Taj took a deep breath. That surprise wouldn't slow Ib in taking what he wanted, or in doing what he wished with Jinger.

The vision ended when Ib entered his workroom with a thick, ancient book. What did he plan this time? Taj gazed into the blue-black sky. It mattered not how Ib executed his plan, unless the female died, the result had always been the same. Now he would attempt to either steal the magic from Jinger or force her to bear a child. Either way, he would dispose of her when he had accomplished his desire.

In the past Taj had been forced to bear witness to Ib's efforts to increase his magic, to the burning and destruction of life. The sorcerer never gained enough, was never satisfied. Like a sickness, Ib craved more and more.

Ommi nudged Taj's clenched fist with her cool nose, then when he opened his fingers, slid her head under his palm. Absently, he rubbed the silky fur between the firefox's ears, the movement giving him comfort as well. "Have we time to prepare?"

The negative response sank to heavy dread in his belly. In the past he'd felt sorrow for those Ib used, but little more beyond the helplessness that haunted his dreams. The thought of the sorcerer touching this winged woman, of causing her pain then stealing her joy and her life churned like acid through his veins.

He jerked his gaze to Ommi and stared into her glittering black eyes. "So soon? I had hoped... no, I will." Taj didn't know how the firefox seemed to understand Ib's plans and machinations. He'd often wondered what his mother might have taken from the sorcerer before he transformed her. Whatever that magic or charm may have been, she'd been able to protect Taj, even before his father banished him from the castle.

Now Taj charged himself with the protection of another. First, she must come to trust him, else any words he may say against Ib would lose urgency. He'd provided food and comfort for her. Watched over her now. Surely those things would tally in his favor.

Ommi gave a soft yip, nuzzled his palm then bounded into the forest. Ib would know his mother had encountered the winged woman, but Taj agreed it would be best if she were nowhere near should Ib attempt to manipulate Jinger. The firefox's presence enraged the sorcerer.

As did his own existence. In days past, whenever Taj had encountered Ib, the sorcerer's anger and disappointment would burn over Taj's skin and fill his veins with shame. As though he had been at fault for thwarting Ib's desires. Long years of such suffering finally ended when Taj realized the folly and falsehood of those thoughts and no longer hoped to please his father.

Despite Jinger's claims she could care for herself, under the sorcerer's power she would be as fragile as a midnight flower's bloom. An easy conquest. Unable to bear the thought, Taj eased to his feet and retreated into the forest to pace the circumference of the clearing. His presence would anger Ib, but Taj couldn't leave Jinger alone. He wouldn't leave her side. That much, at least, he knew deep in his heart.

He jerked to a stop and rubbed his chest. In his heart? What power did the dainty woman have to make his chest ache, to freeze the breath in his lungs? Make his arms strain with the need to hold, to comfort? Shaking his head did nothing to clear his thoughts.

When he'd reached the age of a man, Ib had sent him dreams and visions of women, of lust and desire, of power and pleasure. He understood the physical responses of his body, knew of the pleasures between male and female. Thankfully, his father had tired of the game long ago, and now seldom filled Taj's dreams with ghoulish images of pain-laced threats. He'd learned to defend himself against the dreams—most of the time.

Setting himself in motion, Taj continued prowling under the trees. Simply gazing at the woman caused those pleasure feelings to caress him while awake. This was a fact. A fact he could store away and deal with at another time. He must be aware of his expressions, careful of how he reacted to Jinger, for there was no doubt Ib would know and punish them both.

The punishment he would bear willingly to keep Jinger from harm.

Calm distance was imperative. While Taj needed to remain close to her, he would not allow his emotions to escape his tight control. When sunlight again filled the clearing, he would tell her of the danger. He'd convince her to return to his home, for safety only. Perhaps together they could discover how to prevent her from falling under Ib's control.

Plan set firmly in his mind, Taj returned to the edge of the clearing and sat against a rough-barked tree, resting his forearms on his bent knees. Trying to keep his gaze averted proved impossible. Giving in to the need simply to look at Jinger, he sighed and watched her sleep.

The night grew darker as time passed. The fire collapsed into glowing embers. Still he watched. And thought. When the pale light of the rising sun chased the darkness further under the canopy of leaves, Taj rubbed his gritty eyes and stood. He cupped his hands under a trickle of water from the rocks then scrubbed his cold, wet hands over his face. He was no closer to solutions or understanding.

Let the day bring what it would.

CHAPTER
NINE

Ib hovered over a massive stone cauldron centered in his workroom. Concentrating power into the creation of the cauldron then filling it with sea water had taken the night. Though the circular room had no windows, he sensed the rising of the sun and glanced at his hands. His power lay dormant, overused and cold. A day in the tower would regenerate his command over his abilities and allow him to complete the spell work.

Although not completely. To finalize the conjuration he must first plant a child within the woman then bring her to the cauldron. According to the text, once he spoke the incantation, water would rise from the cauldron to cover the woman, bringing the child to birth within a matter of days. A second spell would rapidly grow the child to an age where he could harvest its magic.

Then he would free himself of this prison and absorb power from other worlds. Tendrils of pleasure quivered along his muscles.

He rubbed his hands together and the friction warmed his fingers. Enough time for that pleasure once he had taken the woman. A deep chuckle rumbled in his chest. Ages had passed since the last time he sought to woo a woman, and he looked forward to stealing the affections of this one from his son.

Ha. His son. The faded scripts claimed the spells of sacrifice would be successful only if the child was born of a willing union. His son would be expecting him to appear this day to steal away the woman. Ib snorted. So he would wait a day or two before beginning his seduction. Ib smiled, closed the ancient text and placed the volume in a deep crevasse in the wall. Stone oozed over the hiding place. Ah yes, both his son's apprehension and his own anticipation would serve his magic well.

Weariness dragged at his muscles. His fingertips had turned coal dark. He'd never before encountered magic that sapped his strength so completely. Once free, the world of the cauldron's spell would be the first he visited. Imagining the power to be gained there, he paced from the workroom.

In the great hall, he paused before the tapestry. His incompetent son remained near the winged woman. Good. Let them await his pleasure. He would watch and time his introduction to the most opportune moment.

At the bottom of a steep, winding stone staircase he rubbed the fingers of one hand against his palm. Finally a bit of warmth seeped into the tips, enough to call his servant.

"You will guard this doorway. None shall pass until I return. Do you understand?"

A single nod. The creature pulled a long knife from a ragged leather scabbard, sat cross-legged in the doorway and rested the blade across its knobby knees.

Ib turned toward the stairs and drew a deep breath.

He didn't fear intrusion—except from the firefox. He let a small smile stretch his lips. She'd remain in the forest to assist in building useless defenses against him. The visualization of her destruction drew him up the steps and gave him energy to climb a portion of the way to the tower room.

Exhausted, straining muscles slowed his steps. The faint flickers of his remaining magic faded until he was forced to crawl up the final worn steps.

Drawing deep, harsh breaths he struggled to the center of the room and onto a low, ornately decorated bed. His head resting on a thick, soft pillow, he sighed and spread his arms to lay with his palms facing the faceted, clear crystal roof. Light from the rising sun cascaded rainbows about the triangular room.

Ib lifted his head to watch the rainbow of light concentrate at two points on the smooth plastered wall. Blazing white-hot light slithered across the floor and up the foot of the bed. He adjusted the position of his hands. At a whispered command thick leather bands trapped his wrists and ankles to hold him in place.

Blinding light filled his palms. Shards of crystal agony pierced his hands, sent fire to boil the blood in his veins. He arched from the bed. Twisted against the bindings. Screamed until the small room filled with echoing sound. With a grunt he collapsed against the mattress, writhing, fingers stiff and curled toward the light.

The pain lessened and he knew he hadn't been given enough. Hadn't taken enough power from the sun. More. He must have more. This day would not be enough. Nor two days. He needed to be filled. Overfilled. Overflowing with power to make the ancient magic succeed.

Ib took a deep breath and spoke a strained command.

The crystal roof shifted to follow the movement of the sun, maintaining a constant stream of power-filled light to his hands.

Pain sliced through him as though knives scored his veins with each beat of his heart. He screamed, collapsed panting, his smile a grimace of bared teeth.

Power was worth any pain.

Consciousness jolted through Ib bringing him fully awake. Testing his senses he detected the last faint bit of sunlight sparkling through the crystals above him. No straps bound him to the bed but the dusty remains of leather tickled his wrists and ankles. An odd scent teased his nostrils, an odor similar to burned hair. He opened his eyes and turned his head to one side.

Coal dark shadows covered the walls with a pattern of remembered flames. Layer upon layer of char encased the room. The signs of success were good. The gathering should have been successful, but he waited before testing his power. On rare occasions he'd been denied the sun's gift.

He lifted and squinted at one hand. Soot caked the lines crossing his palm. Good. Another sign. He made a fist. Surprise arched his eyebrows. Staring at the ends of his fingers, he twisted his fist back and forth. Laughter burst from his parched throat. The sun, magnified by the crystals, had granted him much more than he imagined. In transferring power to him, the fire's magic had burned away his fingernails.

A small sacrifice to those who had shown him the way of magic. Of fire. He bowed his head, offering a miniscule portion of gratitude. For how much thanking did a soon to be dead god need? In truth, it was he, Ib, who now held the power, the skill, and the resources to bring others fully under his control. To use them to discover the way to leave this cursed world.

Ib lifted his head, scraped the tender tips of his fingers through his hair and took a deep breath. How long? How many times had the sun risen, flowing the heat and flame of magic over him? At least three days, for he'd experienced a double day of gathering before—a snarl curled his lip—before the djinn foiled his plans by bearing him a weakling son who controlled no magic. That gathering, however, had given him the power to transform the bitch.

This time he would finally destroy the firefox and her son. Then he'd take the winged woman. Using the spells from the ancient book, she'd swiftly grow him a new sacrifice. He'd escape this dismal, green world and find glory where there were men to worship him.

Nodding, he rose. Waves of dizziness swirled through him and he fell back on the bed, throwing ash into the air. He must take care for a short while to allow the burning within him to settle. Uncontrolled, those fires could bring him to weakness as rapidly as he planned to discover a new path to freedom. Grumbling against the forced slow movements, Ib stood, took a short step and balanced himself with an arm outstretched against the wall. Fire's truth, he felt weaker than he'd been when he'd entered the chamber.

By that same truth, limiting his expenditure of power for a short time, he would be stronger than ever before.

The plans he'd dreamed while caught in the gathering would come to fruition. Today patience would serve him well.

He took the stairs slowly, steadying his balance on each step. Halfway down the steep, winding staircase, he jerked one finger toward the wall. An instant later his dull, plodding servant appeared from a recess. "You have done well guarding the tower. Now, go place a table and the cushioned chair before the tapestry. I would see how the lovely visitor to this world fares. Bring me food and drink. Do you understand my instructions?"

A jerking twitch served as the creature's affirmative answer. Ib waved the servant away and continued his laborious journey from the tower.

CHAPTER
TEN

T he rising sun's light filtered through the heavy tree canopy and sparkled across the spring's softly bubbling surface. Jinger pulled the blanket over her shoulder only to have the comforting warmth slip away with the movement of her wing. She'd fought that same issue all night and repeated attempts at magically hiding or even reducing the size of her wings continued to have no effect. True fairies must have other ways to be comfortable enough to sleep. Maybe she simply needed to adjust and become accustomed to this part of her.

She hadn't slept much, waking often to unrecognizable night sounds. She really did dislike camping. Nature was okay, as long as she could go home and sleep in her own bed.

Taj hadn't slept either. Every time she woke, he'd been watching her, although his gaze skittered from hers when she opened her eyes. She sensed the moment he left the clearing to pace in circles through the trees. His actions made her feel strangely safe and protected.

She enjoyed how he made her feel, all tingly and pleasantly out of sorts. If her focus wasn't on exploring this world to find her way home, she'd focus on him. Explore him. Every inch. Her face heated and she chuckled.

Then sobered to berate herself. She needed to keep her mind on the important things—survival, finding a portal or a way to create one, and remembering details to tell the Alastriona so no others would fall into this world without a way home.

Pressing her lips together, Jinger wrestled her way out of the tangle of the blanket and her wings and sat. Despite her curious nature, she really wasn't cut out for actually exploring new worlds. Still, she'd make the best of the situation and her time here.

With Taj.

Summoned by her thoughts, he appeared at the far side of the spring, arms laden with fruit and bread. Her stomach rumbled and she cast her gaze to the sky. He'd think all she did was eat. Flying used more energy than she normally expended, so fueling up was a good idea. She offered him a smile and gestured him closer. "I won't bite."

Taj's brows drew together and one side of his mouth tilted in question.

Jinger mentally chastised herself. He took what she said far too literally. She gestured again. "Come closer, Taj. That's all I mean. I'm happy you brought breakfast. Won't you eat with me?"

His expression cleared. He skirted the spring and sat before resting his burden on the blanket Jinger spread between them. He handed her a small, bright red fruit. "Eat. We must leave this clearing for a safer location."

"Leave? Why? Safer? Are we in danger from wild animals?" Clasping the fruit to her chest, she peered into the forest.

"Danger, yes. Animals, no. Eat."

Great. He was even less talkative this morning. Determined to find a way to draw him out, Jinger followed his example and peeled her fruit in silence. She hadn't had much experience with uncommunicative people. With her family, there were few opportunities, and even her quieter cousins were still gregarious. How to get Taj to say more than a few words at a time might be difficult, but she was up to that challenge.

"So, Taj, what is the danger if I stay here? I mean, this is a quiet glade. I have clear water, and although there isn't much shelter if the weather changes, I'll be fine."

Taj took a deep breath and closed his eyes. Jinger grinned down at her fruit. She definitely recognized his expression as exasperation with her chatter. She got that a lot. Maybe he'd start talking just to keep her quiet. She continued to fill the silence. "What kind of fruit did you bring me this morning? Where did the bread come from? Oh, is that where we need to go for safety? Where you live? I'm not sure your home will be any safer for me."

Oops. That might not have been the right thing to say. She kept her head lowered and peeked at him through her lashes. The tingles of awareness caused by simply sitting next to him made her rethink her statement. He might not be safe with her. In fact, she rather hoped not. First, though, she had things she needed to accomplish that day.

"Jinger." Taj's serious tone drew her attention. "Yes, you'll be safer at my home. There is fresh water and protection from the weather. Rain falls nearly every day.

At times the storms rage, twisting trees and destroying the forest." He started to say more, but pressed his lips into a tight, flat line.

"What else? What are you keeping from me? If you don't tell me, I won't go. Simple as that." She crossed her arms and glared at him. Her lips twitched at his resigned expression. "Besides, I need to look for the portal today, the gateway. If it's still in the sky, I should practice flying. I haven't used my wings much lately so I need to strengthen my muscles."

"I doubt the gateway will return."

"You're sure?" The heavy weight of fear settled deep in her belly and she set the fruit aside.

"A second opening of the gateway in the same location is rare. I've only seen it happen," he paused and she watched his eyes move as he searched his memory. "Perhaps twice. An opening so soon after the one a day ago is possible. With little or no warning, being at the right place isn't an easy task."

"Warning? So there is a way to know a gateway is opening?" That would be a good start. Maybe if she found her way to another place, another world, she would be able to create a portal home. Hope warred with fear and she forced herself to calm her breathing to contain both emotions.

Taj shook his head. "Not a warning, more of a feeling. Here." He touched the center of his chest. "A vibration?"

She stared at how his long fingers splayed over his tanned skin. His palm cupped slightly, drawing his fingertips across his chest. At her side, her fingers mimicked the movement. If she didn't touch him soon... No, keep on track. Focus. Patting the ground at her side, she retrieved the fruit, finished removing the peel, and took a bite. The juice would bring moisture back to her mouth.

After she swallowed and cleared her throat, she nodded. "I understand. The energy of my portals is a combination of magic and electricity. It tingles."

"Electricity?" Curiosity sparked in his dark eyes.

He didn't know about electricity? Well, probably not. So far she hadn't seen anything resembling technology in the forest.

Taj surged to his feet. "Eat. We must go. We will return to the beach first. Then go to the place of safety."

"But—."

He smiled and the world brightened. The colors of leaves and undergrowth, the flowers and fruits intensified. The light blue sky shimmered. This manifestation was more than just her attraction to him. The thought faded and she sighed. His smile had created a single dimple in one cheek. She loved dimples.

He held his hand out to her. "I understand your concerns and what you believe you must do, just as I know this land. Might we compromise? Do you remember the way to the sea?"

Silent, she pointed, hoping she'd chosen the correct direction.

"Good. Fly there now and I will join you on the beach. If the gateway returns, we'll know. If not, the trek home won't take long." As though smiling was unusual, his lips flattened. "Then you will tell me more of this electricity."

At least he was talking more. Jinger stood and tipped forward a bit. Darn wings, how long was it going to take for her to become accustomed to them? She chuckled. "I don't want to leave you behind. I can fly pretty fast."

His smile returned. "And I know the pathways of the forest."

"Oh, a challenge? A race, then?"

"A race, Jinger."

She adored how he said her name, lingering over the syllables as though he was tasting them. Blinking, she glanced toward the sky. What a silly, trite, and romantic thought. She needed to get her head out of the clouds and her body into them. Her muscles protested but lifted her easily from the ground. She hovered over the trees at the edge of the clearing and waved.

"I'll be waiting for you at the beach, Taj."

Taj planted his feet firmly in the white sand, shaded his eyes with his hand and waited for Jinger. He'd followed her progress to assure she didn't lose herself, then raced ahead to be waiting for her on the beach. Before Ib had transformed his mother, they'd raced together and played hiding games. He'd won the races then, too, but suspected only because his mother slowed on purpose. The hiding games had served him well as practice for avoiding Ib.

Taj had gauged Jinger's earlier speed with the position of the morning sun. Worry was tightening to a knot in his belly. She should have arrived by now. Unless somehow she—no, there, low over the trees. Flying backward?

He chuckled then frowned at the unusual sound. In less than a day she'd made him both smile and laugh. He'd done neither for so long he believed he no longer had the capacity. These uncommon reactions made him relax his vigilance. Lowering his guard was dangerous when, at any moment, Ib might manifest a way to steal the woman away.

Despite his misgivings, Taj couldn't keep the smile from his face as he watched Jinger rise and lower over the trees. She'd been confident she would reach the sands first, so he knew she was looking for him. The thought centered in his chest and he rubbed absently at a spot above his heart. Anticipating the surprise on her face when she finally turned and spotted him, Taj planted both hands on his hips and waited.

He'd taken only four breaths before she noticed and sped toward him. Sunlight sparkled off her rapidly beating, translucent wings, surrounding her with a shimmering halo. She waved, tilting her body, then wavered as though off balance. The speed of her advance sent Taj back a step.

Jinger flung both arms in front of her. Her eyes grew wide. She ducked her head. Twisted her body. Shouted a warning and slammed into Taj.

Without thought, he wrapped his arms around her to cushion her fall. The warm sand turned brutally hard against his back and scraped a patch raw on one shoulder. Jinger landed heavily on top of him. Breath burst from his lungs.

Hands against his shoulders, she pressed until his grasp at her waist loosened then she straightened her arms and looked down on him with wide eyes. "Why didn't you move?"

She didn't appear damaged, but he asked, "Are you hurt?"

"What? Oh, no. Well, maybe rumpled a bit. I couldn't slow down. I told you I need practice." She patted his shoulder. "I didn't hurt you, did I? I really didn't mean to bowl you over like that."

Tiny grains of sand dug into the raw spot on his back, but hurt? No. Her pats turned to soft stroking. Aware of the places where her body pressed against his, he shifted.

"I should get off you, shouldn't I?"

Her weight a delight, Taj shifted again and caught back a groan as she settled against him. The open beach was dangerous, and with her, like this, he was far from alert to anything but her. What harm could there be in a few moments like this? He flexed his fingers against her hips.

She caught her breath. "I think I'd better."

He offered no resistance, rising himself as soon as she slid from him. A strange disappointment settled over him and he covered the reaction with a stern expression. "You will need to be more careful."

"I couldn't slow down fast enough. My muscles were aching so I got a little out of control. I guess I need more exercise." She glanced sideways at him. "And more practice."

His smile escaped before he could call it back. "Yes, you do. We shall walk now and you will fly when you're rested. My shelter isn't far. We can stop at the fishing pool to obtain our next meal." He paused as a possibility entered his mind. He wasn't accustomed to taking another person into account. "Unless you don't care for fish."

She shrugged. "I haven't had it too often, but I can't

say I don't like it. I'm pretty sure I can't clean a fish, though."

"I could hunt." He'd hunt food for her even though he disliked the flavor of game. A wild hen perhaps. For Jinger, for her smile, he'd be willing—.

"Oh, no. That's not necessary. Fishing will be easier. Let's just get through today and see what happens after that." A grin lit her face. "As long as you do the cooking."

With a nod, Taj forced himself to walk forward, leaving Jinger to follow. Distance. He needed distance from the allure of the woman. In the past his dreams had been caught under the spell of Ib's torment when it pleased the sorcerer. He supposed his father found pleasure by inflicting him with sensual dreams. Until this day, Taj hadn't given the lingering physical effects much thought. Until Jinger.

The odd lassitude under his jittery skin confused him. His responses to the dreams had been predictable and pleasant, for the length of time they'd lasted. Nothing more, nothing less. Yet now, after the softness of her body pressed to his, he ached to return to the warm sands to discover more. Of her smooth, pale skin. Of the touch of her wings against his hand, his chest.

He shook his head and stumbled in a dip in the sand. Becoming distracted by thoughts of Jinger, distracted by anything, would lead to disaster. He needed to remain aware of their surroundings, alert to any indication Ib may be near. Once they reached the protection of his home, he could relax.

But first, he'd promised Jinger fish for their meal.

The tide hole held a plenitude of creatures ideal for eating, but if they delayed the tide would return and allow the fish to escape. He quickened his pace.

A breeze cooled his left side so he glanced toward the open sea. Jinger floated next to him, her wings moving lazily, disturbing the air. She grinned. "You're walking so fast, I couldn't keep up. Besides, this should strengthen my muscles without straining too much. How much further?"

A rough circle of stones and cast off shells surrounded the pool only a short distance ahead of them. A distance he could cover in the time of seven deep breaths. "A few moments only."

"Oh, Is it where those rocks are?" At his nod, she fluttered her wings to rise higher and shaded her eyes with her hand. "Is it okay if I fly ahead and meet you there?"

She wouldn't be out of his sight. There had been no signs indicating Ib's manipulation. Taj relaxed his shoulder. The sorcerer would remain in his castle for at least another day. Despite how Ib treated those he brought to this land, he was a creature of habit.

Taj would have a day, perhaps two, without the need for excessive worry. Should Ib begin sooner, Ommi would make Taj aware, so he nodded. "Yes."

"See you there." With a wide flap of her colorful wings, she bounced through the air. Transfixed by the sight of her flowing hair and the tight material encasing her lower body, Taj slowed. Stopped. Stared at the beautiful distraction until she reached the tide pool.

He quickened his pace, pushing his feet deep into the loose sand. Best catch their meal then take Jinger to safety. He had no other experiences to compare to this day, and realized he shouldn't depend on Ib's past behaviors.

Jinger sat on a flat rock, swishing her toes through the water. Sitting beside her, he leaned to one side and tugged a long sharpened stick from under the rocks. He rested the spear across his lap and studied the lazy movements of the fish. The creatures were slow this morning. It wouldn't take long to spear a large enough fish to provide their meals for a day or two.

"While I fish, would you gather some of the shelled sea dwellers from the underwater crevices in the rocks?"

"Is there something I can carry them in?"

Without thought, he ripped off his vest and handed it to her. "This will work when you fold it into a pouch."

"Um, okay." She fumbled with the material but was unable to fashion a suitable bag.

She was very appealing when frustration colored her face a faint pink. He took pity on her, retrieved his vest and rapidly twisted it to a carrying pouch. The smile she gave him after she studied the simple folds was worth much more than he, or his actions, could ever imagine.

Fluttering her wings to keep the tails out of the water, she bent to her task. Taj moved to stand in the center of the pool, but kept the spear resting against his shoulder, watching her. He couldn't turn away from the enticing sight. Nor did he understand why he felt so compelled to study her movements and memorize the lines of her body.

"Looks like we'll only have shellfish for lunch." The tones of her low chuckle sent shards of longing low in his belly. "Or do I need to do the fishing, too?"

With a grunt to acknowledge the accuracy of her statement, Taj turned his back to her and hefted the spear. Tiny fish darted around his feet, nibbling at his ankles. Ignoring the tickles, he focused on a larger, fat fish with sparkling rainbow colored scales. Reaching the flesh through those scales was difficult, but the mild flavor when roasted was his favorite meal.

The fish darted through the warm water staying on the opposite side of the pool from where Jinger splashed. Barely rippling the surface of the water, Taj slid one foot forward. His slow, precise movements cornered the wary creature. One sharp jab and he lifted the heavy fish on the end of his spear. He turned to Jinger with a satisfied grin.

Eyes wide, she set her bundle of shellfish on a stone and clapped her hands. "That fish is huge. Amazing."

Her praise heated the back of his neck and he cleared his throat. "It will provide meat for two or three days."

"Especially with these." She patted her bundle. "I'm not sure what these are, clams, oysters, or something I've never seen before, but I'm sure you know how to make them taste good."

Not trusting his voice, Taj gave a sharp nod and stepped from the pond. He slid the fish to the sand and returned the spear to its hiding place. "Wait here a moment."

He jogged to the tree line and tugged a length of thick vine from the base of a tall tree. When he turned back, he paused. Jinger stood beside his catch, eying the final, dying flaps of the fish's tail. Sunlight highlighted the golden strands in her hair, brightened the colors of the wings she'd folded against her back. With the halo of light surrounding her, he couldn't see her expression. Or tell if she even looked at him.

Yes, he knew. She watched him. The touch of her gaze was as though she stroked her fingers over his chest. Uncomfortable, yet filled with an odd rush of power, he returned to kneel by the fish. With an economy of movement, he strung the fish on the vine to carry it more easily, and stood to offer Jinger his hand.

He stared at his fingers. What was this? What was he doing? Before he pulled back his hand, she touched her fingertips to his palm, then pressed her palm to his and entwined their fingers.

CHAPTER
ELEVEN

Delighting in the strong warmth of Taj's hand, Jinger grinned at his stunned expression. Obviously he'd never held hands with anyone. She was his first. Her heart beat rapidly. How many other firsts might she experience with him?

Reality made her smile falter. He said his mother was a fox, a magical fox, but an animal, nonetheless. Jinger didn't understand the how or why, but had Taj been raised without human contact? Hadn't he ever had a parent hold his hand? The tickle of impending tears made her wiggle her nose. Her clan was large, accepting and sometimes overly demonstrative in their love. She couldn't imagine having no one.

The thought she could be someone for him skimmed through her body, intensifying her awareness of the man.

"We should leave the beach." Fish swinging from the vine rope, Taj gestured away from the tide pool.

"Lead on, McDuff."

He tilted his head. "What?"

"Sorry. Lead the way, Taj. Do we have far to go?" Her stomach rumbled and she pressed the bag of shellfish against the sound. "Oops, looks like I worked off breakfast already."

Taj's chuckle was low and seemed to surprise him. He slung the fish over his shoulder and tugged on her hand, guiding her across the sand and into the thick forest.

Remembering her lessons with the Alastriona, she attempted to pick out easily identifiable trees and small rock outcropping she could use later as reference to retrace her steps to the beach. Taj's warm hand, his broad back when he angled to walk in front of her, even just discovering the wonders of this new world, distracted her focus. She shrugged off the niggle of concern. She could always fly above the treetops and find her way. This new freedom of flight was delightful in many ways.

As she followed Taj's sure steps, she attempted once again to call on the magic to hide her wings. The best she was able to accomplish was tucking them closer to her body.

Truthfully, she was a bit uncomfortable. The breadth and height of her wings teased her concept of the space she occupied. When she thought she'd ducked far enough to avoid a low hanging branch, the rounded top of her wings snagged against the leaves. Or the narrow tails caught on bushes and stones. She huffed and pulled against Taj's loose grip to turn and release a wing. Again.

"Jinger? We're nearly there."

"No wonder fairies are usually tiny," she grumbled under her breath. "Then they fit." Free, she faced him and rearranged the awkward bundle in her arms.

He offered a hesitant smile that didn't quite chase the doubt from his dark eyes. The crease between his brows tempted her to touch and smooth away his concerns. Then discover more. Pressing her damp palm against her thigh, she nodded. She wanted his man, but there were more important issues for her to face. She nodded a second time and he turned back to the path.

True to his word, the twisting path gradually widened, opening near the edge of an oval cerulean pool. A gentle flow of water fell from an outcropping to dance across rounded boulders before bubbling into the pool. A small building constructed of stone and wood stood on the near side of the falls. Created from branches and leaves, the roof sloped low to protect the doorway and a single window.

To the other side of the building, a raised circle built of stone held the charred remains of a fire. A woven vine hammock swayed between two trees. Jinger grinned at the sturdy tree stump with a bowl and cup next to the hammock. All Taj needed was a big screen. She'd be sure to ask for a movie instead of a sporting event for their snuggling time.

Snuggling with him in the gentle sway of the hammock held more appeal than it should but she didn't care.

Taj watched her, waiting no doubt, for her reaction. She smiled to ease the tension holding his shoulders stiff and square. "You live here? It's beautiful."

Silent, he took the shellfish from her and lay them and his catch next to the cook fire. "If you wish—"

A sharp yip from the top of the waterfall jerked his gaze from her. The firefox leapt from the rocks and landed before the cabin door. Taj knelt before her, listening to her growls and yips. The soft rumble of his one-sided conversation drew Jinger closer. Curious, she tapped one foot and wished she understood fox.

Even without understanding, she turned to study the tiny pond to give Taj and his mother privacy. Where she'd spent the previous night was a beautiful glen, but this area, with the song of water splashing over rocks and the quiet chattering of birds, rivaled Faerie. Taking a step closer to the swirling water, she stared at the ripples of her reflection.

Other than her wings behind her head, she didn't look different. She gave a soft snort. How could she tell anything when her reflection wasn't steady? Rather like the beat of her heart when she looked at Taj.

She cast a quick glance toward the hut. Taj nodded then entered the dwelling. The firefox strolled to her side and sat. Resting one paw on Jinger's foot, she watched the water. A gentle thought like the whisper of a voice passed through Jinger's mind. She wrinkled her nose in confusion and the fox gave a sharp yip. Sensing the animal expected something from her, she focused again on the pool.

The reflection of the fox cleared then the water calmed to mirror smoothness around them. Keeping her lip tucked between her teeth to contain the rush of her curious questions, Jinger glanced from the water to the fox. The red and white head bobbed before the firefox indicated the water with her black muzzle.

Behind their reflections a series of pictures formed, flashing rapidly from one to another. A beautiful woman with flame-red hair, a shadowed figure, a baby, the sun, darkness. She sensed pain, joy, horror, seduction, tears, laughter.

Too fast. She couldn't follow the progression if there was one. The fox was trying to tell her something, but she didn't understand. Even concentrating and leaning closer slowed the images minutely, but not enough. Finally she sat, wrapped her arms around her bent legs and rested her forehead on her knees.

"I'm sorry. I know you want to show me, but I don't understand. I've always caught on slower than everyone else. It's difficult to concentrate. Because I'm half-fairy, my thoughts can be scattered. Sometimes I don't take things as seriously as I should." Unbidden, the thought her excuse was just that, an excuse, jolted her upright. Scattered thoughts were a part of her, like her wings. She needed to stop making excuses for who she was.

Comfort flowed through her reminding her of her mother's love. Tears burned her eyes. She dared not cry and let the doubt and fear of her situation take hold. She pressed her fingertips against her closed lids and drew a deep breath. Ommi's cold nose nudged her arm so she hugged the fox to her side and accepted the offered comfort. "Thanks. I'll try to do better."

A soft, alto voice filled her mind. "In time, young one. What you need comes in time."

Jinger dipped her head to peer into the fox's intelligent dark eyes. "Was that you in my head?"

Ommi blinked, yipped then eased from her side. Seconds later the firefox leapt from rock to rock up the side of the outcropping and bounded into the sky. After circling twice above the clearing, she disappeared.

Before Jinger returned to listing her faults, another presence moved to her side and sat. Stashing away her doubts, she smiled at Taj. He held a length of cloth in a loose bundle on his lap. Woven in shades of green as numerous as the trees and plants surrounding the clearing, the fabric looked silky and soft. Her fingers twitched with the need to discover the texture. Then move on to explore the smooth, firm chest of the man.

Taj cleared his throat. "I apologize for not considering your needs."

Heat flared along her veins to center with an odd tingling sensation low in her belly. Her face felt hot. He couldn't read her mind, could he?

His words halting, he continued. "Ommi created this for you. She says your clothing is stiff and dirty from the sea water. She says... you should bathe. I have prepared the space. While you... while..." The movement of his adam's apple when he swallowed fascinated her. As did the tint of bronze across his high cheekbones when he continued.

"Bathe. Yes, while you bathe, I'll prepare a meal. Come." He rose with fluid grace and held out his hand for her.

"A bath would be wonderful. But I should help with the meal."

A grin pulled at one side of his full lips. "You gathered the shellfish. It's enough."

Even with his help she felt awkward and clumsy as she rose but the feelings faded when he kept her hand in his to lead her toward the hut. Once they passed through the low doorway, the room opened into a larger space than seemed possible from the outside appearance. A bank of square openings across the back of the building filled the space with light and highlighted the sparse furnishings. A single chair, some shelves, a wide table, and an even wider bed.

Coverings and cushions similar in appearance to the

cloth Taj held crumpled in his hand were scattered across the surface. A curtain of fine, colorful netting surrounded three sides of the bed while a thick loop of rope held the fourth panel open. Even though the luxury called to her, she turned her back on the bed that belonged in a sultan's haram rather than in a simple stone lodge.

The bathing space she now faced was spectacular as well. Fist sized, rounded stones had been mortared together to form a deep tub. At one end the stones fit over an open grate where the remnants of a fire smoldered in glowing coals. Faint whisps of steam rose from the clear, hot water.

Hot water would soothe her aching muscles. All she needed were a few jets to make the water pulsate and swirl. Still, this was more, so much more than she'd ever imagine in Taj's primitive world. She stepped closer and dipped her hand in the water. The perfect temperature. "This is wonderful."

Taj dragged the chair closer, draped the fabric over the back then pulled a length of rougher material from a hidden storage space and piled it on the chair. The tips of his ears flushed deep red. "I have no need of privacy here, so there is no door."

"Oh, well, I..." Privacy wasn't on the top of her list at that moment. Once she settled into the water, she had a feeling she wouldn't care about much of anything for a while. With that bed, being prim and proper around Taj certainly wasn't an idea she planned to pursue. Pursuing him, on the other hand, might be fun.

"I will remain outside." He backed toward the door, froze then moved to a low shelf under one of the windows. "Ommi claims you will appreciate these petals in your bath." He dropped a handful of light blue blossoms in her palm and dashed away as though chased by a frightful monster.

Well, she was no monster, but she did have a good idea why he was so nervous. Those possibilities could certainly be explored later. First, she'd relax and wash the salt from her body. After her soak, she'd rinse out her jeans and shirt. Hopefully she could find a good place to hang them so they wouldn't take too long to dry.

She cast the blossoms across the surface of the water. When the petals hit the warmth, they released a soft fragrance reminding her of vanilla and lavender. After considering a number of ways to enter the tall tub, she moved the chair closer, stripped quickly and used the chair to lift herself high enough to sit on the edge. When she sank into the water the fragrant warmth covered her to her chin. Perfect.

Except for her wings. She couldn't remember if she'd ever taken a bath with her wings exposed. Attempting to recline comfortably against the sloped end, she sloshed water over the edge of the tub. Finally, with her wings curled slightly around her, she sighed in comfort and closed her eyes. She'd get someone to build her a tub like this when she got home.

Attuned to every slight sound, every movement and slosh of water, Taj barely breathed until Jinger settled. He kept his stiff back toward the doorway and concentrated on cleaning the fish without slicing his fingers on the sharp scales. Although the pain would serve him well to remember the dangers of his world for the woman.

Despite his mother's assurances, he didn't trust that Ib wouldn't appear outside the protective barriers of Taj's home. Or that the sorcerer wouldn't somehow influence Jinger and cause her to leave the safety Taj provided. Ib was unable to cross the barrier, but his influence over a person's mind slipped easily past the firefox's protection.

Jinger sighed again, the sound easing over Taj like a caress. He set the nearly cleaned fish aside. Behind his closed eyelids he imagined her in his tub. How did the dusty surface of her wings appear when wet? How would they feel? How would she feel if he touched her skin? Soft as the flower petals he gave her, or softer still, as only she might be? Would she even allow him the honor of touching her?

His inner vision grew sharp and focused. Even distorted by the water she swirled with her hand, her body called to his, her dancing fingers beckoning to him. He mumbled a harsh curse and forced his eyes open. His imagination created too clear a picture of Jinger, a picture his senses and his body struggled to ignore. More splashing and his eyes drifted closed. Still now, she lay back, her body visible in the clear water. Except for where the flower petals floated, hiding that which he shouldn't wish to see.

Temptation. Ib had used such tactics in the dreams sent to torture Taj's nights. Perhaps Ib was closer than Ommi knew, for the sorcerer had many ways, knew ancient, forgotten spells. It was possible he'd discerned a way around the firefox's magic to torment his son in his waking hours.

Taj shook off the thought and returned to cleaning the fish. There was no reason not to trust his mother's knowledge, but he would remain vigilant. The sudden appearance of a dream come to life was suspect. He would find a way to thwart his father's schemes and temptations as in the past.

If Jinger was no more than she seemed, a magical soul pulled into Ib's trap, he would protect her until she found a way to escape.

He wanted nothing more.

An ache blossomed deep in his chest. Liar.

CHAPTER
TWELVE

Delightfully clean and relaxed by her soak, Jinger leaned forward to glance out the doorway before exiting the tub. Taj wasn't within sight, but she heard the obvious sounds of cooking to the left of the door. While soaking she'd tried to make a few decisions. Leaving this world seemed impossible, but she'd keep trying. If there was a way in, there would be a way out. She would find that way.

Until then, she'd explore both the world and her attraction to Taj. The world so she could give an accurate accounting to the Alastriona and Gowthaman. The librarian would find great delight in adding another circle to his wall-sized drawing of their known multi-verse. She adored the quiet, often somber faerie, she just didn't understand his love of discovering something new in ancient books.

Despite her cousin Breanna's skill at fighting and joy in exploration, the two shared a true, lasting love. As did all those in her clan who had chosen mates. A cloud of sadness settled over her shoulders. She was young yet, there was time in the long human years of her life to find a grand love. To experience a soulfire with another. To be loved and love in return. Despite how her mind flipped from idea to idea, always seeming to follow a sparkling new thought or concept, her emotions were far different from a normal fairy's.

Gentry and human blood flowed in her veins as well and deep in her private thoughts, she ached for something solid and real. A stable relationship. Young in fey years she might be, but in human years she was old enough to know what she wanted. It was just... hard... when everyone around her was so much in love. Time and time again she'd told herself she'd find that special happiness. What good was positive self-talk when you really didn't believe?

Jinger blinked and shook her head, chasing away the dreary thoughts. Where had all those maudlin thoughts come from? She wasn't ever...no, she had to take that back. She'd been sad beyond her understanding when Chance had been killed and his body lost in the World Between Worlds. That sadness had drawn her to the beach where she found the bottle and ended up here.

Did those emotions have anything to do with being drawn here? With being unable to leave? She slapped her flattened hand against the water. The idea was entirely ridiculous. Not worth considering. Not when she had a man to discover.

Rising from the water she tested another of her decisions. The magic needed to make her wings retract or form a portal or even start a fire hadn't worked, so she hadn't attempted anything else. Inherent magic was a part of her, a heritage from both of her parents. She'd just become so accustomed to living in the human world and behaving as a human, she'd ignored the magical, fey parts of her. Beyond a few simple tricks when she'd been a teenager, she hadn't tested her abilities and had no concept of her strengths and capabilities.

Concentrating, she focused on the towel. The fabric remained still. A slight noise from outside caught her attention and she abandoned her attempt at bringing the towel to her.

Yep, she was her father's daughter, all right. A fairy with a short, easily distracted attention span. Dad had overcome that particular issue and ruled the fairy peoples with wisdom and concern. Maybe she just needed a grounding force, someone to calm her overactive thoughts, like Mom did for Dad.

Taj was calm, grounded. She covered her mouth with her fingers and giggled. But did he ever have any fun? Having to survive on his own, did he even really know what fun was? Teaching him might be a delightful activity. There were many, many different ways to have fun. Hopefully encouraging him would be good for both of them.

Scrambling from the tub and steadying herself against the slippery rocks, she reached for the towel After she'd dried her skin, and fluttered her damp wings, she eyed the finely woven material of the garment the firefox told Taj she'd need. Well, she had to wear something other than a towel. She caught back a low chuckle. At least for now.

Jinger held the garment at arm's length then twisted her fingers in the silken fabric. A sigh gathered in her chest. She loved to explore textures and this cool, smooth weave delighted her. Having this touch her body, caress her skin when she moved... How would it feel if Taj touched her with this gliding fabric between them? A shiver of delight traveled her spine. Cherishing the feeling a moment, she squinted at the material.

How was she supposed to wear this?

A long, wide length ended at a rounded opening edged with silver threads. Beyond that the fabric split into three panels that came together and joined the front panel about halfway to the hem. Loops of gold held a thin, silver sash, the fringed ends brushing the floor.

Jinger straightened and held the outfit against her body. Ingenious. Hoping she had figured out how to properly clothe herself, she bunched the material and slipped the opening over her head. After a brief struggle to fit her wings between the panels, the hem fell nearly to the floor. Knotting the sash, she wiggled her shoulders to settle the material and released a long, slow breath.

She'd never wear jeans again.

Okay, that probably wasn't practical, but if she could feel this sensual, this beautiful every day, she would. She blinked and shook her head, sending droplets of water dancing from her hair. Being able to feel like this could only be a dream. A temporary break in the usual, everyday aspects of life. She drew the sash between her fingers. She'd enjoy this sensual luxury for as long as she could.

"Jinger, your pardon?"

Unable to capture her startled squeak behind her hand, Jinger closed her eyes and let her shoulders droop. Caught up in the clothing, in a piece of delightful, sumptuous material, she'd forgotten where she was and the dangers she could possibly face at any moment. Would she never learn?

From beyond the doorway, Taj cleared his throat. "I don't mean to startle you. The food is cooked."

His footsteps retreated, paused, then continued. The rustle of him settling next to the fire drew Jinger from her doubts and recriminations and to the doorway. She brushed at her shoulders and straightened the sash before stepping from the building.

Taj lifted his gaze. His eyes widened, then the lids lowered and he dipped his head. Wondering at his reaction, and his thoughts, Jinger crossed the clearing and knelt at his side.

He shook his head then scrubbed one hand through his hair before looking at her. "You can be nothing but a dream. I—"

Being compared to a dream, was like a dream come true for her, fulfilling a wish she'd made as a young girl. Maybe it was midsummer here. At the fear rising in his eyes, she bit back a grin and her irreverent reply. He'd been alone all his life. She needed to remember that fact and be patient even though patience was far from one of her strong points. For Taj, patience would become her virtue. For Taj.

"You said the food was ready? I'm really hungry." Her stomach not so subtly reinforced the truth in her statement.

He spread his hands indicating the clearing. "I have no fine table, nor cushioned chairs for your comfort."

"That doesn't matter. I've eaten around a campfire before. The fish smells heavenly. Can we eat now?"

Once Jinger arranged the flowing material of her unusual clothing and the awkward weight of her wings, she settled under a shady tree a few paces from the small fire and held out her hands. Taj handed her a shallow wooden bowl and took a step back as though nervous about her reaction.

Subtle aromas rose from the dish and her stomach announced her hunger with a loud rumble. "This smells fantastic. I can't believe you made this over a campfire."

Questions dulled his eyes and he squared his shoulders. "This is how I live. It is what I know. Would you have me eat raw fish?"

Steadying the bowl in her lap, Jinger concentrated on holding back a laugh. The distaste curling his lip reminded her of the first time she tried sushi. She wasn't a fan, either. "No, of course not. But many in my worlds do enjoy sushi."

Silent, his full lips formed the word before he shook his head. "I can't imagine how one would enjoy uncooked fish."

The distaste in his expression deepened and she was unable to contain her chuckle. He smiled in response. Ah, that reaction was worth a discussion of raw fish. In fact, she'd be tempted to try sushi again if his smile was her reward. She adored his expressive face.

Dragging her focus back to the bowl resting on her knee, she attempted to decipher the aromas. At least the tiny portion he'd given her didn't smell like fish. A more plentiful pile of the shellfish balanced next to a mound of vegetables and what she guessed must be some sort of round grain.

Their knees almost touching, Taj sat beside her and handed her a gourd spoon. Conscious of how he watched her as he waited for her to sample her meal, she poked through the grain and scooped up a bit along with a flaky bite of fish. Her hand shook under the intensity of his gaze. Birdsong fell silent, even the fall of water over the stones nearby softened, as if nature held its breath waiting for her reaction.

Another foolish thought. With some effort, Jinger restrained the desire to roll her eyes at herself, took the small bite and chewed. Amazing flavors burst over her tongue, salt followed by a flare of heat and spice. The barest hint of sweetness cooled her mouth and she swallowed. "Wow."

"Wow is good?"

At her nod, the tense lines of Taj's shoulders relaxed and he lifted his own spoon. They ate in silence but after he set their bowls aside, the questions swirling through her mind would no longer remain silent.

"That meal was..." Suspicion narrowed her eyes but still, she could discern no evidence within him. She took a chance. "Magical."

Other than a dimming of the brightness in his dark eyes, he gave no indication of hiding abilities from her. She leaned forward to watch the muscles of his face. "Like the bread yesterday."

He grimaced and drew the corner of his lip between his teeth. Then he sighed. "Ommi said you would question this. I have no magic, but for minor talents which allow me to survive. I am able to create bread. Discover flavors in plants to make my meals more appealing. Start a fire. Simple things, yet even so, I seldom use these abilities. If Ib senses an unusual use of magic, he takes. He destroys. I have no doubt he knows my mother showed me these things. But I have no wish to bring his further anger down on her by the frivolous use of magic when I can do a thing without."

Well, that was the most words she'd heard from him at one time. He'd get along well with Breanna's husband. Gowthaman also had strong beliefs about frivolous magic.

Jinger bit her lip to keep silent. The fairy side of her nature meant frivolous was part of her make up. Drawing a deep breath, she set further questions aside. "I once had something similar to your fish at an Asian restaurant in the human world. Yours is much better." She folded her hands to keep from touching him. "Oh, great. Now that I've thought about that place, we need fortune cookies to end our meal."

A deep line centered between his brows. "Cookies?"

"A sweet treat at the end of a meal. The best way to describe a cookie might be it's like a really tiny loaf of your sweet bread. But that's not right for a fortune cookie. They're crispy and folded."

One of his eyebrows arched but confusion remained in his expression.

"Oh, how to explain this." Jinger glanced around the clearing until her gaze landed on a low, multi-stemmed plant near the path. The circular shape of the bright, yellow-green foliage would work. She pointed. "Could you bring me one of those leaves?"

Taj's expression softened and Jinger straightened her spine. That look. She'd seen it far too many times when others humored her even though they thought her ideas were foolish. She crossed her arms and stared at the ground.

"Jinger?"

"What?"

"I don't understand. Have I made you angry? I will bring you a leaf, but they are bitter unless cooked for a lengthy time. Not sweet like your cookie."

Now she was being silly. Taj was inexperienced in personal relationships, and he hadn't meant to be demeaning. "I'm sorry. You've done nothing. My leaf? Don't look so concerned. I'm not going to eat the leaf."

Taj gathered a leaf and returned to sit cross-legged facing her. She pinched off the thin, woody stem then folded the leaf in half. Holding the two ends of the folded edge, she brought her fingers together. Not perfect, but a fair representation. "A fortune cookie looks something like this, only, um, puffier. There's an empty space in the middle for the fortune."

"How large are these cookies?"

"A little bit smaller than this."

The skepticism in his expression flattened his lips. He took the leaf, unfolded and refolded it several times then held it to the sun. Sticking the tip of his finger into the now open, rounded side, he shook his head. "A fortune resides here? I've seen the fortune Ib hoards in his castle. Even the smallest jewel wouldn't fit within one of your cookies. Fortunes in your world must be extremely small."

Jinger chuckled at his confusion. He shrugged and grinned in return. She explained, "Not that kind of fortune. More like a proverb, a wise or silly saying. They're just for fun. The last one I got was 'You make every day special'. Not very exciting. So sometimes we'd play this game where everyone reads their fortune and ends by saying 'in bed'.

Taj's gaze darted toward the low, stone building. Heat burned up Jinger's neck and over her cheeks. Oh, that bed...his bed. Had he imagined them there, too? Lying together on the silken fabrics, cocooned by curtains as finely woven as spider webs?

No, now was not the time to go there. Fighting the shimmer of awareness flowing through her, Jinger cleared her throat and tossed the leaf aside. "Tell me about Ib."

The sudden request grounded Taj in reality and returned him from his wayward, confused thoughts. Barely able to look at her, yet compelled to gaze upon her beauty, he turned his face from the temptation she'd offered with her strange fortune cookie game.

No matter how he prevaricated, her determination made him realize he wouldn't be able to deny her the information she sought. He disliked bringing a discussion of his father to the warm, pleasant day. To any day.

No time would be appropriate for this discussion. Ommi claimed Ib had retreated to the highest tower, but there was no guarantee the length of time he would remain ensconced there.

Taj shifted. How much should he tell Jinger? All, and frighten her? It was good to be frightened of the sorcerer. Perhaps less than all, but enough to keep her safe? Yes. That would do for now. He would keep her at his side, she would never come upon Ib alone and defenseless. Though should they encounter the sorcerer, Taj could offer her little protection.

"Taj?"

"I know less of Ib than you believe."

"Okay. Tell me what you can. I already know he's your father and he believes you have no magic, except for what little you use to survive. I'm assuming he's the one who transformed your mother?"

Deep sadness welled in his chest, along with the familiar guilt. If he'd been born with magic—.

Jinger touched his arm. "I know what you're thinking. But if Ib is that cruel, your mother wouldn't have been safe, no matter what." She paused and peered into his face. "I'm right, aren't I?"

"Ommi has often said the same. But it is difficult to accept. I barely remember when she wasn't the firefox. For a short while after the transformation, Ib kept me with him. He was waiting for me grow closer to a man's age, hoping my magic would then appear. Once again I sorely disappointed him. One day he set a task for me in the forest. When I returned, the castle had been barred to me. I couldn't enter and he laughed at me from the tower."

"That's horrible. I can't imagine how that must feel. So then he left you alone?"

This he hated most to admit for he'd had no control. "Not long after he banished me, I began to have strange dreams. Many were frightening and Ommi was unable to comfort me. She told me the sorcerer took pleasure in sending me dreams and in sensing my reactions."

A strange shadow filled Jinger's eyes. She opened her mouth to speak but snapped her lips together instead. Attempting to decipher her flowing expressions, Taj watched her closely. She took a deep breath. "Do you still have these dreams?"

"Many seasons have passed since the last one. Over time the dreams changed." The tips of his ears heated. "To those more suited to torment a man. Over time I learned to fight his interference. Perhaps he became bored when I didn't respond as he hoped."

"Can he send dreams to others?"

Had Ib already visited Jinger's dreams? Hoping it was not so, Taj nodded. "I believe he can. Although as I have been alone, there has been no one to ask."

Again Jinger appeared ready to speak. Instead she gave her head a tiny shake and grinned. "I can't imagine being alone for so long. It's difficult to find alone time within my family, whether you're a blood member of the clan or not. My family, my large and exuberant family, accepts everyone. There's a place for anyone no matter what your abilities or skills. As long as you have a good soul, it doesn't matter who, or what, you are."

An odd sensation settled in Taj's chest. Welcoming, like a bright flare of hope. "That is something I am unable to envision. Would they accept my mother?" Then, because he had the perverse need to know, he asked, "Me?"

She gave him a look of mock exasperation. "Of course. There are many magic welders in my family, and more in the worlds they rule. It wouldn't surprise me if somewhere there's a spell or charm or something that could release your mother from that enchantment. I have cousins who love that kind of research. If there's a way, they'd find it."

The brilliance of her smile filled the clearing and chased the remnants of heavy sadness from his heart. For such a thing to happen was too much to hope for, yet her conviction gave him hope. He didn't need much for himself. He wanted little. To return his mother to her rightful form in a welcoming place would do much to negate these many years of solitude and struggle.

As though she understood his thoughts, Jinger scooted closer and placed her hands on his forearms. "I believe I'll find the way out of here, and if you wish, I'll take you with me. You and Ommi. I promise."

Such a thing was beyond any promise, but he would allow her to believe it could be as she wished. "In return I give you this promise. I will keep you safe until you find your way home."

Her gaze on his face, she tilted her head in a manner that had him leaning toward her, drawn closer by her sparkling blue eyes and the slight parting of her lips. He sensed no magical allure but couldn't stop himself if he'd wanted. A slow blink hid her eyes from him and he paused.

"How do..." She sighed and her expression turned wistful. "How do people here seal a pledge? Do you shake hands?"

His confusion must have shown for she chuckled. "Spit in your palms before you shake hands?"

That was a disgusting thought. He shook his head.

"Or maybe, do you conclude a deal with a kiss?"

"A kiss?" What was that odd hitch in his voice?

Bracing her hands against his thighs, she rose to her knees and leaned closer. The floral scents from her bath swirled around them and as he inhaled, he lifted his hand to touch the smooth skin of her cheek. "I don't know if any here have ever made a 'deal' for which an agreement was necessary."

"I think this is completely necessary." Skimming his chest, her hands rose to his shoulders. Heat blossomed under her touch, spreading to his neck and face. Then lower where his body responded as it had to Ib's dreams. This torment, similar, yet so different, he welcomed. Wanted. Ached to truly experience. He slipped his fingers through the silken strands of her hair and cupped the back of her head.

"Taj, I need to kiss you."

Need. Yes. He hadn't realized that since he'd first seen her, he'd hoped for this moment. Now, his mind was unable to draw upon any thought but her, of her hands against his skin, his fingers buried in her glorious hair. No words. Nothing but the need for more.

She pressed her cheek to his, her breath tickling past his ear. "Taj?"

"Jinger."

Her arms slipped around his neck and she leaned fully against his chest. The brush of her lips near his mouth set his skin to trembling. Then he was falling.

Jinger yelped.

His shoulder scraped against the worn bark of a log. The remains of their meal spilled from the bowls broken under his back, cooling his skin. Jinger landed hard on his stomach and lay with her forehead pressed against his chin.

"Damn." She tapped her fist against his chest. "Damn, damn, damn. Stupid wings."

She attempted to lift herself from him but he'd clenched his hands and her hair had tangled through his fingers, holding her in place. Her slender body shook and she made soft sounds against his chest. Panic rose, chasing away the desire.

"Jinger? Are you hurt?"

She shook her head, but her shoulders still trembled and her breaths came in soft gasps. Taking great care, he untangled his fingers and lay with his arms at his sides. "What did I do?"

"Noth...nothing. It's me. My stupid wi...wings."

"Then why do you cry? Are your wings damaged?"

"I'm no...not crying." She wiggled and slid to his side, tugging on her clothing until she angled to face him. Moisture glistened in her eyes but her mouth stretched in a crooked smile. "I'm laughing. Damn wings. I just can't get accustomed to the weight and I overbalanced."

Three days later, Jinger woke with a smile. She stretched and rubbed her cheek against the silken throws covering the bed. She'd been surprised to discover this simple luxury in such a primitive place. The only thing that would have made the nights better was if Taj had spent them with her instead of stoically sleeping in his hammock.

Well, that and she really wanted the stupid dreams to stop.

Each night she'd dreamed of the powerful man who insisted she make her way to his castle—for her own safety. Some scholars would say there must be some deep, psychological reason for her dreams, but she'd never paid much attention to those who claimed to analyze the dream world. Even Catori, who traveled into dreams on drum quests, ignored those intellectual pundits.

Then there were the legends claiming fairies didn't dream. Ha! She'd been dreaming all her life, silly little things she supposed fit with who she was. Or what the non-magical world thought she was.

Curling to her side with one hand under her cheek, she worked through the last dream. The shadow shrouded man continued to encourage her to find him but this time he'd been more intense, stopping just shy of demanding. Then suddenly, the dream had been gone, leaving her shivering despite the heat emanating from her skin. She'd never had a dream affect her physically. Maybe heat was a part of this land's reaction to her magic.

Tangled in the satiny bedding, Jinger lay still a moment then huffed out a frustrated breath before struggling to crawl from the bed. Giving the light coverlet a jerk, she freed her wings and sat, drawing her bare toes across the cool stone floor. Yes, she was frustrated. Frustrated with dealing with the awkwardness of her wings. Frustrated with her lack of progress in discovering a way to open a portal to home—or to any other world. And doubly frustrated with Taj.

Since their near kiss at the campfire, he'd kept his distance. Sort of. He remained polite and solicitous, assisting her when she asked, but rarely coming close to her otherwise. It was as though he'd erected a wall between them and only the barest of cracks in the mortar allowed interaction beyond daily necessities. She hated that wall.

More than willing to explore the obvious attraction shimmering between them, she'd tried subtle, and not so subtle, hints and actions. At least he didn't jerk away when she touched his arm. Although the stone-like tightening of his muscles was just as bad. Today, she'd leave him completely alone. Let him stew in his own desires. She knew he had them, she simply couldn't figure out what held him back.

Besides, she needed some alone time. Even if Taj wasn't with her emotionally, he was physically. Always on the other side of the camp or waiting on the beach while she exercised her wings. Watching her as if afraid she'd disappear.

From what little he'd finally told her about his father, it made sense. Ib was an expert at taking whatever he wanted and didn't care who he harmed. She understood the debilitating agony of waiting for something horrible to happen. She'd been a tiny child when the over-whelming evil of Feidhlim had finally been destroyed and eliminated from her family. Then Lucidea's uncle had been taken to the World Between Worlds by an ancient fire elemental. That evil hovered over their family for twenty years.

Chance had died destroying Brandr Ur. She blinked away the sting of tears. Seven years since then, and it still hurt. She pressed her palms over her eyes and took a deep breath. Now she was lost to her family as well. While the Alastriona had surely tracked her to the beach, she doubted there would be any evidence of the portal that dragged her here. Who, or whatever had imprisoned Ib in this world wouldn't make his escape easy.

She had to find her way home. Or at least some way to send a message or a signal. Or something.

This latest dream spurred her to finally make a deci-sion. Today she planned to do some exploring on her own. Take time to think. Alone. Without Taj's eyes constantly on her. She wasn't sure why time alone seemed so important, but perhaps she was reluctant to take any chances with him keeping track of her like an errant child.

Taj had been delightfully protective of her the past few days. Today she wanted to find her own way. Today she needed to take risks. Especially since he refused to search in the direction she felt she needed to go.

That was interesting in itself. Taj made a point of always keeping his back to what she sensed might be south in this world. It seemed to her he felt if he ignored the direction long enough, whatever bothered him might disappear.

This glen wasn't that far from the place he'd marked as the furthest he'd taken her. He'd made marks on the tree trunks, telling her the forest was dangerous beyond his markings. He'd repaired small stone cairns when they came across them. She'd asked and he'd said they also marked boundaries then refused to say more.

She sensed the piles of stones held small magics, more of ability he refused to accept within himself.

Sounds filtered into the low building. The thud of a pot against a stone. The soft hum of song from Taj as he prepared breakfast. She grinned. He didn't realize he hummed when he concentrated. Maybe that was part of the greater magic she'd sensed but he continually claimed he didn't have. She wanted to ask Ommi, but the firefox hadn't returned. Jinger hoped her inability to decipher the swift images the animal had sent to her mind hadn't chased Taj's mother away.

For the first time since she'd come to Taj's home, Jinger dressed in her jeans. For her plans, she needed to be able to move as freely as possible. As much as she loved wearing the flowing silks, today called for practicality. Pausing in the doorway to gather her courage, she watched Taj. His economical movements had become familiar, the kind of familiarity that settled deep in her chest and made her smile. Familiarity that spoke of home, contentment... of love.

Love? Surely not. Jinger retreated into the hut's cool interior. She was completely in lust with Taj. Simply thinking about him tightened her breath and sensitized her skin. Maybe she needed to offer him stronger encouragement. Or make the first move. One more successful than that aborted kiss. Maybe if they had sex she'd get him out of her system.

A peek around the doorframe gave her a view of how his loose pants tightened when he bent forward. He straightened and reached to one side, flexing the muscles in his back and arms.

No, once would only feed the need for more.

But love him? She'd only been in this world four days, and the odd situation probably made her emotions dance the same way sparkles danced in his eyes when he smiled.

She stared at the thatch ceiling and shook her head. Some old psychological theory probably explained her reactions. She'd detested the strictures of psychological study in school and saw no reason why every action or reaction had to have some deep seated reason. Shouldn't life just be... life?

And love... simply love?

Members of her family had a history of falling in love quickly, with lasting, successful partnerships that put romance novels to shame. Why should she be any different? No other man—be he human or one of the fey races—had captured her interest the way Taj did.

But the circumstances concerned her. With any luck,

she'd be leaving soon. She'd promised to take Taj with her. What if it wasn't possible?

She wrapped her arms across her chest and clasped her shoulders. The personal hug did little to lighten the recurring, sobering thought. Coralie had been willing to stay in the World Between Worlds with Morghan, leaving behind family and friends to be with the one she loved. Breanna had said much the same about staying with Gowthaman.

Ducking her head and rubbing the back of her neck Jinger considered that option. Would she be able to do the same for Taj? Stay here and never see her family again? She wasn't as strong as Coralie or Bree. She needed family. Her family.

She and Taj could become a family here, but it wouldn't be the same.

Nothing had a hold on Taj to give him a reason to stay in this world. Except his mother. If Taj and Ommi were prevented from escaping with her, surely her family and the Alastriona would find a way to rescue them. Just like they had helped Coralie bring Morghan back from the World Between Worlds.

So much to consider. Too many options and possibilities. She could barely keep her thoughts centered on one problem. Taking some time alone would allow her to weigh the options and make decisions beneficial to both her and Taj.

Strengthening her determination, she stepped into the clearing and spread her arms as if to capture the sun streaming through the narrow opening in the leafy canopy. The light warmed her face, chasing the odd heat of the dream from her skin and thoughts.

The clearing was oddly silent and she lowered her

gaze to Taj's hammock. Empty. The cook fire was banked with the pot he used for cooking set at the edge of the coals. Concern drew her brows together. He'd been working here moments ago.

She was accustomed to his morning greeting when she stepped from the building. Panic rushed to fill her chest. What happen? Where was he?

Taj crouched at the edge of the spring watching, but not seeing, the bubble of water cascading from the rocks. After the past night, he no longer discounted Jinger's dreams as only a wish to return to her home. Ib had visited him with a disturbing dream this past night as well.

Much time had passed since the last time his dreams had been so evilly directed, and he'd hoped his father had grown tired of tormenting him. This dream, however, instead of tempting Taj's body with pleasures he would never know, had caused him a pain that lingered deep in his chest.

Even more disturbing was the thought Ib might have sent the same dream to Jinger.

The sounds of her waking this morn had invaded his solitude. Made him twitchy as though insects crawled beneath his skin. He'd left his food preparations to find calm within the music of the dancing waters. Today he discovered no peace here.

Solitude lost its appeal the moment she fell from the sky. In less than a hand of days, he'd grown accustomed to her presence, attuned to the sounds she made, the strange words and expressions she used. The situation was odd for he hadn't realized he could miss things he'd never had.

Ommi was no help. His mother only laughed when he'd voiced his early concerns. But then, she'd always been full of joy despite her transformation and Ib's continual attempts to destroy her. He wished he could remember her better as she had been. The beautiful, red-haired djinn who had smiled down on him in his bed, who had sung to him of other worlds, other times.

With a start, he dropped the small stone he'd been twining through his fingers. The songs flooded his memory and he sighed with the loss. How different his life would have been if she'd been allowed to lead him, to show him the joy and teach him the songs. What kind of a man might he have become?

Jinger was much like his mother had been, full of joy, laughter and song. Even when Jinger spoke, her words lilted with happiness and music. Her laughter cascaded thrills of awareness over his skin, heating and cooling him at the same time.

Like the evil intent behind it, the dream resurfaced, turning his thoughts dark once again. In the dream he'd heard Jinger's soft sounds of pleasure. But her cries of passion hadn't been for him. In the dream Ib had seduced her. And she had allowed him to touch her, caress her skin. Pleaded for more.

Taj snatched up the stone and hurled it across the spring. The pebble bounced against the rock with a sharp crack then tumbled into the water.

"Wow, you've got quite the throwing arm, Taj."

Jinger's soft voice, so close behind him, froze his muscles for a moment. He'd heard her hovering in the doorway, but so lost in his thoughts, hadn't noticed her crossing the clearing. She was dangerous to his senses— in more ways than he cared to examine.

He angled his face toward her. "Good morning."

She crossed her arms and tilted her head, studying him. Then she shrugged. "Okay, don't tell me what's got you attacking the outcropping.

Attempting to ease his expression to a bland, emotionless demeanor, Taj matched her shrug.

With a chuckle, she sat on the tree trunk stool next to him. "Oh, don't look so amazed. When I pay attention, I can often sense when others are upset, or have some-thing on their mind. Especially when it's something they don't really want to talk about. And since you don't want to talk, let me."

Her tone, though light and musical, had a serious note riding below the surface. He sat at her feet and rested his open palms on his knees to keep from touching her. Deep in his mind, he wondered if she would respond to his touch, his caresses, as she had to Ib in the dream. He drew in a deep breath and forced the dream from his thoughts.

Jinger had dressed in her tight, blue trousers—jeans, she'd named them—and he wondered at her choice. She'd seemed so pleased with the flowing clothing Ommi had provided for her. Now, she sat staring into the spring much as he had done, twisting the hem of her shirt in her fingers. He waited.

She spoke softly, almost as though she spoke to herself alone. "I've been here for five days. Once you brought me here, to your home, I haven't explored beyond where you've taken me. Only seen what you've allowed me to see. I need to know more about this place."

Facing him, she leaned forward and rested her hand on his shoulder. "I *need* to know more, Taj. That means, I've got to *see* more. I've found no clues or hope for a way home in the areas we've gone. I need to expand my search."

Knowing what her next words would undoubtedly be, he tensed.

"I know you want to protect me." She patted his shoulder then drew back her hand. "And I appreciate that more than you can know. I'm not sure how well I'd have done on my own. Yeah, okay, I do know. I would have—had been—failing miserably. Thank you for helping me."

"Jinger, I would do—."

"I know. That's why you need to allow me to explore on my own today, to discover what I can on my own. Honestly, Taj, you're a bit of a distraction." The fine pink blossom of her blush covered her cheeks.

Fascinated, he stared for a long moment as the color deepened. Until she looked away and the meaning of her words eased past the pleasure of simply looking at her. Alone?

"No. You cannot wander about alone. There are dangers you don't understand."

"I know. Taj, I really do know how to take care of myself. I just think I might see something, discover a way, or at least a hint of what I need to do to go home when I'm focused. I need to do this by myself. I get distracted easily."

Yes, he needed to distract her now, keep her safely at

his side. "Then we shall search together and I will remain somewhat distance from you."

She cast her gaze to the sky and twisted her lips as though she tasted something sour. "Yeah, like that'll work. No, Taj. I need to be by myself. Just for a while. A few hours. Then we can talk about what I may or may not have discovered this evening at supper."

The determination in her expression sent a chill of fear and foreboding skittering down his spine. He had no doubt she'd dreamed last night. The foreboding flashed into rising panic. Did she want to find Ib? Believe Ib could help her? Or make remaining here pleasant?

He bit back the questions. "You shouldn't be alone."

"So you've said. Many times." She leaned back and crossed her arms. Even with the defiant posture, the morning sunlight highlighted golden streaks in her hair encouraging him to touch. The spark in her cerulean eyes nearly drew him to his knees to take her in his arms. The thin line of her lip invited kisses meant to soften the fullness and bring a smile.

He blinked. His dream had affected his judgement. "What of the dreams? Did you dream last night? Did Ib visit appear?"

An emotion he couldn't catch passed through her expression. "And if I did?"

"He is able to control through dreams. I've told you of my younger days."

She shrugged one shoulder. "He didn't control you though, did he? Only sent dreams to torment and make you believe you were flawed. Worthless. When will you see that's not true. Dreams from Ib are *not* the truth."

Standing, Jinger stared down at him and shook her head. "You're not going to change my mind today. I'm

exploring on my own and I'm starting in that direction."
She pointed.

He followed the graceful sweep of her arm. "No.
Don't go that way. It's to—"

"Dangerous. Yes, so you've told me. I don't sense
anything different there than I've seen anywhere else.
Taj, you need to trust me. I won't be gone for long. I'll tell
you everything I discover. If I feel like I'm in danger, I'll
be really careful and come right back."

That wouldn't be enough. Once Jinger crossed the
boundary Ommi had set when she made this home for
him, Ib would gain the upper hand. The forest grew
darker and more mysterious in that direction. Taj had
survived the dangers, the traps and tricks set there.
Barely. Jinger would be destroyed.

He rose and matched her crossed arm pose. "No. I
won't allow it."

Her eyes wide, she took a step back. Then she drew
her brows together and a new fire danced in her eyes.
"You don't *allow* it? You don't *allow* me to go wherever I
want? You don't... Taj, you don't have any control over
me. I am a free being. I make my choices, for good and for
bad. Hopefully the majority are good. When they're not, I
face the consequences of my actions and decisions. Not
you. So no, you don't *allow* me to do or not do anything.
Do you understand me, Taj?"

Anger pulsed from her with each harsh breath. He
would never have imagined his sweet Jinger to have such
a temper. She was wrong. He needed to make her see
reason. His anger rose in response. "I know this land. All
of the land, the dangers as well as the places of safety.
You've been here a few days. How much can you know?"

"How much? Well, not as much as I should. Since you

won't *allow* me to find out. No, I don't want to put myself, you, or anyone in danger. Sometimes you have to face unpleasant things, those dangerous options and situations, in order to understand the whole of something. Sometimes you need to know the truth. I need to know. Why is my going in that direction so dangerous?" She shook her head. "You don't understand why I need to know."

"I do understand. That is why—"

"No, you don't. My magic is different than what I've seen here. You don't know what might be a clue or mean something to me. I could see something you pass by every day that makes sense to me. Helps me figure out how to get home. You distract me. I can't pay attention to what's around me when you're near. I might miss something that's important."

He opened his mouth to speak and she lifted her hand with a jerk to stop his words.

"*Don't* say any more. Just don't. And don't look at me like that. I understand the unknown always carries a touch of fear. If I learn something about the danger I have to face, somehow that makes it seem conquerable."

A tiny grin softened her lips. "I sound like a combination of Gowthaman and Nightshade."

A jolt of nearly physical pain pierced Taj's heart. Who was this Gowthaman? This Nightshade? Why did he care? He took a step toward Jinger, desperate to make her understand.

She held up both hands, palms facing him and shook her head. "Don't try to intimidate me into doing what you want. I'm going. I don't want you to follow me. Do you understand me, Taj? Do. Not. Follow. Me. I'll be back this afternoon. I know enough to find my way back."

"Jinger, be reasonable."

Her laugh carried tones of bitterness. "Reasonable? I've been reasonable for the past days letting you take me only where you thought I should go, to see only what you thought might be important. Now I need to discover things for myself. There's sure to be something I missed. Or a clue that can only be found where you don't want me to go. If you don't tell me..."

Her brows lowered again. "Is that it? Is there something in that direction that you don't want me to see? Something that might help me find my way home? Please don't tell me you want to keep me here. You'd better not be trying to control me."

Control her? To do so would make him no better than his father. A sour weight filled his stomach. Did she believe he was so deceitful? He was nothing like Ib. Yet he was unable to control his temper when he responded. "Go, then, foolish woman. Don't expect me to come to you when you have lost your way."

Her eyes grew wide then narrowed. "Don't worry about that, stupid man. I can find my way just fine. I'm taking the rest of last night's bread with me."

He huffed out a breath.

"Don't snort at me, Taj. I'm taking a water flask, too. See, I know what I need. I'll see you when I return."

"Unless I choose to wander off alone and lose myself in the forest." He blinked. His thoughtless words made no sense.

"Yeah, like that would ever happen. Fine. You go pout somewhere and I'll discover what I need to help me return to my world. Then you won't have to be concerned whether or not I'm acting responsibly or if I'm safe. You won't have to think about me at all."

She turned with a swirl of her wings, stomped to the hooks outside the door to the lodge and tugged at the sack containing the remains of the bread. She slung the strap over her shoulder and settled the bag against her hip and positioned the water flask on her opposite side. With a glance back over her shoulder, she shook her finger at him, then strode from the clearing.

Astounded by her actions and accusations, Taj jerked to face the pond, giving her disappearing form his back. He glared into the trees at the opposite side of the clearing. She was a fool. Going in that direction only led her closer to Ib.

Because Taj hadn't told her the whole truth.

His anger dissipated and he dropped his gaze to the ground at his feet.

Perhaps that's what she wanted. If she'd dreamed of Ib, perhaps she found the sorcerer appealing. Certainly he was more able to assist her in discovering a way back to her world. At least, that's what his father would promise. Taj knew what Ib wanted, and shuddered at the lengths he would take to obtain that desire.

Taj turned toward the lodge and shook his head. Jinger would no more wish to participate in Ib's plans than she would wish harm upon another. Even if the sorcerer offered her the desire of her heart, she would see past the empty promise to the true malevolency of the man. She was smart, she did understand the danger inherent in facing the unknown. He relaxed the tight set of his shoulders.

Although he'd had occasional disagreements with his mother, he'd never experienced such a swing of emotions. He attempted to categorize how he felt. Anger. He understood anger, although why he'd become so angry with Jinger remained elusive. Fear. He feared for Jinger's safety. Hiding beneath that was another fear he hesitated to examine. She might no longer need him. Pride. Jinger was a strong, capable woman. Stubborn perhaps, but so was he.

He had been overly protective. She'd seemed so unprepared to face this world, so innocent, and he'd only wanted to see to her safety. Being close to her for these few days, he'd learned differently. While her arrival here had caught her unaware, she did have skills and talents that would keep her safe. She would have found her way without him.

The thought made him sad.

He looked into the clear sky. There were dangers in the forest other than Ib. Nodding to himself, he made a plan and marked the sun's position. Once the sun reached the point of midmorning, he'd go after her. This would both give her time to explore as she desired and show his trust in her abilities. But not allow her to wander too far.

He couldn't simply remain here waiting for Jinger to return. His imagination would create dire possibilities and his anger would return.

He'd use the time to fish and clear his mind. If luck was with him, he'd have a variety of sea creatures with which to create a thick stew for their evening meal.

He would welcome her back with a peace offering. And an apology.

FOURTEEN

I b jerked from his contemplation of the thick tome of ancient sea-magic. A wave of awareness burned along his skin and he smiled. The winged woman had finally tired of his worthless son and entered a part of the forest he could sense. The feeling wasn't strong, so she was still a fair distance from the castle. He'd encourage her closer.

The dreams he'd sent to her hadn't had the immediate effect for which he'd planned. She should have come to him two days ago, after he'd returned from the tower. He'd spent the time since then wisely, increasing his knowledge and reviewing the spells and formulas he needed as well as the prophetic terms of his imprisonment. He rubbed his hands together and relished the power created with so simple a gesture.

Soon, he would get a child on the woman. He rested his palm against the brittle parchment pages of the book. Then use this spell to speed the gestation and birth from months to hours. Dangerous for the woman, of course. She didn't matter, only the child of her womb was needed for his escape. He laughed. Soon he would be free. Retaliation and ultimate power would be his.

He needed to know exactly where the woman was and the tapestry was too slow. Unable to comfortably pass beyond the castle walls while maintaining his full power, he was forced to wait for her to come to him. How to ensure that happening quickly?

Ah, yes. The unicorn would do.

Leaving his workroom, he strode along the empty hallways and descended a narrow, spiral staircase to the lowest level of the dungeons. Memories of screams and torture had seeped into the stone and as he ran his fingers along the rough wall, he smiled. He hadn't been down here often since his son had fled to the forest with the bitch fox.

He paused and pressed both palms to the lintels of a narrow, barred doorway to access the full memory. The boy's screams had faded, his tears dried and he'd curled into a small, weak ball. Ib had towered over him, hand hovering above the crown of his son's head, drawing life and power—such as it was—from the young body.

Until the firefox intervened.

Ib glared at the scars marring his arm. The bitch had nearly bitten through his wrist. Then she'd taken the boy and disappeared. He should have killed her when he had the opportunity, before *her* power had grown by birthing a worthless boy.

He backed away and continued lower. No matter. Soon he would have another opportunity and would not make the same mistakes. His plan was set, his future secured. All he needed now was the woman.

At the base of the stairs lay a single cell. Should she

think to defy him, this would be her home until she offered herself to him.

Damn the need for her to be a willing partner. He would need to stoop to her level and woo her. Ib shook his head at the folly and waste of precious time. He would be kind and offer the fulfillment of her deepest wishes. Perhaps he would find pleasure in the task and her willingness.

He drew in a deep breath filled with anticipation. The true pleasure would come when he denied her those wishes, stealing her hope along with the child.

A winding passage ended at a thick, wooden door set in a deep recess of stone. Razor sharp pulses of power pricked at Ib's skin. To pass through this barrier meant a minor loss of the heat that gave him the ability to create his magic. His days in the sun chamber had filled him until his skin could barely contain the powerful energy. The loss caused by the barrier would be barely noticeable.

The pulsing pain was a mere tickle compared to his experience in the sun chamber and he relished the indication of his growing strength. He easily opened the door and entered a shallow cave. Beyond the narrow, rock fissure, the forest stood in the light of the sun. A breeze that seldom reached the undergrowth tossed the upper tree branches.

Ib scowled. The forest had grown closer to the castle until the undergrowth disguised the mouth of the cave and further hid the doorway. Perhaps the passage of time indicated here wasn't detrimental. If he could direct the woman here, the ease with which he could bring her into the castle would barely test the weakest of his abilities.

He thought a moment. A storm. Yes. If she was alone

among the trees, the violence of a storm would encourage her to find shelter. The unicorn would bring her here—to safety.

Creating a mental image of the single horned equine, Ib sent out a magic-filled call. At first emptiness answered him, then came the faintest of refusals. So, the beast still thought to challenge him.

Ib arched one eyebrow at the insolence, decided against punishment for the moment then pressed the tips of his index fingers together. By touching the tips of his thumbs he created a triangle and spread the rest of his fingers wide. Electric power sizzled from fingertip to fingertip before concentrating in the center of the empty triangle.

He blew a gentle breath through the space and spoke the unicorn's name. Drawing his index fingers and thumbs together he completed the call. A dark spot throbbed just above his hands. The unicorn's denial.

"You shall come to me. You will do as I command."

The spot pulsed once, growing larger, then popped from existence.

Ib gave a single, satisfied nod. "Your challenges are feeble, my old friend. I don't know why you bother." He leaned against the doorframe and waited. Moments later the beast ducked its head to enter the cave and stood before him, nostrils flaring.

"There is a woman in the forest."

The unicorn's head dipped in acknowledgment.

"You will bring her here. To me."

The length of the unicorn's mane shimmered in the dim light as it shook its head.

"You will. A storm comes. She will need protection

from the weather. Bring her. To defy me brings punishment."

The unicorn curled back its lips, silently laughing at him. Ib drew the fingers of one hand into a loose fist to collect power. But before he unleashed his anger and punishment, the unicorn dipped its head again.

Ib called back the magic. Still, the beast continued to challenge him, dared him to strike, to destroy. What the beast wished for, he would not give. "Do not defy me."

The unicorn backed from the cave and disappeared into the forest. Despite the beast's disrespect, Ib knew it would comply with his wishes. A prisoner like himself, the unicorn had nothing to lose. Except for the young, still hornless unicorn hidden deep in Ib's dungeons.

Ib rubbed his hands together and grinned. Now, it was time to create the storm.

J inger stomped through the trees until the clearing
disappeared behind her, then continued at a rapid
pace until she felt far enough away to have proven
her point. Then she stopped, turned back and
listened. Taj could move silently through the trees and
underbrush, but still she cocked her head to listen for a
long moment.

When nothing but the rustle of leaves and movements of the few creatures that lived in the forest tickled
her ears, she relaxed. He might follow her, but as long as
he kept his distance, she would consider being okay with
that. Maybe.

Her anger had faded and she reprimanded herself for
being such a bitch.

No, she amended. Not a bitch. Just someone who
stood up for herself and claimed her own decisions and
actions. Nightshade would be so proud of her. Even if she
was reckless in taking off on her own and marching in a
direction where she might meet the sorcerer.

Adjusting the bags at her hips and tossing her hair back over her shoulder, she turned in a slow circle.

There wasn't any indication this part of the forest was well traveled. That made sense if Taj was the only large being living here, and he obviously didn't come in this direction. So, she'd make her own path. The undergrowth wasn't terribly thick, nor the tree branches low enough to snag her wings, so going forward should be fairly easy.

She glanced up through the canopy of thick leaves. Not a whole lot of sky to use to gauge her direction, and her personal ability to stay the right course wasn't always dependable, but she'd do her best. Then she studied the tree trunks around her. What was the trick she'd been taught when camping? Ah, there was a soft, mossy growth on most of the trunks that appeared to be thicker on one side. That meant if she used the thicker moss as a guide, she could keep going in a consistent direction.

That problem solved, she chose her direction and stepped forward.

During her trek, Jinger had to frequently remind herself of her purpose in exploring the forest, otherwise she was distracted by the beauty surrounding her. She hadn't thought many animals or birds lived in this land, but when she was silent and careful with her movements, they appeared to her as if recognizing no threat from her.

One particular insect, another of the moth-like creature with bright green wings larger than the spread of both arms, had her frozen in awe. She had no idea how long she stood watching how it moved those marvelous wings, catching bits of sun and shadow to keep it nearly hidden on the broad tree trunk. At one point she caught herself moving her wings in exactly the same manner then chuckling at the action. But the movement felt good, easing the strain of trying to keep her wings still. Perhaps her wings weren't meant to be at rest when she wasn't flying. She'd have to ask about that when she got home.

Home. That single word brought her back to her personal mission for the day. Exploration and discovery. While discovering something about herself was a good thing, it wasn't the focus she needed. So she left the intriguing moth behind and continued deeper into the forest.

The bright yellow and orange blossom of a plant cascading from an overhead branch caught her eye. She moved closer, then immediately backed away from the small pile of dead insects and small birds lying beneath the flower. Danger hiding within beauty. She gave herself a mental pat on the back for observing and recognizing an obviously poisonous plant. She was getting the hang of this nature stuff.

But she still hadn't discovered anything new that might help her. Not yet. She'd go a bit further then start back to Taj's clearing. She needed to apologize for how she'd acted and what she'd said. Well, maybe not for what she said, but how she'd said it. Her family encouraged strong women who spoke their minds. But frowned upon hurting others when doing so.

Since Taj had spent his life pretty much alone, he wouldn't have much experience in arguments and friendly disagreements.

Besides, she did understand his concerns and shared the need to be careful. She drew her attention back to her

critical observations of the land, trees, rocky outcrop-
pings and wildlife.

A few minutes of walking found her mind
wandering again. Nothing was different. Same tall foreboding trees with the same mossy growth. Same
sunlight beating down through the occasional breaks in
the branches overhead. Except the air had changed.
Instead of cool breezes, the occasional bursts of light
wind were hot, like off the desert sands. The air itself
grew stifling, and the stillness between those breezes
became oppressive.

Light sweat formed on her forehead so she patted at
the dampness with the hem of her shirt. Curious about
the change in temperature, she kept moving forward,
noting how with each step the air seemed filled with
more heat. Taj hadn't mentioned there was a desert, nor
did the air carry the moistness of a tropical jungle. She'd
experienced many different weather conditions in a
number of different worlds but nothing felt similar to
this strange heat.

She'd ask Taj when she returned. There was probably
some good reason for the weather changes. She'd feel
silly for being concerned and a little bit frightened.
Forcing a laugh that sounded weak, she decided it was
time to retrace her steps and admit the loss of spending a
day with Taj.

The thought of seeing him made her grin. She'd find
a good way to apologize to him. He might not be ready
for makeup sex, but a little cuddling could be in order.

A streak of light burst across the sky, branching into a
multitude of tiny, jagged, crackling spears of lightning.
The boom of thunder lingered quivering in her chest.
Great. There hadn't been a storm, or any kind of weather

other than bright, sun-filled days since her arrival. She was a half a day's trek from safety and a dry roof.

Lightning cascaded around her, sizzling across the treetops, blocking her path. The roar of thunder grew from a distant growl to an overpowering rumble that surrounded her then pressed her back. Every time she took a forward step, either lightning or the nearly physical thunder pushed her back a few paces.

Intending to escape the strange trap, she spread her wings. Wind swirled around her, lifted her, then tossed her to the ground like a discarded tissue. Okay, this was starting to feel personal. Lightning bright and rapid as a strobe light burst around her. The wind howled an obscene harmony to the thunder and she covered her ears.

The thought she should have listened to Taj helped her remain calm. She'd chosen this path, she'd deal with the sudden, dangerous weather. If she had to sit under a tree hoping against a lightning strike until this was over, she would. What other choice did she have?

The soft rustle of undergrowth to one side drew her attention from the sky. Some animal seeking shelter from the storm? As long as the creature didn't appear dangerous, she'd share the area. Whatever it was lived here, so it should know how to deal with the storm. She'd follow its lead.

At least it wasn't rain—

As though answering her thought, a deluge of uncomfortably warm water fell from the roiling clouds. Drenched within seconds, she wiped ineffectively at the water pouring down her face. The upper edges of her wings curled over her head but did nothing to keep the rain from her eyes. Wrapping her arms around herself, she shrank back against a tree and resigned herself to a long, wet wait.

The undergrowth parted and a horse stepped into view. Jinger gasped. No, not a horse. A unicorn? A flash of lightning highlighted the silver swirls of the single horn. Deep azure eyes filled with intelligence, and sorrow, watched her.

A unicorn. Here. A real, live unicorn was standing in the rain watching her. Despite being a creature of fantasy and folk tales herself, having a mythical unicorn right in front of her held her speechless. Should she go to it? Would it run away? She wasn't a virgin after all. Maybe that was something someone just made up. Maybe.

She lifted one hand and held it out with her palm facing the sky. The slight depression filled with rain-water so she tipped her hand to let the water drain away. The black unicorn was huge, the size of a draft animal. It lowered its head and stepped closer. Despite its size the silver hooves were silent against the forest floor. When it pressed a velvety soft nose against her skin, Jinger sighed. She couldn't wait to tell her cousins about this. Bree would be so jealous. They'd pretended to be wild unicorns when they were children.

The unicorn sidled closer and snuffed at her neck. Then it took the shoulder of her shirt between its teeth and tugged, making her step to one side. A second tug, another step. Cautious, she touched the silky mane. "Do you want me to go with you?"

The unicorn bobbed his head, an affirmative answer if she'd ever seen one.

"Are you taking me to someplace out of the storm?"
Another head bob.
"Somewhere safe?"

Instead of answering, the unicorn turned those sad eyes to her.

"I don't mean to question you. I'm sorry. I... I've just never encountered a unicorn before. You're very beautiful."

The unicorn huffed and gave her a look so full of distain she bit back a chuckle. Taking her shirt between its teeth again, the unicorn pulled her a few steps further. The wind at her back pushed and batted against her. "Okay," she muttered to herself, "I get the point."

She patted the unicorn's nose. "I'll follow."

The sadness deepened in the animal's eyes but it turned and walked away without another glance. Confused, Jinger followed. While the beautiful creature seemed intent on taking her somewhere safe from the storm, it also appeared to regret doing so. The odd combination of action and intent kept Jinger's mind busy, so she paid little attention to her surroundings or the direction of the path.

Not that she would be able to see and remember much. Slashing rain poured over them, the wind continued to buffet her and tear at her wings. She wrapped them tightly as she could and tucked them close to her back, hoping to protect them. While strong and pliable, a fairy's wings could be damaged past repair as her father's had been. Now that she was becoming accustomed to their weight and presence, she needed to keep them safe from harm.

Time lost meaning as she walked beside the unicorn. Thunder, deep as the largest drums pounded, insisting her heart beat the same rhythm. Lightning cracked and burst over them and Jinger's hair lifted and swirled in the charged air. The storm was getting worse. Hopefully the shelter wasn't much further.

A tall rock wall emerged through the driving rain. Dark rivulets of water poured down the stone, dancing around protrusions and cascading into tiny waterfalls. She'd find it fascinating if she wasn't feeling nearly drowned. She followed the unicorn along a narrow path at the base of the cliff, skirting the accumulating pools of rainwater until the animal paused at a dark, narrow opening in the rock.

A cave. Shelter. Jinger patted the unicorn's arched neck. "Thank you." She moved to the front of the animal and stroked her hand down the long, elegant face. The unicorn touched its horn to the top of her head. A blessing? She'd just received a unicorn's blessing. She couldn't wait to tell—

With a gentle nudge of its velvety nose, the unicorn encouraged her to enter the cave.

"Won't you come in with me?" Leaving the amazing creature out in the storm didn't seem proper.

But the unicorn shook its head in obvious denial and backed from her. After one final, deeply sorrowful look at her, it turned and galloped into the storm.

Still standing in the rain, Jinger lifted one hand as though to call back the unicorn, then covered her heart with her palm. A tight edginess, the feeling something wasn't quite right seeped into her consciousness. Like the movies said, now she had a bad feeling about this.

Maybe she shouldn't enter the cave. She was soaked and couldn't get any wetter. Walking in the rain had never bothered her.

Clutching a rounded stone set shoulder high in the cave's entrance, Jinger paused a moment. Lightning speared from the sky. A massive tree a few feet from her exploded. She ducked, protecting herself from the burning debris. Another crack. A second tree burst into flame. Lightning struck the stone much too close to her hand. Rain was one thing, aggressive lightning another.

She retreated into the dark cave.

The storm had turned the bright day to twilight and that muted light fought to illuminate the small cave. Wishing she had the ability to create a small glow in her palm, Jinger shrugged and, keeping her hand against one wall, paced a few steps into the growing darkness.

Just beyond where she stopped, the cave opened into a space the size of a small room. She blew out a relieved breath. At least there didn't appear to be other passageways leading away from the cave. She shrugged away thoughts about what creatures might be taking shelter or making a home there. That kind of thinking would be enough to send her back outside to take her chances with the storm. Maybe it was that concern that had made her wary before she entered the cave.

Telling herself to relax, she forced a laugh. She'd wait out the storm then return to Taj's clearing. She hadn't found anything helpful for making her way home. But she'd had an adventure of her own, with no one watching over her. Except for the unicorn.

A unicorn. She'd met, touched, and been helped by a unicorn. The gentle expressions in the animal's dark eyes conveyed much she didn't understand. Sadness and regret. Why would it regret showing her the way to a safe harbor from the storm?

She glanced around the small cave, discovering a knee high flat stone on the far side of the entrance. A good place to sit and wait out the weather.

She had no idea how long she sat there cross-legged, elbows on her knees and her chin cupped in her hands, watching the storm. Her mind wandered from one inane thought to the next and she celebrated the opportunity to release the concerns for what might happen next for a short while.

When would this storm end? There was no indication of the rain slowing or the dangerous lightning easing. Thunder continued to shake the ground. At least the cave was solid.

A dull thud, like something heavy hitting the ground sounded behind her. She scrambled to her feet to face the noise. She jerked into a semi-crouch and wished for a weapon. Even a stick like the one she'd carried from the beach.

A plume of dust rose from the dirt floor filling the air. A sneeze tickled Jinger's nose and she rubbed at the irritation with her fingers. The dust settled and the cleared air revealed a deeply inset, arched opening filled by a dark, wooden door.

A doorway that hadn't been there a moment ago. Like the portal that ripped her from a world she knew to this place. She backed away until her back pressed against the uneven stone wall then inched toward the cave entrance. Not again. She wouldn't be taken again. She couldn't get pulled anywhere else. She wouldn't. If she got lost further along a twisting path of unknown worlds, how would she ever find her way? The chances of anyone being able to track her movements would shrink to nothing.

The stone at her back shook with the rumble of thunder. Danger waited out there, but at least she understood the dangers of a storm, of the wind and lightning. She had no idea what lay beyond the door—or what might come through the opening at any moment.

Her heart stuttered, matching the vibrations in the rocks. The intensity swelled through her. A zap of ozone filled her nostrils. With a sharp crack, the cave entrance collapsed. Darkness. Total. Complete. Darkness.

Jinger caught back a scream and scrambled through the dark, tripping over jagged stones. She fell painfully, jarring her knee and scraping her palms. The pain was nothing compared to the fear of being trapped.

Trapped in a dark cave, in a world she didn't know or really understand. Trapped and alone and...helpless. Tears burned behind her closed eyelids. At least she thought her eyes were closed. It was so dark. Too dark.

The sudden weight of all she'd experienced the past few days crushed down on her shoulders. Confidence fled and she sat silently in the dark, her fairy nature fighting the hopelessness that stole possibilities from her. She didn't even want to think any more. The darkness was devoid of hope.

"Taj," she whispered.

As though the speaking of his name held magic the darkness faded from her mind. Not much, but enough to allow her to take a deep breath and discover the rational amidst the hopelessness.

"Taj," she said more loudly. Once the storm was over, he'd come looking for her. She knew that fact as surely as she knew her name. Even in the rain-washed landscape, he'd be able to track her path. If he came across the unicorn, perhaps the animal would lead him to the cave as well. Working from each side of the cave-in, they'd create an opening large enough for her to crawl through. She'd be free.

The shroud of darkness wrapped silence around her. The stone no longer shook from the force of thunder and lightning. Which was worse? The total dark or the lack of sound. She hummed softly to assure herself she hadn't ended up in a void of some kind.

The vibrations of her throat froze. Is this what it was like in parts of the World Between Worlds? Gowthaman didn't talk much about his times there, but she thought she remembered him saying something about a lack of sensory stimulation. If only she'd paid more attention.

A crackling sound jerked her head to one side. Maybe toward where the doorway had appeared before the entrance collapsed. She couldn't be sure. She shrank back and strained to see through the inky darkness.

The sound repeated. Louder.

A thin spot of light appeared high on the wall making her squint. The bright line split and traveled to the sides and down, outlining the door before expanding to fill the entire area. She shielded her eyes with her hand.

The brightness faded to a dim glow surrounding a tall figure before spreading outward to fill the cave. The figure remained still. Then as if it knew the instant her vision cleared, moved to the center of the cave. She blinked the final blurs from her vision. A man held out one hand to her.

Jinger eyed the offered hand before lifting her gaze to the man's face. He couldn't be the man from her dreams, could he? The face was similar, yet his expression was more intense and calculating.

He smiled broadly and his expression softened. "At last you found your way to me. You are safe now and you are welcomed. Let us come to know each other without the separation of a dream. Come, then, and enter the sanctuary I offer you."

When he assisted her to her feet, the heat of his hand startled Jinger for a moment. She was chilled from the storm and the cool air of the cave. Of course his hand would feel warm. She shrugged away the concern.

His gaze was heated as well when he glanced sideways at her during their long, silent climb up a steep, winding staircase. Caught up in her thoughts and trying to understand the strange storm and how she ended up with this man, she wasn't inclined to speak. Neither did he fill the quiet with useless words. That was okay with her.

Her knees ached when at long last they reached a wide, flat landing with another heavy door fortified with metal bars crisscrossing the wood. He paused with his hand on the latch. "I am Ib."

He pulled open the door and gestured to a grand hall decorated with lush fabrics and intricately carved furniture. Jinger peeked around the edge of the doorway before she entered the space. A massive fireplace dominated one wall, but only a small fire burned brightly in a trough centered on the hearth. A low table with covered dishes sat between a pair of overstuffed chairs before the blaze. Even more inviting was the fleece-lined blanket draped over the arm of one chair. She shivered and rubbed at the chill bumps on her arms.

Ib canted his head to indicate the room. "Welcome home, Jinger."

SIXTEEN

P leased his prey didn't balk at entering the recently created hall, Ib remained near the doorway while the winged woman wandered a short distance into the room. He'd learned much from his time in her dreams and surprised her by knowing her name. He knew the words to say, the tricks of seduction to apply, and he would use that knowledge in time. First, he would put her at ease by seeing to her comfort.

"Please, Jinger, sit by the fire and warm yourself. There is food on the table should you be hungry."

She nodded then turned in a slow circle studying the room. He'd used the colors that had filled her dreams to fashion the hangings and upholstery. Even the minimal use of power for such frivolous trappings had rankled, but from her wide eyes and half smile, the effort was successful.

There was still much to do before he could properly entertain his guest. "I fear I must leave you alone for a short while to attend to important matters. And to your safety. Rest and refresh. I will not be gone long."

"Ib?"

The questions hung heavy in her use of his name. Some he could answer now, others would wait until a more auspicious time. "Yes?"

Wet and bedraggled, she stood in the center of the hall and spread her hands. He sensed words forming in her mind that never reached her lips. After a moment she lowered her hands to her sides. "Thank you. I didn't know how I was going to get out of the cave."

"And I apologize for not coming sooner to your aid. But as I have said, I have much to attend to. If you will excuse me?"

"Oh, of course. Yes. I'll be fine. Thank you again."

"Jinger." With a bow he gestured toward the fire then turned and crossed the hall. Once through the far door, he drew a deep breath and snapped his fingers. His servant emerged from the stone wall, its dull eyes lowered in proper respect.

"Guard this door and do not let the woman pass."

Ib waited until the servant positioned itself at the hinge side of the door and stretched one arm across to the other side to clutch the latch.

"Good." Ib whirled and strode down the hall, grimacing at the frippery he'd placed there to impress the woman. If—no, when—he was successful in planting a child in her, he would release the power used in such a foolish way. Once gathered and returned to him, he would begin the spell from the ancient text.

He rubbed his hands together, stirring the power. One last thing he needed to do before beginning his seduction. If the firefox appeared in the castle now, she would ruin his plans. The bitch was tricky, so he needed to think as she might. Discover any cracks in his magic before she did. He'd attempted barriers before, and she'd always found the way through.

This time he placed no barrier to tempt her curiosity. Since time flowed differently in his castle than it did in the rest of this prison world, he would use time to his advantage. He would further alter the difference. Speeding the passage of time within his walls would serve his purpose in multiple ways. Should the fox gain entrance, she would discover only the past, moments that had already happened.

To the woman, his seduction would seem to take many days, but he could have her in his bed this night. And thus a child by the morrow. Anticipation halted his steps and he lifted one hand to stare at his spread fingers. Five days. He would be free within five days.

Yes, he had much to do. Plans to complete, his library to store in a way he could carry the tomes and scrolls with him, the destruction of his son and the bitch firefox. This was a good day, a day turning to magnificence. His magnificence.

In his workroom, he sat at the scarred table before the thin window and glared at the sun—both the giver of his power and the representation of his hated enemy. Once he obtained freedom, he would surpass the supposed fire god who abandoned him here. Ib had given much thought over the eons to the punishment he would mete out to his tormentor.

The time grew near to set the price Brandr Ur would pay.

CHAPTER
SEVENTEEN

Taj set off for the beach. Fishing had always had a calming effect on his scattered thoughts and emotions, but he had the suspicion this day's fishing would find him no closer to understanding himself. Or Jinger. Or his reactions to her.

At first, when he'd only watched over her, he'd thought to be no more than that, a protector and guide to someone drawn unwilling into this world. Those thoughts had lasted barely a day.

When he'd presented himself, he still had the best of intentions, but once he allowed Jinger into his home, into his life, something had changed.

He desired her.

He understood desire, but had never thought to feel such attraction, such need and wanting outside of Ib's dreams. He thought Jinger felt in a similar way about him for she often touched him for no reason or sat too close at the fire. When she gazed at him with wide, deep blue eyes, she drew him to her much like an insect drawn to the fire.

Was she as dangerous to him as the fire was to the unknowing insect? He huffed out a breath and tugged at the sticky, sap covered vine tangled in his hair. Yes, she was dangerous if just the thought of her made him heedless of his surroundings. The forest was rife with dangers to the unaware.

He'd allowed her to stomp off alone, into the forest, in a direction that held even more danger. The direction leading to Ib's castle.

Taj turned on his heel to retrace his steps, stopped and shook his head. No. He would honor Jinger's determination and not follow her until the sun reached midmorning. No harm would come to her, for he doubted she'd explore far enough to come within sight of the sheer rock foundation of the castle. She was easily distracted and there were many beautiful plants for her to admire.

Beautiful and dangerous.

After their confrontation, he realized she would be both dangerous and beautiful when extremely angry. He hoped to never face such anger from her. But if he did, he considered ways to return the smile and wonder to her face. To bring back the joy sparkling in her eyes. Perhaps he would be lucky enough to discover how when she returned.

To that end, he turned once again toward the beach. Instead of fishing, he sat and watched the sea, allowing his mind to ramble along with his runaway emotions. He just couldn't seem to gather his thoughts concerning Jinger into a coherent plan. Did desire do that to a man?

A cool wave intruded on his solitude. He frowned at the wet sand left behind by the retreating sea. The tide didn't normally reach this high until after midday. He jerked to his feet and stared into the sky. The sun had peeked and was beginning the downward path to the far horizon.

Too much time had passed with him lost in his thoughts.

The rumble of thunder sounded in the distance and he glanced toward the high cliffs beneath Ib's castle. While rain fell nearly every day, the only storms this land knew were of the sorcerer's making. The fact he was brewing one now boded ill for the land.

And Jinger.

Surely she was wise enough to return to the safety of his lodge with the first hints of a weather change. He turned, intending to race home, but Ommi bounded onto the beach from under the trees.

When she stood before him, he crouched to touch the top of her head. "Mother?"

The firefox drew a deep breath and stared into his eyes. The progression of images and near verbal communication flashed through his mind. Ib was building a storm larger than any he'd created before yet keeping the focus near the cliffs. Ommi insisted they find and remain in a sheltered area until Ib's temper tantrum blew over. Ommi laughed at that thought.

"Jinger has gone exploring."

At Ommi's thought question, Taj felt as he had when a small boy and had to confess to a wrongdoing. But he had done nothing wrong this day—except argue with Jinger and allow her to walk away unprotected.

"She entered the forest in the direction of the castle. I could not stop her, Mother."

Ommi gave a sharp yip, turned and raced toward the trees.

"Wait," Taj called.

Ommi skidded to a stop then wheeled in a circle. A low growl rumbled from her throat.

"I..." Taj had no excuse for his actions. Lost in the wonder Jinger brought to his life, he'd ignored the depths of depravity that delighted his father and how zealously Ib pursued any magical female drawn through the gateway. He'd wrongly hoped since Ib hadn't taken Jinger immediately, she was safe.

He'd been a fool, many times over. And now, he'd allowed Jinger to travel even closer to Ib's lair. The brewing storm took on new meaning.

"He'll use the storm to drive Jinger to him."

Ommi gave an affirmative yip.

"Go, I'll follow." The fish lay forgotten on the sand as Taj raced to the edge of the forest and leapt to climb onto the low branches of a tree. His speed was greater through the canopy. His mother took to the air, the swirl of colors filled with dark intensity flowing behind her. Silent, he moved through the trees following her lead, each leap, each swing punctuated the mantra pounding in his head.

Let her be safe.

At a sudden blast of cold air, Ommi tumbled head over tail backwards to slam to the ground. Taj dropped beside her, hovering protectively until she shook off the daze clouding her eyes and stood steady.

"He'll block you in the air. On the ground?"

She cocked her head to one side and sent an impression of shrugging her shoulders.

"We go on." If his mother wasn't able to proceed, he would. Even if he had to crawl, he would find Jinger and bring her to safety. Ib would not have her. This time his father would not win.

Lightning streaked across the sky. Thunder roared, shaking the ground. Cold rain, the drops sharp as ice and driven by the wind, stung his skin. He and Ommi hovered under the meager protection of a broad-leafed tree. This storm would damage the land, cause trees to fall and the streams to overflow. Bright light sizzled the air around them, the sharp cracks of electricity lifted the hair on Taj's head and made his mother's fur stand on end, softening the outline of her body.

He gasped out a sound, part laugh, part sorrow. Jinger would find Ommi's appearance delightful. She could find joy in the smallest of things. There was no joy in this storm, only danger. "I must go on. Wait here until the lightning stops."

With a snort, Ommi gave her opinion of staying put and stepped from under the tree.

Lightning split the closest tree. Another strike burned a patch of dried grass not an arm's length from where she stood. Taj wrapped his arms around her and cradled her against his chest. "No, Mother. He knows we're here. We'll wait until he grows tired of this game, then find Jinger. He won't waste power holding us here for long."

Images flowed through his mind and he sighed. "I understand. Neither do I wish a delay in searching for her, but if one of us is destroyed now, what chance will she have? I ache with the need to move, to run, to find her. Yes, and to hold her, keep her from him. Keep her safe for as long as I'm able. We'll wait, watch. As soon as he tires of this game, we'll find her."

Ommi pressed her nose against his neck, nuzzling as

she had when he was but a small child. Until that moment, he hadn't realized how much he missed the contact, the acceptance and love a simple touch could show. He moved from the tree trunk yet remained under the minimal protection of the leafy canopy. He would keep himself and his mother safe.

Ib hated wasting power, so the storm wouldn't last. Soon they could continue through the forest and find Jinger.

He cradled the firefox in his arms and scowled at the driving rain.

EIGHTEEN

The incantations needed to speed time within his castle were similar to the one Ib would use to speed the gestation and birth of his child, but much simpler. Within a few short moments he had set the time factor in motion. He stood at the window watching the world around him slow until the flashes of lightning crawled across the sky like bright worms. Even if the firefox made her way through the storm, she'd never discover an opening in the flow of time large enough for anyone to enter the castle.

Ib gave a satisfied nod, locked the workroom door behind him then stood before a mirror he'd placed in the hallway. For eons he hadn't needed to consider his appearance or what his facial expressions might reveal. Now both concerns were of supreme importance. He brushed at the flyaway strands of his white hair and patted them back close to his skull. He practiced a smile, a look of concern, and finally an expression of hopeful joy.

Satisfied he hadn't lost the skill to use appearances to

persuade another, he smoothed his tunic and knee length vest and returned to the grand hall. His servant remained exactly where he'd been instructed to stay, one long arm guarding the door.

"You have done well," Ib said softly. "Return to you place until I call again for you."

The creature turned so his back pressed against the wall. The whisper of the stone receiving it made Ib smile. Such a handy way to keep an underling close by. He kept the smile in place and opened the door.

After Ib left her alone, Jinger warmed her hands at the fire, then curled her legs beneath her on one of the chairs. The soft cushions molded around her body, even offering slight dips and curves for her wings. Delightfully comfortable, she tugged the heavy throw over her lap and up to her shoulders. Her clothing had mostly dried, now, finally, she was getting warm.

Even though her stomach complained, she was unsure whether it was wise to eat. So despite the spicy aromas wafting from under the metal covers, she'd ignored the dishes on the table. Instead, she'd studied the room and found nothing frightening, nothing to cause an alarm to sound in her mind. She didn't sense any magic directed toward her. Still, the warmth and comfort of the room lulled her and she fought a losing battle as her eyelids drooped.

The sound of the door scraping across the stone floor brought her back to full awareness.

Ready to jump to her feet the moment any danger

appeared, she tensed, clutching the chair's arms. She'd heard enough stories from Taj to know despite the apparent good will and friendly gestures of her host, there may still be danger lurking, waiting for her to become complacent.

She just couldn't quite match the things Taj had told her about his father to the man who'd come to her rescue at the cave. Yes, appearances were often deceiving, but she didn't sense any ulterior motives from him. If only that tiny niggle of fear would ease and the prickles of danger would leave the back of her neck alone. She often doubted her own common sense. Maybe the sorcerer was manipulating her. She needed to be more careful.

Ib entered the room, a soft grin making him seem younger. Even a bit appealing. She blinked then rubbed her eyes. A glamor? She assumed this man had no fey blood—at least not that she knew. She knew so little of this world and Ib, so perhaps he had the ability to cast a glamor over himself. Or was the magic somehow influencing her observations?

Calling on the lessons she'd learned as a young child, she gathered her magical abilities and gave a gentle shove. The resistance hovered a moment at the edge of her senses, then faded. Ib's eyebrow arched and his grin grew wide. Had he been testing her? Or was he surprised she recognized the feel of glamor? Giving her no other indication to his thoughts, he crossed to her and sat in the other chair.

He glanced at the undisturbed cloches on the table. "Aren't you hungry? It's well past midday."

She would have given a negative response, except her stomach chose that moment to grumble. According to her belly, she needed to eat constantly. Holding back the need to roll her eyes at herself, she shrugged.

Ib chuckled and lifted the cover from one dish. "I eat no meat or fish, so I fear all I have to offer are grains, vegetables and fruits. If you prefer a meal filled with spice and heat, try this." He replaced the cover and lifted another. "For a milder dish, these root vegetables are delectable. Please don't fear me or what I have to offer. I yearn only for your... pleasure."

Pretending to study the plate of vegetables, which smelled delicious, she considered his words, his tone. He was flirting with her.

This Ib was far different from what she expected. The man Taj had described was evil and ruthless, taking rather than offering. She'd never been able to see a clear projection of Ib in her dreams. She'd only seen a blurry figure and heard his light, tenor voice. Now that voice offered her comfort and more.

The comfort she was okay with—until she returned to the forest and her search for a way home. And Taj. She took a small, empty plate and added a small portion of each of Ib's offerings, smiling in thanks as he lifted the dome from each plate. The mixture of fresh, cut fruit was exceptionally tempting.

"May I speak with you while you eat?" Ib asked.

Maybe he had some thoughts on how she might be able to reach the portal once it opened again. Or how to open it. She'd let him talk, then she'd have a ton of questions for him. "Of course."

"You have been in this world for a number of days."

She nodded and took a bite of the spice laden vegetables. Oh, so delicious. "This is really good."

With a bland smile, Ib waved away her praise. "It is

sustenance. Perhaps you have not eaten well in the forest."

Now he was blatantly fishing for information. The stories Taj had told her about this man made her wary. As well as a bit proud of herself. For once, she wasn't taking someone she'd just met at face value, wasn't trusting him right off even though he had come to her rescue. She matched his noncommittal smile. "I had some luck finding ripe fruits and clean water."

"Hmm, I see. You met no others in your time here?"

Ah ha, he did want to know about Taj. Eventually she might tell him, but for now, let him guess. Maybe that would keep him a bit off kilter until she figured out more about him. "Oh yes, a black unicorn with a silver horn found me in the storm and led me to that cave."

A double line appeared between Ib's lowered eyebrows. "I see. Then it is a good thing I sensed the rock fall and your presence."

"Yes. Thank you again."

"Jinger, there are others in the forest, other beings who are dangerous. Who have no love for me. Should they know you are now under my protection, the danger to you increases. Tell me, did you not encounter a man?"

Heat blazed across her cheeks. Damn her fair skin and easy blushing. Evidenced by the satisfaction filling Ib's expression, she'd be unable to talk her way around this. So she nodded and promptly took a big bite of food to give herself a few moments to come up with an answer that wouldn't endanger Taj.

Ib drummed his fingers against the chair's padded arm in a mesmerizing rhythm. She forced her gaze away and reached for a tall, clear glass of water. Ib tried another, subtle control magic. She deflected his attempt.

He was a sly one. So, she'd answer his question, at least enough to make him think he was gaining control over her. She'd been trained by the best in the Alastriona and by Nightshade. She could do this.

She also decided she would leave as soon as she possibly could. That niggle of awareness, of fear, returned to caress the back of her neck with fine prickles. Only when she was with Taj would she feel safe again.

"Yes," she drew out the word. "I did."

Apparently satisfied, Ib leaned back in his chair and steepled his fingers before his chest. He tapped the tips of each matching finger in slow succession. Inwardly, Jinger rolled her eyes. He didn't expect her to fall into his trap so easily, did he? Yeah, he did. He thought she was a simple creature, not up to his level of magical sophistication.

She probably wasn't, but she wasn't defenseless either.

"I feared it would be so since you did not find your way to me sooner. That... man... is my son."

Jinger gasped and covered her mouth. All those times she and her cousins acted out plays for the family now came in handy. She grinned behind her hand, then sobered. This was no game.

Ib continued, "I fear I failed with him. When he was but a boy, he became crazed and obsessed with the false idea I wished to destroy him. He ran away, and somehow made a home for himself in the forest." He sighed and glanced at the fire. "I have never understood what made him hate me, why he fled when I wanted nothing more than to watch him grow into a man."

Making her eyes wide, Jinger sat her plate on the table and waited until Ib looked at her again. Firelight burned in his eyes, masking any true emotion she might have discovered there. But how did his eyes reflect the fire when he no longer looked in that direction? A wave of heat flowed over her, memories and future possibilities merged.

She shook her head. He was attempting to control her mind again. What did he really want from her? Why did he cast Taj in such a pitiful light?

"I've heard rumors of the fantasies my son has concocted about me. How I make him dream of horrible things, or of a life he is unable to live. How I destroy others to increase my power. For yes, I am a sorcerer, trapped by another in this world."

"Trapped? By another sorcerer?" Interesting.

His lips flattened. "Had it been another magical being, I could have fought, and won. No, this being claimed to be a god."

The prickling at the back of her neck traveled down her spine. She rubbed her neck but couldn't chase away the dreadful premonition.

"A god?"

Ib snorted. "A pretender. One not worthy of our time or words. Tell me of yourself, Jinger. Of the world you come from."

Loath to tell him much, she shrugged. She'd keep her explanations to one world only. "Obviously, I come from a world where there is magic. But there are areas where there isn't much magic. So, in order to keep those who don't believe in magic secure in their beliefs, I often go about without my wings."

"Ah, such a beautiful part of you. I cannot imagine why you wouldn't wish to always have them." His gaze moved leisurely over her wings. She felt the caress and forced herself to keep from leaning into the sensual feeling. Oh, he was a tricky one.

"They'd make quite a stir in that non-magical part of the world." The story of how her father's wings had been forced into the open when he'd visited a human renaissance faire had always been one of her favorites. She loved how her cousin Jayse had concocted a cover story about the wings being part of a trial run of the special effects for a fantasy movie.

A wave of sorrow washed over her. She'd be home soon. There would be a way.

Perhaps if she told Ib how she got to this world, he'd be satisfied. "The day the portal to here opened—"

"Portal? How you arrived?" At her nod, Ib continued, "I call it the gateway."

"Makes sense. Anyway, on that day I was spending some time alone on a beach. It was the anniversary of my cousin's death." The sorrow rose with fierce determination this time, and her vision blurred with tears.

"No, my dear, don't cry." Ib rose and offered her a square of silky cloth. "I've made you sad. We need talk no more this evening. I will show you to your room."

Dabbing at the lucky tears, Jinger froze. Her room? No, she couldn't stay here. She had to get back to the forest. Taj must be frantic with worry. Unless... no, he wouldn't forget about her just because they'd had an argument, would he? She really didn't know him that well. Since she'd stomped away in the direction of... here. Oh, no. She'd ruined everything.

"Jinger? What can I do to ease your sorrow?"

Unable to think of an easy answer, she shook her head. Ib took her hand and caressed her fingers. "Your day has been filled with horrible events. Come, you will rest and we will speak again on the morrow."

"But I should go back..."

"Nonsense. You will not go back to that ruined cave. Nor will I allow you to roam the forest in the dark of night. There are things far more dangerous than one misguided man living there. You will rest here in safety." As he spoke, he drew her across the wide room to a short hallway.

"As it is only my servant and myself in the castle, and our rooms are opposite this hall, you will be safe and undisturbed."

He ushered her into a small room dominated by a canopy bed. Thick, fluffy blankets covered the mattress. Soft, draping fabrics flowed from the canopy to puddle on the floor. She'd dreamed of such a bed when she was a little girl. Now she preferred the silken pillows and covers of Taj's bed. She shoved that memory and desire to the back of her mind. If she didn't keep her love for Taj hidden, Ib would somehow use the knowledge against them.

She stepped further into the room. A wooden stand with a lamp cast a soft glow over the room. Through an arched doorway, she saw an ornate metal bathtub.

Ib spoke close to her ear. "I have cast a small magic over this room. Should you need anything, hot water in the bath, a lighter covering, a darkened room for sleep, all you need do is speak into the lamp and your wish will be provided to you."

"I... thank you." She sensed no deeper magic than he claimed within the room. She was so tired. Tomorrow, after a good night's sleep, she'd find her way from the castle and back to Taj. Lulled by the thought, and curious about the lovely room, she thanked Ib again.

He backed from the room and with a soft smile, shut the door.

Jinger stood in the center of the room for a long moment, concentrating on discovering any other magics Ib might have hidden within the room. She paced the perimeter then glanced with longing at the tub. She was still cold. Returning to the doorway, she touched the multipaneled wood door. An odd vibration rubbed against her palm. So, despite his assurances, Ib had magically locked her in the room.

He wanted her complacent but took no chances she might try to escape. Although anything was possible with the sorcerer, for some reason she thought he was really trying to make a good impression on her. Nor would he risk her compliance by invading her privacy. At least, not yet.

Tomorrow might find him with a different mindset. Especially when she demanded he show her the way from the castle and back to the forest. She'd been a fool and underestimated Ib's masked power.

Tonight, she'd take advantage of the luxury. But she wouldn't be foolish with her actions. She stood by the lamp. "Lock the door from the inside as well."

A swirl of power rose from the lamp and flowed toward the door. Arching her eyebrows, she waited until she sensed the magic take effect. Her request might not keep Ib out, but hopefully would provide a warning if he did return.

She spoke again to the lamp. "I'd like the tub filled with hot bathwater."

The sound of rushing water came from the other

room. Jinger moved to the doorway and watched the tub fill from an invisible tap. The warmth emanated from the water in a rise of fine steam. The tub wasn't as deep as Taj's, but it would do just fine.

Taj. Was he looking for her? Or had her anger, their anger driven a wedge between them? She crossed the room to a single, extremely narrow window and peered into the darkness. Lightning still flashed, but if the thunder roared, the sound was muffled by the thick castle walls. Rain streamed down the rippled glass.

Taj. Be safe. If you're out there, be safe. I'll be back as soon as I can. I'm so sorry I didn't listen to you. Taj, I...

She wanted to say the words to him in person, not just in a wishful call from her mind. She loved Taj and she needed him to know. No matter how he might feel about her.

She didn't believe one word Ib said or implied about Taj. On the other hand, was everything Taj told her about Ib the truth? Or was Taj's truth stretched to create a history he could justify? Even among fairy folk and the gentry there were cases of post-traumatic stress concerns and forgotten memories. While it had always seemed strange to her, she'd seen examples of the debilitating pain and in both Gowthaman, and Searlait of the Alastriona.

No, Taj's behavior didn't coincide with anything she'd experienced or read about.

However, the smarmy vibes she sensed from Ib told her more than anything else about him. He was dangerous, and she needed to be extra careful.

The steaming water called to her. The momentary thought that Ib might be watching her stalled her hands as she started to undress. She forced away the thought.

The sorcerer would do as he wanted and until she learned more, there was little she could do to prevent his spying. She didn't need to make it easier for him though.

She asked for candlelight. The brighter ambient glow dimmed and a row of candles appeared to edge the tub. Very nice. She slipped into the warmth and sighed.

While she relaxed her body, her mind would be active. By morning she needed to have a workable plan in place for dealing with Ib and leaving the castle.

Because despite his overly kind and considerate attentions, she didn't doubt she was nothing more than a prisoner in a luxurious cell.

Ib resisted the urge to spy on his *guest*. The winged beauty held more power than she imagined, and he hungered for a taste. Taking her body would bring him a pleasure he'd long forgotten Taking her magic would be ecstasy. Finally taking her child would be the ultimate fulfillment of power. He would finally have the means to escape and force the pretender fire god to meet his challenge.

Retiring to his bed chamber, Ib stood for long moments at the window, watching the storm that continued to rage over part of the forest. He sensed his son and the firefox mired deep in the center of the wild winds and driving rain. Sending sleet to add to their discomfort would bring him joy, but he'd already used more power than he'd thought necessary to create the storm and bring Jinger to him. He'd let the storm fade naturally and deal with the would be rescuers later. If they survived.

Should they live, by the time they arrived at the castle, the winged woman will have given birth to his child and he would be deep within the magical processes needed to access the gateway and escape to another world. So, let the storm rage, he would rest easy that night.

Angling to peer at the horizon, he gave momentary thought to once again climbing the stairs to the crystal tower. He'd never called for power while he still held such glory in his hands, or before he was depleted.

He didn't need to expend much power to convince Jinger to come to him. So, he would wait and draw naturally from the sun each day. He would have no difficulty maintaining the level of powerful magic he needed. If he required time in the chamber before escaping, he would climb the stairs. Until then, what he had was enough.

Before retiring, he held up a palm sized clear crystal and spoke a single word. The woman's room pulsed into view and the focus settled on the bed. She slept on her side, those glorious wings spread across the bedding behind her. Desire settled low in his body and he arched his brows at the sensation. How long had it been?

He knew. Not since the djinn, his powerless son's mother, not since that bitch had he truly desired a woman. For a moment a deep fear sparked in his chest. If he desired the winged woman as well, would her child also be worthless?

He shook his head at the folly. His magic was at peak power. All he needed for success had been provided. There was no question, no doubt. This child would be the means to his freedom.

The storm continued to rage, keeping Taj and Ommi sheltering beneath the broad leaves of a squat tree. Thunder shook the ground, threatening to loosen the boulders high on the distant cliffs. Lightning flashed across the sky in jagged ribbons of blinding light, striking land and trees near them. Their tree refuge kept them safe.

Taj felt something nestle close to his hip. With Ommi cradled against his chest, he glanced down. A tiny creature, no larger than his hand, curled next to him. Soon a second joined them, followed by a line to even tinier young. He grinned. "Welcome, friends. We're happy to share this shelter with you.

Ommi stretched to touch noses with the first animal then glanced into Taj's eyes.

"Of course, Mother, any who wish to take shelter here are welcome. No, I don't understand why the lightning doesn't strike this tree, but I'm happy to take advantage of the boon. I hope Jinger has discovered a place of safety as well."

The need to move and fight the storm to find her grew strong, but Ommi placed her paw on his shoulder and shook her head.

"I know. Should I leave now, the storm would throw the entirety of its force against me. Ib has created a more powerful storm than I've experienced. Do you think he may have lost control?" If Ib lost control of a storm, then perhaps we wasn't as powerful as he claimed.

At the fox's negative head shake, Taj released a slow breath and resigned himself to wait. However long the rains fell, however long lightning pierced the sky, he would wait. Then, he would find Jinger, confront his father, and return with Jinger to the less dangerous areas of the forest.

He'd thought himself patient. Another misconception about himself Jinger had shattered.

The undergrowth parted between two trees near their sanctuary. A long, dark head appeared and a long, silver horn sparkled in the afterglow of a lightning strike. Taj arched his eyebrows as Ommi leapt from his lap to greet the unicorn. He hadn't seen the animal for so long, he'd thought perhaps it had perished. Before Taj escaped his father, Ib had often shown off his pleasure and power while torturing the elegant beast.

The unicorn crossed to Taj and bent one foreleg to kneel. It touched its horn to the damp grass. Raising its head, the unicorn's dark eyes shone with unaccustomed sorrow. In the same way his mother communicated with him, the unicorn sent a flurry of images to his mind.

Jinger. Alone in the storm. Ib, a cave, a command. Then Jinger again, the softness of her hand upon the unicorn's neck, the thankfulness in her eyes when it led her to a cave. One last glimpse of her with one hand lifted in farewell.

"You did this for Ib?" Disturbing the tiny family, Taj jerked to his full height and glared at the unicorn. "Why?"

Head lowered, the unicorn huffed once. More images. A deep, terrible sadness. The anger fled from Taj and his shoulder slumped. "You have a young one?"

The unicorn nodded.

"Ib has taken her and holds her in terror to make you do as he wishes." No question, for Taj knew this to be fact. His father was no different than he had been, except, perhaps, he'd become even more cruel. Taj touched the unicorn's forelock. "Now he has taken Jinger as well. I don't know how to win against him, but I will. Once I find Jinger, we will bring your young one with us from the castle. As well as any others we discover there. This is my vow."

Ommi added her confirmation with a sharp yip.

Taj glanced up at the storm through a small break in the overhead branches. All he needed now was some idea of what to do. His initial anger had faded to a dull roar at the back of his mind. Anger would only get him so far, for Ib knew how to manipulate his anger, a skill he'd practiced often enough since Taj was a boy. He needed to find a place of calm within himself to discover a plan. Taj glanced from his mother to the unicorn.

"If there is any help you can offer me, any knowledge of Ib or his plan, I have time now to listen." He fought to make his grin not a grimace. "With the storm, Ib provides us time to plan against him."

O n the third day of her captivity in Ib's castle, Jinger woke confused and blurry. She lay in the comfortable bed staring at the canopy attempting to make some sense from her disordered dreams.

In her dreams, a storm still raged outside the castle, although from her window the sky had been clear for two days. Through the storm, the dream, she'd heard Taj call to her, begging her to take care, to not listen to Ib. Telling her he would find her soon.

Then Ib had entered the dream, a kind Ib, not at all as Taj had described him. He'd shown her his home, offered her fine meals, music, friendship. His brightness shoved Taj to the shadows and she'd begun to wonder what was real.

She sat and scrubbed her hands over her face. No, that part was real. Over the past days Ib had catered to her wishes, smiled and chuckled at her wonder of his home. The perfect host. Until yesterday.

He'd become more insistent she follow his suggestions. His smile had been flat, he laughter tinged with... evil? Yes, that was what she felt oozing through the air between them. But then he'd been kind again. In the dream.

It was becoming more difficult to tell what was real, what she imagined, or what she hoped. Ib used subtle magic on her. She was sure of it but hadn't been able to recognize the enchantment as it happened. Each hour spent near him made it more difficult for her to resist.

She wasn't even sure anymore why or what she tried to resist.

Remain strong, Jinger. I'm near.

Taj? His voice was faint, so distant. She fisted her hands. Was it truly Taj, or another effort by Ib to keep her off-center, disoriented?

She chose to believe in Taj and moved her lips without making a sound. "I'm trying. Hurry."

A soft chime sounded. She grimaced and slipped from the bed. Ib waited for her in the grand hall and if she didn't appear soon, he would order the creature he called a servant to fetch her. She'd tried to ignore him the first morning and the slimy being popped out of the wall, grunted at her, then wrapped long fingers around her wrist and tugged her from the room.

The second morning had been worse. The servant had unceremoniously tossed her over its shoulder and carried her to the hall. Not wanting to experience another encounter, she rushed through dressing and was waiting at the door when the second chime rang. The door unlocked and swung open allowing her to leave.

The hallway wasn't any better than being locked in a room. The one time Ib had allowed her to wander the castle without him, she'd tried opening every door she found. Not a single one budged even an inch. She hurried toward the great hall, paused to run her fingers through her hair, then entered.

Ib sat in his usual chair by the fire but her chair had been moved from across a low table to next to his. The upholstered sides touched. She hugged herself, rubbing her arms. He was obviously ready to go beyond the many hints he'd spoken the past two days.

Unfortunately she didn't think she was as strong as she hoped.

"Ah, there you are, my dear. Come, break your fast and tell me what you wish to do today."

She wanted to go home. If not to her own world, then to Taj's clearing. Not the answer she dared give to Ib's overly interested expression.

She paused, curled her thumb under her chin, and tapped her forefinger against her jaw. The typical thinking pose wouldn't delay her need to answer for long but might buy her a few moments.

When Ib's eyes narrowed, she continued to the table and sat, leaning away from the sorcerer. "The sun is bright today. Could we go outside? Does your castle have gardens we could visit. I do enjoy flowers."

She watched him from under her lashes while she reached for a small, stone bowl filled with cut fruits. His eyes unfocused for the briefest of moments. One of his fingers stirred the air. He was casting a spell. Then he turned to her with a smile. "Of course, my dear.

While she ate, Ib picked at a bowl of fruit. He never seemed to eat much and she wondered if he'd added some sort of charm to the food. No longer hungry, she returned her half-full bowl to the table.

Ib arched an eyebrow. "You are not hungry this morn?"

She shrugged. "Not really. I could use a good dose of sunshine though."

He smiled slowly, his dark pupils grew larger, and a spark of fire lit his eyes. The desire was powerful and she leaned toward him, wanting... wanting what? The spark faded but the allure continued to draw her closer.

"The sun. Ah, yes, my dear. I, too, enjoy basking in the powerful light of the sun."

His emphasis on power made her pause. Maybe going outside wasn't a good idea after all. She'd hoped to discover some way from the castle, perhaps through a garden gate. Now she wasn't sure she wanted to leave.

Jinger gave herself a mental shake and shoved at the tendril of magic teasing her thoughts.

Ib reached for her hand, rose and drew her from her chair. His hand rested at her waist for a long moment while he stared into her eyes. She tried but couldn't tear her gaze from his. His warm palm slipped to the small of her back, encouraging her closer. He was going to kiss her.

No, he wasn't. Jinger angled away from his touch. She fought to control the rapid beating of her heart, calm the shortness of her breath. How was he doing this? She didn't want him. She wanted Taj. There had to be some way to leave the castle, to escape. Today she would discover the way.

A frown soured Ib's expression and he huffed out a mumbled curse. A second later his smile had returned and he turned toward a doorway she'd never noticed before.

More magic to keep her contained and confused.

"Come, my dear Jinger. To the gardens." He held out his hand but when she refused to take it, his lips flattened and he walked away. "Follow, then, if you wish."

He led her through a series of large, open spaces. She sensed how magic had changed the rooms so gave up trying to remember the way back. Why was she able to recognize and understand this but not how the sorcerer manipulated her emotions?

They entered a large room where one entire wall was covered with a detailed tapestry. Jinger stopped to study the finely woven scenes. Ib returned to her side.

"This is beautiful," she said.

"Yes. It is a depiction of the land around my home." He hesitated. "Around my prison."

"You mentioned that before. That a being... a fire elemental, was that it?" She'd try and get Ib to talk more. Maybe she'd discover a clue to her escape.

He rested one palm against his chest and sighed.

Jinger fought the urge to roll her gaze at the overly dramatic action. She asked a dangerous question. His answer might help her find her way home. "And you haven't found a way to escape?"

Bright light sparkled again in his eyes. The air around them grew warmer. "I have. To do so, I need your help."

"My help?"

"Come, we will talk in the garden."

He walked away, obviously expecting her to follow. Jinger considered staying right where she was, but curiosity overcame her minor act of rebellion. She wanted to know, yet was afraid to find out, how she could help such a powerful being. She hurried to catch up with his long strides.

Filled with a bounty of fresh, fragrant blooms, the garden was a nearly perfect match to her favorite space outside the palace in Faerie. Here the colorful flowers were slightly duller, the feel of the air oppressive even with a light breeze. So close to her memories, yet not accurate. Like the canopy bed. A handful of other items around the castle that reminded her of home. Had Ib somehow searched her memories to create these things?

More than just invading her dreams, he'd invaded

her mind and taken from her without permission. Stolen her memories to use for his benefit. How could she have been so stupid to not recognize this sooner?

Any lingering false attraction to the sorcerer died and she was able to see past the glamor he'd cast over himself and the garden. She couldn't let him know she'd somehow broken through his spell so she glanced around the area. By squinting she could still see the spell-casted flowers. "Oh, this is beautiful."

Ib guided her to a bench and they sat. He took one of her hands and held it between his palms. She fought to restrain a shudder at the appearance of his fingers. He had no fingernails, only blackened, burned skin. She made herself look at his face. His skin was taut over sharp bones. While filled with the actual blaze of fire, his eyes were dead. His smile exposed browned teeth, the incisors sharp as fangs.

Afraid her expression would give away her reactions, she angled her head to gaze out over the dead garden. "Thank you for showing me this. You said I can help you escape?"

"You can."

Fearing she was taking a huge risk, she sighed. "I would like to return to my world, too."

"Ah, then, my dear, we are in accord. We can assist each other."

"I don't know what I can do. Anything I've tried to reach the port—gateway has failed. And then it disappeared." She didn't have to fake the tremor in her voice. "Along with my hope."

"There is a way. We must combine our magics."

Jinger shook her head. "Sounds good, but my magic doesn't work in this world. I haven't been able to do anything. Start a fire. Form a portal. I can't even hide my wings like I usually do."

He stroked the edge of one wing. "I don't see why you would want to hide such a beautiful part of you. Your inability is not surprising. This land, where we are held, suppresses magic."

"But you can—"

Ib tightened his fingers against her wing. "I have been trapped here eons upon eons. Uncounted ages of time. I had to relearn my skills. Study and sacrifice. In my study I discovered the way. I am unable to complete this magic alone. I need you."

A premonition skittered down her spine. Attempting to ignore the cold fear, she asked, "What do I need to do."

"Bear me a child."

I b leaned closer to study the emotions flashing
through the woman's expression. With little true
companionship over the ages, he didn't understand many of her thoughts. He did recognize revulsion
and the flash of pain when he crushed the edge of her
wing in his fist.

She slid away from him on the bench and lifted her
hands with her palms facing him. "Wait…a child…what…
I can't stay here that long. I need… Are you crazy?"

"It is the only way." He released her wing and eased
closer, taking her hands. "The birth will not take long.
There is a magic—"

"You want me to get pregnant, then you want to use
magic on my unborn child?"

The loathing in her expression pleased him. He
wanted her willing, but not so much to be compliant
under his hands. Only enough to satisfy the prophecy.
She wasn't required to know the entire procedure. "It has
been foretold that the birth of a child will aid in my…our
escape."

She tried to pull her hands from his and he tightened his grip. Her eyes narrowed with pain. "How? How can a baby help?"

He would ignore that question. "I only know that if a child is born from a willing union—"

"Willing? I'm not going to have sex with you. Not now. Not ever."

"Ah, my dear, I do believe you are mistaken." He rose and dragged her to her feet. Her resistance gave him strength and hope. He would get a fine child on her. A worthy sacrifice. She would never know for the spell would take her life as she gave birth, adding to the child's power. He smiled and she cowered, pleasing him greatly. He would enjoy his time with her.

However brief that may be.

Trying to rip her hands from his, she struggled, planting her feet solidly against the stone pathway. Her head shook from side to side in denial. "I won't."

"Ah but, my dear, you shall. To be willing you must only beg for me to take you."

She straightened and laughed once, a harsh sound of denial. "You're delusional. I will never beg you for anything. Let. Me. Go."

"You will. And soon. I grow impatient and tired of this game we play. Come, allow me to offer persuasion.'

He wrapped her in a cocoon of magic stilling her movements then dragged her across the garden. At the far wall, he pressed his hand to the stone and opened a narrow doorway. Not even his servant knew of this space, so he would be free to 'persuade' Jinger as he desired.

He released the magic binding her and shoved her into the tiny, circular room. The whitewashed walls created a false brightness to the space. Her wings brushed the wall as she turned once in a circle then rushed for the door.

With a. flash of light, Ib positioned himself in the doorway and lifted one fist. She barreled into him, her lowered shoulders bringing her lovely face level with his fist. He would not hit her, but if she caused the injury herself, he would use the pain.

She fell at his feet, her eyes wide with shock. She touched her fingertips to her cheek, then to her bleeding lower lip.

Ib crouched before her and curled his finger under her chin. "What a shame, my dear, that you damaged yourself. No matter. When you come to me, I shall accept you as you are."

"You'll be waiting a long time."

"I think not, Jinger."

He rose, backed from the room and secured the door. The heavy thumps of her fists against the wood made him grin. He thought a moment, then touched a crystal imbedded in the wall activating the full power of the room. Imagining how the space filled with blinding light, he passed through the garden and chased away the glamor from the dead plants. No need to waste energy on foolish things.

It shouldn't take long for her to call for him and beg for release. To beg to bear his child. No being had held out long against the blazing white pain.

The thought brought a lightness to Ib's step as he crossed the great hall and entered his workroom.

J inger sat cross-legged on the floor, her face in her hands. Trying to rush past the sorcerer had been stupid. Now she'd have a bruise and a split lip to show for her foolishness. Battle scars. She grinned and winced at the pain. Not productive battle scars, but still. She'd tried.

Now all she had to do was wait out whatever Ib had planned for her. Wait until Taj found her. She hated to think it as being rescued, she so didn't want to be the helpless maiden in the tower some guy had to rescue. But she couldn't deny the fact she couldn't escape by herself. Ib was too powerful, and she had next to nothing to fight back with.

No magic. Barely practiced fighting skills. Not very logical thinking and planning skills. She sighed. Positive thoughts only. Being negative never helped. She lifted her head from her hands.

Bright light pierced her vision and she closed her eyes tightly. Where had the overly bright light come from? She squinted one eye open and immediately closed it. It was like being an inch away from a spotlight.

She scooted back until she ran into a wall and, hoping the small distance helped, tried opening her eye again to a space that was more than white. It was as if the room was made of pure heat and light.

Hot, sharp pain pierced her retina before burning into her brain. Physical shards of light pulsed agony through her mind. Pressing the heels of her hands against her eyes, she curled forward. She bit her broken lip hoping the pain would help her fight the need to cry out, to beg for an end to the pain.

She would not do that. Ever. Ib would not win.

Hurt. So bad. A whimper escaped. Tears trailed fire down her cheeks. Fearing she'd be burned, scarred, she lifted the hem of her shirt to absorb her tears.

Taj. She needed Taj. Think of him. Remember the cool diffused light of his forest home. She tried, but each thought brought a blast of even brighter light until her inner vision danced with starburst sparkles. *Taj, help me.*

Jinger? Be strong. I'm coming.

T b sensed the setting of the sun and frowned. He'd expected to hear the woman's screams, her pleas for release long before the day had passed. His frown deepened. The bitch hadn't gone and died on him, had she? Closing his eyes, his mind traveled through the castle walls to the light oubliette. He heard the harshness of her breathing, then the soft undertones of her voice.

Pleading. His shoulders relaxed and he allowed himself a small smile of satisfaction. He listened closer.

Slamming his fist against the text he'd been studying, he growled. The bitch was singing. He pushed his senses closer to see. She'd covered her eyes with cloth from her clothing as well as her hands, then wrapped her wings around herself. And she defied him by singing.

Perhaps the song was a form of magic she attempted. He leaned forward and tilted his head to listen more closely.

...nothing bring me down...

What words were these?

...because I'm... happy...

The light had addled her brain. It mattered not. As

long as she was willing. He lifted one hand to summon his servant then dropped his flexed fingers to the table. If he sent the creature to fetch the woman, it would know about the oubliette. That didn't matter now. Ib would be free of this prison within a handspan of days.

He called the servant, gave instructions, and returned to searching the text. Should Jinger remain unwilling, he would be prepared. He remembered a spell that would work. Heedless of the aged, brittle parchment, he flipped the pages. Ah. There.

He gathered what he needed into a metal bowl. He would only use this tactic if she still refused to come to him willingly. The expense of energy would be worth the end result of a son to sacrifice.

When his servant reported the successful transfer of the woman, Ib began the long trek to the deepest dungeon.

T he sound of wood scraping against stone intruded on Jinger's misery. Was Ib returning? Her wavering song faded and she curled further in on herself. The last she'd heard Taj say—or had it been only her imagination? The words, 'be strong' were hopeless. She wasn't strong. Her ability to fake it had disappeared in the pain-filled white light.

Even so, she would not do as Ib wished.

Rough hands grabbed her and she was unceremoniously lifted and draped over the servant's broad shoulder. She recognized the moldy scent of the creature and supposed she should be thankful for the jarring steps that carried her from the tiny room. She didn't trust the cooling of the air around her and kept her hands firmly over her eyes.

Bright spheres of colored light danced behind her closed lids. Had the light damaged her vision? Even though her eyes continued to water, they also felt dry and scratchy. She tried blinking but that only made the scratchiness worse.

Concentrating on how the creature's bony shoulder poked into her belly with each step, helped her focus on what might happen next. Although she dared not think about what new form of persuasion Ib planned.

How long was this creature going to carry her? Thank goodness she'd barely eaten anything earlier. How long ago had that been? She'd lost all sense of time, of direction, almost, she feared, of herself. Only trying to remember and singing silly songs about happiness had kept her from being lost in the pain and the light.

Finally the servant grunted and bent forward to drop her to a hard stone surface. At least this stone was cool. It took one of her hands and snapped a metal cuff around her wrist. With the clink of chain, he extended her arm, lifting her wrist above shoulder level. This was more what she imagined being imprisoned would be like. Chained to the wall. Probably in a dungeon deep under the castle.

She caught her split lip between her teeth. If both of her hands were chained, she wouldn't be able to keep her eyes covered. What if this was a trick and the light returned. She tried twisting away from the servant. It grunted again, tested the metal cuff, and stepped back. A wet noise sounded then nothing.

"Hey, are you still here?"

Silence answered her. Just as well. After a long moment, she kept her hand over her eyes and eased one open. The colored spots remained, otherwise she saw only dim, shadowy shapes. Blinking to refocus, she opened both eyes and moved her hand.

Near total darkness surrounded her. "Thank goodness," she whispered. Carefully rising from a stone bench and moving around the cell, she ran her hands along the wall to where the chain had been fastened to a thick hook. She discovered nothing that felt like a door.

How had the creature disappeared? A trap door? She scuffed her feet across the floor as far as she could reach. She didn't feel any joints or cracks withing the smooth stone. Curious.

She'd try to locate the entrance once her vision cleared a bit more. If there was time. Ib wouldn't leave her alone for long.

She made her way back to the bench. Dust rose from her movements, tickling her nose. Half expecting to discover the desiccated bones of some long dead creature, she snorted then coughed. Not a smart move.

She hadn't made a smart move since crawling from bed this morning. Now her attempt at finding a way to escape had landed her in the dungeon of the very being Taj had warned her against. The sorcerer was far more powerful than she'd imagined. He should have been throwing off a nearly visible aura or magic. How had Ib disguised the extent of his magic so completely?

Maybe he hadn't needed to, she had been distracted by her thoughts. She'd welcomed Ib's consideration and sympathy and allowed him to rescue her from the rockslide. Stupid fairy. All of that had probably been his plan the entire time.

She sat cross-legged on a low bench, planted her elbows on her knees and braced her chin on her fists. Her entire family would be disappointed in her. And Nightshade? He'd throw one of his famous hissy fits. One of his lectures would be welcome right now. Imagining his directions, she attempted a charm to release the cuff.

The cuff burned with blazing hot magic. Knowing the effort was useless, she still tried every charm and verse she knew but succeeded in only making the cuff tighter. In the past it had always been easy to fall back on magic to solve problems. Here her magic no longer functioned, becoming a useless part of her.

She didn't believe Ib's assertion he'd regained his magical abilities over time. He'd always had some control over his magic here. While she didn't know the extent of his power, she felt confident he'd built on those abilities. She sensed the presence of ancient magic in his aura, spells and powers far older than any of Faerie she'd encountered.

How was she supposed to fight that? How did she keep her sense of self and not become a willing participant in Ib's plans? Knowing she wasn't the first woman in this situation, she shuddered. How many? How many had he taken to his bed?

How many children? What had happened to the children? If this had been going on for the eons he claimed, there would be many children. Where were they? She only knew about Taj.

As he had with Taj's mother, Ib insisted Jinger bear him a child.

Revulsion shuddered through her and she caught her lip between her teeth to keep from giving voice to her fear. The pain and taste of blood from her split lip brought her back to constructive thoughts.

Were there any positives for her now? Understanding the ways of magic in many worlds, the need for consent truly could be imperative here.

She'd never give her consent. He'd never convince her to agree. Never.

A whisper of sound preceded the appearance of the faint outline of a doorway. Jinger huddled into the corner as far as she could. Keeping her eyes closed against the pain the tiny bit of light surrounding Ib caused, she lifted her chin. She might not be able to fight the sorcerer's magic. So she would defy him as long as she could.

"Ah, my dear. I am pleased. Few return from my oubliette. You shall bear me a fine child."

"I will not."

"You still defy me?"

The surprise in his tone made Jinger smile and gave her a needed shot of bravery. "I will always defy you."

Ib made a harsh sound of disbelief and crossed the small cell. He grasped her free hand and the weight of a metal cuff wrapped her wrist. Wrenching her to her feet, he turned her to face the wall. With an echoing clink, both of her wrists were bound to the chain and lifted high above her head.

"I have considered our situation, my dear. I believe I have discovered the means to aid in your decision."

"I've made up my mind. My answer will always be no."

"So you say, Jinger. So you say now." He stroked her wing and she jerked it from his touch. He chuckled. "Such beautiful wings. A shame you had to hide them. I'm sure having them free is a relief."

He turned away and she dared open her eyes before trying to angle to see him. His sing-song tone sent chills along her spine. She reminded herself to stay strong. Nothing he could do to her would make her beg. Stay strong because Taj was coming.

Ib placed a small metal bowl on the stone bench. Humming, he set a series of tiny vials and boxes beside the bowl. With a glance in her direction, he smiled, cradled the bowl in his palm, and began adding his ingredients.

Heavy dread settled in Jinger's belly. Her arms and legs felt like lead. Was Ib draining something from her? Her life, her hope? Planting her feet against the cold stone, she struggled weakly against the chains.

"Struggle if you wish, my dear. There is but one thing which will end this. You need only say the words, 'I come to you willingly'. So simple yet those words will prevent what is to come."

"I... I am not willing. Never will be." Defiance faded with her voice. "What are you doing?"

"You are unaccustomed to your wings. I thought to remedy this concern."

He didn't mean... "No. You're not going to take my wings."

Ib paused his mixing and shook his head. "Take your wings? My dear, you wound me. I only return them to you."

A swirl of pale smoke rose from the bowl. "Remember, my dear. All you need say is 'I come to you willingly' and this will end."

Jinger shook her head and struggled. "Leave me alone."

With a huff, Ib spoke a syllable and the chain tightened, lifting her arms high, stretching her until her toes barely touched the floor. A second word and her back was bared to him. He pressed his hand between her shoulder blades.

His hand was hot and had it been anyone else's touch, would have been comforting. That frightened her more than the expected burn.

He whispered close to her ear. "Only your words, my dear. Only your words."

A stream of cold liquid trailed down her back along the base of one wing. That wasn't too bad.

Shards of pain pierced her back. Each point of pain burned deep under her skin then spread to the tips of her wings. Pressure shoved her against the wall. So much pressure.

Unable to hold the agony at bay, Jinger screamed.

"You must say the words."

TWENTY-ONE

With the storm finally abated, the unicorn led Taj to the collapsed cave entrance. Taj eyed the fallen stone. "Thank you my friend. I will not forget my promise to you."

The unicorn dipped its dark head. Ommi twined around the animal's front legs then sat before it. Taj watched the silent communication between the two while he considered the fastest way to enter Ib's castle. When he'd been young, there had been many small chinks in the sorcerer's magic allowing him to easily leave and return. Once Ib banished him, most of those entrances had closed. Not that he'd ever wanted to enter the castle again.

Until this day.

With a soft snort, the unicorn touched its velvety nose to the top of Ommi's head, turned and moved swiftly along the rock strewn pathways. Ommi paced a short distance from the cave entrance.

"We need to find another way in."

His mother gave him a disgusted took at his obvious

statement then leapt into the air. She pranced higher and faced the rocks creating the foundation to the huge castle. Impatient, Taj watched his mother search the stones. Finally, she gave a sharp yip and moved toward the rocks.

An explosion of clear air tumbled her backward through the sky. Head over tail, she rolled above the trees before righting herself. Taj dashed in her direction and stood beneath her. "Ommi?"

She shook her head and the message to wait filled his mind. "Only a moment. I've wasted too much time already."

He crossed his arms and leaned against a narrow tree. His mother would not have him wait for no reason. This delay made him itchy. He had to enter the castle. Find Jinger before the sorcerer had time to harm her. Each moment felt stretched. He would be too late.

Taking a deep breath, he focused on a calm that continued to elude him. He pushed off from the tree and stalked toward the blocked cave entrance. A symbol scratched on one of the fallen stones glinted in the sunlight. Climbing on one of the larger boulders, he stretched to trace the design.

He'd made this long ago, a sign to lead him back into the castle after being sent on one of his father's tasks. A faster, easier way in—and out—than the gateway Ib commanded him to use. The gap in Ib's protective spell wasn't in this cave, but it was close. He waved at Ommi.

When she landed next to him, he pointed. "There is a way. It will take us directly into the dungeons. We'll search there first."

Ommi ducked her head, then lifted her dark gaze to

Taj. Again her communication was forceful and urgent. "You're sure?"

Ommi nodded.

Ib had somehow discovered a way to alter the flow of time within his castle. "How long?"

The answer was hesitant and he closed his eyes against the implications.

In the few hours he'd hidden from a storm, Jinger had been in the castle over three days. Dread possibilities threatened to steal his determination. Motioning to Ommi, he slid down the boulder. "If hours to us are days to Jinger, we must hurry. Follow me. The distance is not far."

As they followed the discrete markers along the base of the cliff his mother told him the time distortions prevented her from entering the castle. The lump in his chest fell to his belly. He'd hoped for her help in searching the dungeons. Or using her ability to sense Ib to serve as a warning while they were in the castle.

Even her silent encouragement did little to ease his concerns. If he must face Ib alone, he would. He would do anything, sacrifice anything to protect the woman he loved.

Jinger? Be strong. I'm coming.

Small stones and dirt had partially filled the narrow fissure marked as an entrance. Taj barely remembered the opening but trusted his mark and was able to squeeze though. When his mother failed her attempt to break through the time barrier, Taj entered the small cave. There, in the furthest corner was a second narrow opening leading to one of the dungeon levels.

Taj pressed the flat of his palm against the rough-hewn stone wall. Cool. He released a slow breath.

There were no heat markers announcing Ib's presence. He moved further into the near darkness. Along the wall of the dungeon's passageway, tiny bits of flame held in stone bowls cast dancing shadows over the stone. The minimal light drew him further into the dungeon.

Months held in the dim recesses of the dungeons as a child gave Taj intimate knowledge of the narrow, twisting passageways, tiny cells and traps the sorcerer set to ensnare the unwary. This was no place for the light and joy intrinsic in Jinger. She was strong, and filled with bright magic, but was she was strong enough to fight Ib's influence? His love of torture?

Fear for her tightened Taj's throat and he forced a dry swallow. He'd allowed this to happen. He'd been correct in his determination she shouldn't explore alone, so he should have followed her, watched over her. Kept her from entering the castle.

He shook off his recriminations. What was done, was done.

Leaving the uncertainties of the past hours behind, he scanned the walls, the floor, the heavy rocks overhead for traps. Disturbed by the lack of snares, he ached to rush along the passage but held his steps in check. Remembering others who might be held here, he paused at each heavy door, shook his head and moved on.

Near the end of the passage, where five tunnels led away from a central room, he heard the sounds of movement. Pressed against the wall, he held his breath but Ib did not appear. The sounds continued from behind the door directly across from him.

Aware of possible dangers, he carefully cracked open the door. The occupant bared its teeth and stomped a hoof against the stone. The young unicorn. Taj fully opened the door and lifted his hands. "I am Taj."

The unicorn nodded. It appeared nearly fully grown, yet not old enough to communicate easily with him. As long as the young one understood Taj's directions. "Come. It's time for you to leave this place."

Another nod. When Taj backed from the doorway, the unicorn followed. He gestured and pointed down the passageway. "Quickly now. Come."

The animal trotted behind him and Taj winced at the noise the hooves made but knew of no way to avoid the sound. When they reached the small cave, Taj discovered his mother and the adult unicorn digging through the dirt and stone to make the opening larger. It wouldn't take them long before the young one would be free.

"Thank you, Ommi. And to you, my friend. May you and your young be safe."

Leaving the animals to their work Taj rushed back into the dungeons.

There was only one cell where Ib held his most treasured captives.

Taj took the passage with a steep, downward slope. He'd occupied that cell. Dank and musty, the memory of those months tickled his nose and he pinched his nostrils to control a sneeze. The cell was Ib's favorite because for the captive there was no visible exit. Only darkness and even darker stone.

When Ib entered the cell, he had been the only light. He'd held the only power.

At the end of the deep passage, Taj stopped at the narrow door that both mocked and beckoned him. As surely as though the stone were transparent, he knew Jinger was behind that door. His throat tightened with the need to call out to her, his muscles ached to rush to her side.

Standing well back, he scanned the door, the frame, the area surrounding the opening. Nothing... ah, except the tiny, tight spiral of a coiled spring balanced on the lintel. Until he knew the construction of the spring, he wouldn't be able to dismantle the snare.

Three steps brought him to the door. He stood at an angle to catch what little light there was and peered at the spring through narrowed eyes. His brows arched in surprise. Such a simple device, one of the first he'd discovered how to manipulate. This lack of concern throughout the dungeons proved his father didn't believe Taj willing or able to take Jinger from the castle.

With a grim, tight smile, Taj lifted one finger, shuddered, then pressed down against the side of the spring. Tiny bones crunched within the leather casing. He closed his eyes and offered a sorrow-filled thought for whatever creature this had once been. When he'd flattened the spring completely, he stepped back and held his breath.

The door swung open silently. He waited for the count of six heartbeats before stepping into the cell.

Jinger lay curled on the narrow bench against the wall of the dusty room, facing him.

"Go. Away." The rasp of her words cut through his soul. She had every right to deny him after his failure to protect her. But her eyes were closed. Perhaps she thought Ib had returned.

"Jinger?" By the stars, his voice was as raw as hers.

Slowly, she opened her eyes. "Taj? Are you another trick? Another attempt to make me—"

"No. I am not Ib. Hurry. I don't know how long until

he returns. Come back to the forest with me. Please." He held his breath waiting for her answer.

"Taj? Yes. Help me."

Her awkward struggle to rise held him frozen. To crawl from the bench, she turned her back to him. No. Her wings. Her wings were gone.

TWENTY-TWO

Taj had found her. He'd take her from this place. Keep her safe. Jinger made it to her feet, barely maintaining control over her exhausted, abused muscles. She held out her hand. "I think I'm strong enough to get out of here. To get back to your home where it's safe."

Pain rippled down her back and she gasped, falling to her knees. "Maybe I'm not."

Taj knelt before her. "I shall be your strength."

The dim light from outside the cell did little to illuminate his expression, making it difficult to watch his eyes as he studied her. Without her wings would he still... still what? Did he even like her, or did he only feel responsible for her?

"Jinger," he whispered. "I should have protected you from him."

"No, I was the idiot. Get me out of here. Before he comes back. Before he captures you, too."

Taj rose and paced around her. She had no clue what

her back looked like, but the pain brought her images of torn flesh and jagged scars. A bit of warm cloth covered her back and she sighed. He couldn't bear to look at her.

"Wrap my vest around you. It isn't much but will prevent further damage. I have healing..."

She settled the vest over her shoulders and carefully slipped her arms through the armholes. She glanced at the dark bruises on her wrists. Thank goodness Ib had released her from the chains after he'd... after he'd... she sniffed back the tingle of impending tears.

Taj knelt before her again and cupped her cheek with one palm. He touched her abused lip with his thumb. "Are you ready?"

"More than ready."

Rising, Taj lifted her in his strong arms and carried her from the small cell. His sure steps lulled her exhausted mind. Knowing danger could appear at any moment, she fought her lethargy and concentrated on the firm line of his jaw.

The dim corridor grew lighter, the air freshened. Thankful the light no longer hurt her eyes and only a few colored spots remained dancing in her vision, she glanced around a small cave. At a narrow opening, Ommi dug at loose stones. She stopped and backed from the fissure.

Taj angled sideways and ducked through the opening. Here the full force of the sun was too bright so Jinger covered her eyes. Taj moved rapidly down a steep slope, slipping yet never loosening his hold. She surrounded herself with the blessed security and curled tighter against his body. No matter what the future brought, right now, in this moment, she felt safe.

The bright heat of the sun faded and the air cooled.

They'd passed into the thick forest. Taj stopped and after a moment stood her on her feet. Off balance, she reached out one hand and flattened her palm against a warm, soft hide. Her eyes burst open and she blinked rapidly, clearing her vision.

She was leaning against the unicorn.

A smaller, dove gray unicorn approached cautiously then pressed its head under her free hand. She stroked the fairy-silk soft forelock.

"Jinger, the unicorns thank you and plead for your forgiveness."

"What for? I haven't done anything." Petting the animal was calming her, allowing her to release a portion of her fear.

Taj cleared his throat. "Ib commanded the unicorn to direct you to the cave."

"Oh." She jerked her hand from the larger beast. "Oh."

"The task was completed under duress. Ib held its young as leverage. Both beg your forgiveness. Had the unicorn free will, you would have been lead far from the castle."

"Oh." She patted the large animal's neck. "Of course you are forgiven. I know how... hard it is to defy Ib."

Taj continued, "The unicorn came to me during the storm then led me to the base of the castle. The young one was imprisoned in the dungeons. In return for the guidance, I was able to free it."

"Taj, that's wonderful. Thank you." Jinger wrapped her arms around the young one's neck and glanced at Taj. "I hate to think of this beauty in one of those dark, hopeless cells."

Taj offered a tight smile and nodded to the unicorn.

"Even if no agreement had been made, I would have released the young one. Thankfully there were no others." He cocked his head, listening as he did to his mother.

He nodded again. "If she agrees. Jinger, the unicorn wishes to carry us home. If riding does not increase your pain, we will find safety more quickly. We must prepare for Ib's next actions."

Ommi yipped in agreement.

Jinger studied the large beast. "I'd be thankful for the ride, but I'm not sure I can stay upright and mounted. I really don't want to fall off."

Taj's smile softened. "We will ride together." He faced the unicorn. "With your permission."

The unicorn knelt allowing Taj to mount. The young one braced Jinger's side as she struggled to join him. The unicorn was Clydesdale large and she was stiff and each movement ended with pain. Trying to keep the extent of her agony hidden from Taj, she gnawed on the inside of her cheek. The distraction was only partially successful. Finally she sat sideways on the broad back, safely encircled by Taj's arms.

As the unicorn rose to its full height, Taj adjusted her closer to his body. "Although Ommi hasn't been able to enter the castle, she can still sense Ib's presence there. He is deep within the catacombs of his library so we are safe for a short while."

The smooth movement and Taj's gentle, secure hold lulled her to sleep.

J inger didn't wake when Taj dismounted, carried her into his lodge and slipped her arms from his vest to expose her back. Then he backed away and stood helplessly in the doorway, watching her misery. What should he do? What could he do? In the short while she'd been held in Ib's castle, she'd lost weight and bruises marred her skin. He hadn't realized the sorcerer had learned to warp and control time. To Taj, Jinger had only been gone a few hours. For her, many days had passed.

Unfortunately he could imagine what horrors she'd been subjected to. Ib had, without doubt, discovered more ways to harm and disable his victims.

Jinger shuddered and he was drawn closer. Tremors ran along her bare arms and spasms arched her back.

Two long slits, each halfway between her spine and shoulder blades expanded and contracted with her breathing. The glorious teals and purples pulsed as her wings struggled to escape the sorcerer's magical bindings. She'd said in her own world, she often walked about with her wings magically withdrawn into her body. He hadn't thought it possible when she'd told him.

Though Taj's mother had discovered a way, magic in the sorcerer's world otherwise could not be hidden. Somehow Ib found a way, creating magic to restrain what could not be magically restrained. How Ib accomplished this sent dread coursing through Taj. What other power had his father discovered while Taj remained unaware?

Now Ib had damaged the woman Taj loved.

Righteous anger for the lives Ib had abused filled Taj. For those the sorcerer had killed in a quest for power that saw him no nearer escape from this world than he'd been when Taj was born. Taj could do nothing to help those in the past—except his mother—but he would fight for Jinger. Until he could fight no more. Even then he knew his spirit would continue the fight until Ib was destroyed.

A soft moan stirred him from his vengeful thoughts and he returned his attention to the wounds marring Jinger's back. Strips of skin had been laced across the raw strips and pulled tight. Her wings showed through the gaps, appearing soft and otherwise unharmed.

She opened her eyes, met his gaze and immediately broke into tears. Violent shudders shook her as she cried. All Taj could do was hold her close, stroke strands of her tangled hair from her face and whisper gentle syllables of concern and calm. A calm he barely managed when her agony triggered an anger such as he'd never faced within himself. The deprivation and torture of his own past faded to a pale smear of pain.

Ib would never lay hand, or magic, on Jinger again.

"*Jannia,* what can I do?"

Her shoulders jerked once and she stilled, speaking against his chest. "What does that word mean?"

Taj drew his brows together. "I'm not sure. Perhaps I read it when I was allowed in the sorcerer's library. Perhaps my mother spoke it to me in a dream. For me, the word is you. Think of it as an endearment... if you so wish."

Her strangled chuckle blew air across the skin of his abdomen. "My father couldn't think of anything like sweetheart or darling he believed was good enough for my mother. So he calls her 'endearment'. I like *jannia.* Unless we find out it means something awful."

"I would never—"

"I know, Taj. You'll probably get tired of hearing this but thank you for rescuing me."

He'd brought her from the castle. Comforted her as best he was able. He ached to do more. He rested his palm against her side. "I don't know what to do, Jinger," he whispered.

"I know. It doesn't really hurt so bad now that we're not in the castle."

She lied. But he allowed her that falsehood and knelt beside her, repeating his admission of helplessness. "I don't know what to do."

"His magic is more powerful than I expected. I'm sorry I didn't listen to you. I thought I was going into a cave. Then rocks fell and blocked the entrance. Then he came. He was...not what I expected. I tried to be careful. Pay attention and not let him trick me. I didn't do a very good job."

"He is skilled at deception, love." Taj closed his eyes. She was his love, but he hadn't told her. He thought she might feel as he did, but how did one know?

"Taj, will you hold me?"

He stared at her for a moment. Her tentative smile erased some of the worry from his soul. "If that is what you wish. It won't cause you additional pain?"

She started to shrug, then winced and stilled the movement. "I don't know. I could use your warmth. I'm so cold."

He shifted to sit on the mattress and draped his arm carefully around her shoulders. She snuggled closer and rested her cheek against his chest. He sat frozen, still as the stones of the sorcerer's castle.

She sighed. "Ib didn't break me. You won't either."

A startled chuckle burst from his lips and he relaxed, nestling her closer.

"That's better. I don't understand how Ib's touch was both hot and bitterly cold. He's obsessed with heat and fire. And bright light. How is he cold, too? After he touched me, I should be burned to a crisp. Not cold. You're helping me get warm." Despite her assertation, she shuddered again.

"Jinger?"

A series of spasms curled her forward. Taj's hand slipped to the center of her back. Fearing he'd hurt her, he jerked his palm from her skin. She whimpered a denial. Tentative, he slowly returned to gently caress her.

At Jinger's sigh, Taj continued to stroke the soft skin down the center of her back. If his simple tough brought her comfort, then he would continue through the night. He cocked his head to listen, but the clearing beyond the lodge was quiet, only the muffled sounds of small animals and birds disrupted the night.

He trusted Ommi's word Ib hadn't discovered Jinger was gone. That she and the unicorns guarded his clearing. He needed to remain vigilant and wary.

Once Ib discovered the empty dungeon and realized his prey and the opportunity to father a child had been taken beyond his reach, he would know Taj had taken her. In his cruel way, Ib would bide his time, create doubt and havoc in their minds, then come for her. For them. This would be his final battle with the sorcerer. Either Ib would be destroyed, or Taj would perish in the attempt.

While Taj had breath in his lungs, Jinger would not fall again into his father's hands. He made this vow in silence and heard a soft yipping howl from not far distant. His mother knew his thoughts. He sensed her approval and added determination. Together they would fight, the three of them.

Until that time, he would cherish every moment with Jinger. His love for her filled his chest with unusual hope.

Hope? When in his life had he ever felt hope? Perhaps when he had been very young and still believed his father might actually care for him. Even then he hadn't expected love, not like his mother loved him. No matter the form Ib forced her to take her love, care, and protection had remained constant.

Taj had tried many ways to make Ib love him. But the sorcerer loved no one and nothing but himself and his lust for power.

Taj shoved those thoughts away, for they would only bring deeper anger. Now was not the time for anger. Now was the time for care and healing. The need to give to Jinger, to replace what Ib had stolen from her, grew with each pulse of his heart. One of his seldom used abilities could speed the healing of his own minor injuries, but not heal them completely. If he could do the same for Jinger and take away some of the pain, he would count himself a happy man.

He lengthened his strokes along her spine but feared touching the laced wounds would cause her more pain. Until she shifted and his hand brushed the edges of the crossed skin. Her relaxed breathing encouraged him to continue.

Jinger blew out a soft breath. The sharp edges of pain faded from her back. Was this another form of the magic Taj didn't realize he controlled? No, his touch was deliberate and caring, he did understand some of the talents he held within him. But possibly not how to control them. If he were in her world she'd take him to the Alastriona for training. Derrik had a talent for bringing out latent magic and teaching the wielder use and control.

Taj's fingers brushed the edge of one of the stripes of pain. Ib had caused her wings to retract, then bound them somehow. Now her wings pushed at her back, the magic of the land insisting they be released. What had the bastard done to her?

"Taj, tell me what he did. What does my back look like?"

His hand froze.

"No, please, don't stop. Your touch makes the pain bearable."

The caress returned. "I don't wish to cause you further agony."

Biting back an inappropriate chuckle, she shook her head. "He's contained my wings somehow, I only want to know how. Why the pain is so bad." Why Taj's touch made her feel so much better.

Okay, she knew part of why the path of his fingers pleased her. Her spine had always been an erogenous zone. It was for every winged fairy. But the way she felt now went far beyond that kind of pleasure. If asked, she wouldn't be able to explain the feeling. Just that now it was a part of her. Of him.

Taj cleared his throat but his voice remained raspy. "Somehow he has taken bits of your skin and woven it over where your wings are held. Like thin crosses from one side to the other.

The vision of a tightly laced corset filled her mind. A double corset. One restraining each wing. The thought fascinated her and she wished she could see for herself, then thought better of the idea.

"Will it heal that way?"

"I don't know. I wish I held the power to release your wings from the prison of your body."

Her morbid train of thought continued. She needed to know the extent of the wounds. "Would you trace the edges of the strips?"

Again his hand froze. "I don't wish to increase your pain."

"It doesn't matter. I just... just need to know." Her father had damaged his wings in a battle with a Bocan, then given them up completely to be with her mother. Her love for Taj wasn't any less. The realization made her smile.

Taj gave her a concerned, questioning look, but complied with her wishes. His fingers were cool against her now heated skin. "The length of each is this."

His soft touch tickled and she bit back a giggle.

"And the skin crosses like this."

She gasped at an influx of sharp pain but as she had asked, he continued.

"Your skin is crossed here. Here. Here." His voice lowered at each touch, softening, but rasping in her ears. Then he rested his palm over one of the areas and the pain faded to a dull ache. "I would take this torment from you if I were able. Still, your suffering is mine. I wasn't able to prevent Ib from capturing you. From...damaging you."

"I'm not damaged, Taj. We'll figure this out. If not now, then later, when we're in my world."

"There is no escape from Ib's prison. All here are imprisoned as well."

"There's always a way out. I've got to believe that. You should, too. Oh, that feels much better. See, I'll heal."

She forced as much confidence into her words as she could and thought Taj might believe her. Maybe. Maybe there was hope.

He skimmed his hand across her back to another crisscross of skin. The pain continued to fade. Healing skill was present in his touch, even if he didn't realize it. As long as she could function without too much pain, she'd be fine.

After a long moment, he'd touched and eased each binding of skin. He rested his palm at the small of her back and was silent for a long moment. "Jinger?"

"Hmm?" The press of his palm sent sensual awareness swirling through her.

"Nothing." He swallowed hard.

She leaned back just a bit to look at his face. His eyes were closed. His breathing sharp and shallow. His fingers twitched. She drew her gaze down the length of his body, the rise and fall of his chest, the tense muscles of his abdomen. And lower.

He wanted her.

Not like how Ib had wanted. Like Taj wanted. Like she wanted. Dare she take the chance?

She'd never been good at resisting a dare.

"Taj?" She waited until he opened his eyes to look at her. "I know what will make me feel better. Will you help me?"

Watching the sleek muscles of his throat as he swallowed boosted her courage. He nodded. "Whatever you wish. Name your need."

He made this too easy. "My need? You."

The dark arches of his brows drew together. "I don't

understand."

Maybe not, but his body did. She lifted one palm to his cheek. "I need you. To make love with you."

His eyes widened. "Make love?"

"Yeah, you know..." She hoped she wouldn't need to explain too much.

He cast her a wry grin. "Yes, Jinger. I do know. I'm not unaware. But—"

"You don't want to hurt me?"

Covering her hand with his, he shook his head.

"Yes, my back ached with a pain I can't describe. Your touch eased much of the agony. I have another, different kind of ache. Your touch can ease that as well. We can be careful."

"I've told you how Ib would send dreams to me. Many of those dreams were of lust and wanting. His darkness colored those dreams. I will not chance any darkness that could remain within me from those dreams might touch you. What he has already done is far more than you should be subjected to. No, I can't risk more."

He tried to set her aside and slide away but Jinger clung to him. There was no promise of a safe tomorrow for them. This time, this moment was a now or never occurrence. Never was not acceptable. "I don't sense any frightening darkness within you. Someday, I'll tell you how my family withstood battles with an evil who would make Ib shiver in his shoes."

Taj snorted. His disbelief evident in his expression, yet at war with a glint of hope in his eyes. She had to make him believe making love was a good thing. She could shorten her family history to a few sentences. "An evil one of the faerie race tried to eliminate my entire family, saying he wanted to make faerie blood pure. Ha. When he himself carried a touch of human blood. My father had to battle unknown monsters, and a Fir Dhaerrig who stole the kingdom from my ancestor. Then there was a battle fought against an ancient being. A fire elemental."

Something different sparked in his eyes and Jinger caught her lip between her teeth. Fire and heat were Ib's evil calling cards as well. For a moment she considered there might be a connection between the two, then shook her head. Gowthaman had discovered how Brandr Ur's power spread to multiple worlds, so it was possible. She'd access the legends in the Fey library.

When she got home.

When *they* got home. No way would she leave Taj or his mother behind. From the way he watched her gnaw on her lip, she didn't think he'd want to stay here without her, either.

"So, you see, I grew up knowing evil, and experiencing how it can affect someone. And, like my family, I refuse to bow before that evil. Even if you hadn't come for me, there's no way I would succumb to Ib and his magic. I could never do as he wished. I would die first."

"As now I would die to keep you from him."

"Well, good then. We're on the same page."

"The same page?" His frowning concern eased and he smiled.

"Yeah, you know, thinking the same thing."

He leaned closer to whisper, "Do we now think the same thing?"

Her voice lowered as well. "I sure hope so. Love me?"

Without speaking, he closed the distance between them and pressed his lips to hers. From any other man, the unpracticed exploration would have slowed the rise of her passion, but with Taj, it endeared him to her, heart and soul. He may know of such things, but obviously had no practical experience. She hadn't thought to be the one guiding their sexual encounter, and now endless possibilities stretched before her.

Possibilities she intended to fully explore.

TWENTY-THREE

T aj moved to kneel at the side of his low bed and studied her face. Afraid he would still deny her, Jinger scooted toward the middle of the bed and stretched her arms toward him. After a long pause, he smiled, crawled next to her and eased his arms around her. His fingers splayed against her back, but she felt almost no pain. Or if she did, that pain was hidden beneath the rush of liquid desire just under her skin.

She took his face between her hands and kissed him, teasing, coaching, encouraging. He was a quick learner and soon took possession of the kiss, drawing her deeper into passion's spell. His hands skimmed her sides, gathered the torn and burned remnants of her clothing and slowly undressed her.

He leaned on one arm to gaze down at her. She didn't feel exposed or studied, and when she lifted her hands, she didn't cover herself, wrapping them over his shoulders instead. With subtle pressure from her palms, he returned to kissing her. His hands skimmed along her side. Roughened by his existence, his fingers tempted and teased her skin. The delight and rush of desire was like nothing she'd ever experienced. Did love truly make a difference?

She guided his caresses until he discovered his own way. Her way. Their way. She gasped and whispered his name.

Silent, he slipped from the bed. Panicked she turned her face to stare at the ceiling and flattened her palms against the mattress. No, he couldn't stop now. Had she been too eager?

A rustle of fabric and he returned to her side, his clothing gone.

At his tender smile, Jinger's concerns faded. She stroked his chest, his side, the defined muscles of his abdomen that quivered under her touch. Finally she reached for him and his hard length leapt in her hand. A long, slow stroke and then another had him clutching the bedding at his sides. With a groan, she rose to her knees and took him in both hands.

"Taj?"

His hands firm at her waist, he lifted her to straddle his stomach. He cupped her breasts and teased her nipples with those delightfully rough fingertips. His length pressed against her bottom and she tried to scoot back but he held her in place with one hand. His abdominal muscles contracted and he took her nipple in his mouth. The strange thought that Ib must have sent him some interesting dreams shattered at the light scraping of his teeth over her distended nipple.

Her orgasm followed and she collapsed against his chest as he lay back caressing her hair. Her entire body pulsed with delight and renewing desire. Just as he throbbed against her. This time, she wouldn't take no for an answer.

She rose to her knees to tangle her tongue with his then pulled back to laugh when she realized she was holding him in place by his ears. So she kissed the rounded tips and tugged on the lobes with her teeth.

Taj speared his fingers through her hair and offered the same ministrations until they both gasped for breath. Taj's eyes were dark, the pupils huge with need. But a fear he couldn't hide still dulled the sparkle. She didn't know how for sure, but she'd try to release that fear. Release them both.

She crawled backward and perched on his thighs. Now the object of her desire stood before her. She took him in her hands. Taj watched from beneath half-lowered eyelids as she positioned herself to receive him. Trembling with her own need, she paused and waited until he caught his lower lip between his teeth.

He was beautiful wreathed in passion.

With a long, achingly slow descent, her body welcomed him. Overwhelmed with sensation, she groaned. His length twitched and she cried out in joy.

His hands tightened at her waist. He lifted then lowered her as he thrust up into her. Again and again. In the rare seconds she wasn't lost in their passion, she marveled at his strength and delighted in the sensations crossing his expressive face. The desire, the need was there because of her.

Then these sensations weren't enough. She leaned forward, bracing her palms against his shoulders and met his thrusts with fierce determination.

His eyes burst open and wonder filled his gaze. "Jinger? Love?"

Those words sank deep within her, tightening her body, clenching around him. "Love," she repeated.

"Ah." He sighed and held them still, smoothing his palms over her skin and igniting an even deeper fire at their joining. His fingertips met at the base of her spine. The soft strokes danced along the edges of her captive wings then his palms flattened between her shoulder blades.

She sobbed his name and climaxed with a power that shook her soul. He cradled her against his chest. His urgent, whispered words and stroking fingers gave her no rest. Hips rising to hers, he drew her toward another powerful release.

Cracking, like the snap of a small fire filled the air. Pops of sharp pain traveled the length of the wounds on her back. With a power that flattened her against him, Jinger's wings broke free, uncurled then curved to the sides to cocoon them in velvety softness. His marvelous hands and thrusting body froze.

"How?" Taj whispered.

"You. Your magic. I can feel it. Can't you?"

He shook his head.

"Stay still a minute." That had to be the most difficult thing she'd ever asked when their intimate dance continued. When his hips stopped moving, she nearly begged him to begin again. "Concentrate, look inside."

"All I feel is you, love."

"Flatterer. Really, Taj. Don't you feel the magic? Your magic?"

Despite the pleasure of her tight heat, Taj fought the need to arch into her and did as she asked. He closed his eyes and waited. If his Jinger wished for him to do this, he would. Even though the internal search would not

produce evidence of enough magic to account for the
release of her wings. He didn't believe—

A small flame burned in the darkness. He struggled
against the vision. No, Ib would not prevail. The flame
grew larger, the colors brighter, deeper, tinged with a
rainbow. Mother? Then a swirl of teal, a wash of purple.
Jinger.

The clarity and knowledge made him gasp. He was
the flame, and all these, yes, even Ib, were part of him. It
was within him to control the fire, the magic. Nor did he
have to do so alone.

In a flash he understood. His mother had loved him
enough to bind and hide his talent within him to protect
him from Ib. She had allowed him only what he needed
to escape the castle and survive.

Jinger loved him. Her love had freed his magic. Only
with her could he have discovered this and be born again
into his true self, discovering his magical heritage.

It was his love for her then that had broken Ib's spell.
Healed and released her beautiful wings.

He opened his eyes and smiled.

Jinger watched him warily then matched his grin.
"So, you understand?"

"Yes. And no. Right now, it doesn't matter. Only this."
Still wary of hurting her, he captured her complaints
with a kiss and slipped from her heat. He carefully spread
her wings across the bed to each side. Finding a place to
plant his hands took a moment. Then he kissed the
corners of her swollen lips and joined their bodies. It
didn't take long for them to discover the rhythm that
delighted them both.

He'd thought he'd understood pleasure from Ib's
dreams. Had separated the truth from the pain and

degradation. Now, in this moment his understanding became clear and the differences manifested in sensations he'd never imagined. The tight, wet heat throbbing around him as he moved within her. The sensitivity of his skin to the bedding, the tickle of her hair, the smooth caress of her demanding hands. Even the sharp dots of pain as she dug her nails into his hips to encourage him was new, beautiful and theirs.

For there would never be another.

"Taj," she gasped. "Touch my back. Please. Where my wings... meet... skin."

He encouraged her to wrap her thighs around his hips, supported her and sat back on his calves. Maintaining the force of his thrust and retreat, for he could do nothing else, he lifted one hand and did as she commanded. The contrast of textures triggered a powerful need within him. He pounded up into her.

Whimpering, encouraging, she tossed her head and he matched the stroke of his fingers along her back to the speed of his thrusts.

Her body convulsed around him, pulling him deeper. She keened with pleasure. Her wings wrapped tightly around them, the velvety caress vibrating against his skin.

Cocooned by Jinger's body, her beauty, her love, Taj found his first true release, shouting her name.

Much later Taj insisted Jinger soak in the huge tub and she encouraged him to join her. After a wild romp that splashed water about the room, they lay next to each other against the angled backrest. Jinger kicked her feet stirring up tiny waves and laughed. She'd broken through the mile high walls of Taj's defenses and discovered a playful, caring, and loving man.

She didn't know yet how to tell him about the wealth of glittering teal sparkles shimmering around them when they touched.

Soulfire. She'd hoped and dreamed to one day discover the true mate to her soul, the one whose love brought the soulfire into her life. While she'd expected to find him in any of a number of different worlds, she'd hoped to share her love and her happiness with her family.

Taj pressed his lips to her temple. "You think much too loud. You worry you'll never leave this place."

How did he know? Or did her merely guess? Of course she'd be thinking about that. Hadn't that been on her mind ever since landing here? She nodded.

"And you are concerned now how I will react, how my life will be when you are gone."

"No. Not that. You'll come with me of course. Unless..." No, that wasn't an option, was it? "Unless you don't want to."

He curled his finger under her chin and brought her lips to his. "I would follow you to the edge of the world. Of any world. And beyond, should you ask me to. I just don't see how such a thing will be possible."

'There must be a way. Something we haven't thought of."

"Perhaps. If we don't find a way, would you be happy here? Even with the danger of Ib's desire hanging over us? He will never cease his attempts to bend you to his will. Perhaps we might discover a way to defeat him."

Even before discovering her soulfire, there was no chance the sorcerer would be bending anything about her. Now, with Taj at her side and in her heart, there'd be no crack Ib could find to force his will on her. She understood that, as well as knowing Ib would never stop attempting to force his will on them.

Remaining her was not an option.

Entwining his fingers with hers, Taj lifted their hands from the water. "What is this thing?"

"Thing?"

"Yes, don't you see how the color sparkles around our hands? I see it in your eyes, feel the warm tingles against my skin. Is this a thing you brought from your world?"

She took a deep breath. "Yes, I suppose."

"Why didn't it appear before? I've not witnessed this before today."

Another deep breath. "In my family there is often a visual representation of love when they discover the true mate of their soul."

"But," he mumbled, ducking his head. "I loved you before today and haven't seen this."

Now came the tricky part, something even she didn't really understand. "It's called a soulfire. It most often manifests during, uh, when the couple makes love. It doesn't have anything to do with sex, because the love the soulfire represents is far deeper than physical attraction. So much more than just caring for another. Soulfire is special. When it manifests separate from the physical act..."

"Ah, then it means the bond is even stronger?"

"Yes. Stronger. Unbreakable many say. No one in my family has ever attempted to break a soulfire bond. No one has wanted to."

"The mates in your family are all happy?"

"Of course there are times of strife and arguments. Sometimes epic fights. That's how it is when people come together."

A grin tipped his lips. "So when we have... disagreements, we shouldn't worry the other will walk away?"

What was he asking? Did he fear she'd walk away? She'd already said she'd never leave him. Oh, god. Did that mean he thought one day he'd leave her? Was he already thinking to that future time?

"Jinger, please look at me."

She hadn't realized she'd turned away and slowly returned to face his somber expression.

"I was merely curious, for I know little of the interactions and relationships of others. Obviously, I have not had opportunities or good examples in my life."

He looked so repentant, she burst into laughter. Covering her mouth with her hand, she mumbled an apology. Taj arched one eyebrow, moved her hand and kissed her. She forgot the direction the conversation had turned.

Taj ended the kiss much too soon. "Now, we must leave this moment of joy, keeping this..." He lifted their hands again and for a moment they watched their soulfire dance. "...in our hearts. We must prepare for Ib's attack. If there is a way from this world, we will find it. Together. Already you've brought much to my life, shown me more of myself than I believed possible. I find myself believing in new possibilities."

Jinger wasn't ready to leave the safe bubble of their newfound love and soulfire. She pushed off the side of the tub and floated around to face him, straddling his lap. After glancing down through the clear water, she tilted her head in a coy manner. "New possibilities?"

TWENTY-FOUR

I b squeezed, tightening his fingers on the dull creature's slimy neck. Anger lent extra strength to his power and soon the servant's gasping breaths ceased. Silence surrounded Ib and he let the creature fall with a wet plop to the floor. Flexing his fingers, he stalked from the mess. He was better off with no servants to stand in his way, better to trust no one other than himself. Especially when it came to matters of power.

He'd given the idiot one simple order. Watch the female. The fool had watched her. Watched her escape from the dungeon. A feat she never could have accomplished alone. The bitch firefox hadn't been able to break through the time distortion, so that meant his worthless son had been in the castle.

Ib had been close to her capitulation. He'd known she would speak the words and willingly come to him soon. He'd already prepared the potion to speed her pregnancy and the growth of his new son. His better son. A son filled with powerful magic that would be a worthy sacrifice to Ib's power. Now the ingredients taken from his small store of magical components had been wasted, the potency of the spell waned with each passing hour.

Had he been told of her escape sooner, he would have been able to easily rectify the problem and still have a new son for the knife. Now she'd be protected and watched. It would be difficult to catch her alone again.

Finding the way would take time, time he wasn't willing to wager. Though the amount was miniscule, the power he'd collected from his time in the tower drained from him each day. There was no time for a return to the tower. He would find a way to conserve the power remaining to him. The more potent his magic, the more he'd be able to gather into himself from other sources.

No matter who assisted in her escape, the woman would be with his puny son now. Ib chuckled. His son would have no idea what to do with her.

Ib paused and rubbed his chin. Although the dreams he'd sent when the boy was younger may have taken root in his memory. With only that knowledge of lust and power, he might frighten the woman away. Such action would work in Ib's favor. Few men could resist one as comely as the woman he'd chosen to bear his son.

The child would be born into perfection, unmarred, and carrying a wealth of power in a tiny body. Power Ib would absorb and use to his advantage.

Urgency spurred Ib to action. He had no time nor energy to waste creating a new servant, so he would discover the solution unaided. At least there would be no distractions or missteps. For Ib never made a mistake. He would prevail and leave this cursed prison behind.

He allowed himself to smile at his reflection in a dust covered mirror. This day's minor setback would prevent nothing. Success remained in his hands alone. He held his hands by his face, the palms toward the mirror. Golden spirals expanded and tightened in his palms. Streaks of lighter gold pulsed toward his fingertips. He folded one hand to a fist and studied the white-gold markings on his knuckles. He'd been granted an excess of power and he'd use every droplet to destroy anything standing in his way.

Satisfied, he continued to the tapestry room and stared at the slow weaving of the threads indicating his son. No change or movement from the prior days. He poked a finger at the cloth. Curse the magic that didn't allow an accurate and timely representation. Much could happen in the lapse between actual time and what appeared in the wool stitches. The representation was even slower now that he'd altered time within the castle.

Perhaps he should return the castle's time flow to match that of the forest.

No. To do so would waste magic. Matching the times would also allow the firefox to sneak into the castle. What his son did was little of consequence. If the woman hadn't returned to him by now, she would soon. Or be lost in the forest. Either way Ib would discover and retrieve her with ease. He turned toward his workroom and the future.

His future.

S moke and the scent of burning stone billowed from Ib's workroom. Coughing, he followed the foul odor to the great hall. He stuck his head out a narrow window to draw in gulps of fresh air. When the sting of bile left his throat and his eyes cleared he rested across the wide stone sill and stared out over the forest. A sharp stone poked his belly so he turned to the hall and sank to the floor with his back against the cold wall.

Another failure. More wasted time. He shouldn't have taken his anger out on his slow, idiotic servant, for now he had no one to fetch tomes for him or stand as a focus for the magic. Ib was skilled and vastly proficient in nearly all magic he'd encountered, but creating a living creature took too much time and energy. There was nothing for him to do but return to the pattern of his apprentice days and do everything himself.

His foul mood deepened. He knew the spell he wanted, remembered reading and marking it for the future. That future was here and now he couldn't find the old, rancid text. Casting a finding charm hadn't worked, but he hadn't expected it to. Magic to call for an ancient magic was tricky, demanded concentration and a deep pull of power.

The power he had. But his focus continually returned to the woman and his son. Some change had occurred, something had been altered. He sensed the source but refused to acknowledge the possibility. To do so would mean the failure of his plans. That was unacceptable.

As was doing nothing but thinking dire thoughts. He scrambled to his feet, pointed to the remnants of smoke and waved the cloud out the window. Parlor tricks. He needed the deepest, darkest of magics now.

Long ages had passed since the last time he visited the lowest, most secret areas of his library. His servant had come from there and knew the placement of the contents well.

Ib descended the narrow stairs, muttering foul curses. When dim light no longer penetrated the passage, he snapped his fingers to create a steady flame to light his way. The tiny fire hovering a foot before him brought a sense of calm so when he reached his destination, he easily found the scroll he wanted on a stone bench piled with a mix of books and scrolls. With the crinkly hide cradled in his arms, he returned to the workroom.

He fought for patience while he deciphered the tiny, handwritten ancient languages. Thankfully, many years ago he'd studied this scroll, and the memory surfaced rapidly. But the markings had faded to near invisibility in some places, making him question that memory. He made a list of variables and possibilities, created a platter of cheese and fruit to nourish his body, then studied his list.

Accessing the truth of the spell would take a day, perhaps a bit more. He wasn't weary, but the effort would drain energy he wished to retain. So, he would rest during the night and begin under the power-giving light of the rising sun. The waiting chafed at him, but the end result would be worth the extra effort. Instead of harvesting the power of a single magic-child, he would gather the soul-power of three beings. The woman, the bitch firefox, and his son.

Then he would shatter this prison and consume the magic of other worlds.

Ib moved into the waning force of the setting sun and

spread his arms. The rays blessed his skin with vibrant shimmers of magic, fueling him for the following day. He bared his teeth in a wicked grin.

Soon he would challenge the fire god himself. Brandr Ur's anger would be but a shadow when faced with Ib's glory. He would throw down the elemental and take his place.

The so called god?

Let him rule this prison.

The firefox rested beneath a bush at the far side of Taj's clearing, her head on her outstretched paws. Taj smiled. Ommi would be pleased, but not so pleased as he. She had approved of Jinger even before she'd insisted he go to her. He glanced back into the lodge. Jinger slept on her side, hugging the pillow that had recently cushioned his head. He longed to sleep at her side, but understood time was short. Ommi had been patient long enough.

"Mother, what news do you bring?"

The firefox stretched, rose, and stretched again. She shook out her red fur then crossed the clearing to his side. Together they walked toward the pool. He didn't wish to hide anything from Jinger, but should the news be dire, he wanted to tell her gently. His mother's slow ease calmed much of his concern. Perhaps there would be a bit more time to spend learning how to please his soulfire.

Then he would help her find the way from this world to her own and block Ib's passage should the sorcerer attempt to follow. Taj held no delusions. Despite Jinger's assurances, he wouldn't be leaving with her.

Ommi claimed the gateway would open again in the same place, leading to Jinger's world. He knew of no way to reach the heights needed to access the doorway. Except for the power of Jinger's wings. He would watch her fly to the gateway, guard her path from the ground, and be happy.

Until Ib destroyed him.

He could envision no other possible outcome.

Shoving the thought aside, he sat on the ground with the firefox next to him. He watched the ripples on the water, the ever increasing circles from fallen leaves. A change of seasons was upon them and the world would cool when the sun remained low on the horizon. The intriguing image of Jinger wrapped in warm furs upon his bed distracted him until his mother rested her paw on his thigh.

"I know I dream of things that won't be, Mother. As long as I remember these to be no more than pleasant dreams, I will remain a happy man. Did you know of a thing called soulfire?"

He listened to his mother's silent communication and shook his head.

"I don't see how that will be possible. I've never seen such a stairway. Stairs leading nowhere yet somewhere?"

Ommi accented her communication with a series of yips and growls.

"Yes. I understand. This soulfire of Jinger's, what it represents, has freed the magic you bound within me. For that I thank you. No, I could never hold you to blame. What you did was for love. Just as what I must do."

Ommi's low growl made him smile. "I will believe

what you say as much as I'm able, Mother. Don't take me to task when I can't accept the unimaginable without question. We will leave, as you say, before the night falls and search for these stairs. Together. The three of us."

He sensed she wished to argue, wished to stay behind to guard their passage from Ib. Such a stand might delay the sorcerer for a short while, but not long enough to ensure success in finding an unbelievable set of stairs. If they had to fight Ib—and they would—it was best the three of them remained together. He had much to learn about himself and his abilities and hoped Ommi could teach him as much as possible along the way.

"I'll prepare then wake Jinger. She should sleep as long as possible to heal before we—"

"Before we what?"

In a whirl of action Taj was on his feet facing the intrusion, his fists clenched and ready for battle.

"Whoa, Taj. I didn't mean to startle you. Ommi knew I was here. What are we going to do?"

He struggled to pull back the unaccustomed surge of power pulsing in his fists. He might have lashed out at her. He was a danger to her. Like his father.

"No, Taj, don't think that. You could never be like him." Jinger stepped between his outstretched hands and pressed down on his fists until he dropped them to his sides. "This isn't a battle you face alone, you know. Every creature of magic must learn to control the extent of their powers. I thought I'd learned mine, but now I'm not so sure. I don't know if I'll ever stop learning. In a way, I hope not. That means there's always the possibility of something new and wonderful just around the corner."

Ommi gave a sharp yip and Jinger grinned. "Yes, or in an abandoned bottle. Now Taj, what are we going to do?"

He huffed out a short breath. "Look for a stairway of green that reaches to the heavens yet goes nowhere. From the heights of these stairs there may be the way to send you home."

"No."

"No?" What was this woman about? From the moment she'd appeared in his world, she'd claimed the need to return to her home. Was this to become one of those disagreements those who loved faced?

"I only mean no to sending me home. You and Ommi are coming with me." She crossed her arms. "Or I won't go. I'm not leaving either of you to Ib's delusions of power."

"His power is no delusion."

"Perhaps not, but his pride in that power is. Seeking power for the sake of more power is of no help to anyone. Why be granted power or abilities, only to hoard them away and not use them to help others? That's one of those things that even though on some level I understand. But for the most part, I don't. I won't leave you. I see you how you're trying to form arguments. One thing I've learned from my father is to be stubborn when what I really want is on the line."

Taj stood in silence and matched her crossed arms pose, feeling the gathered power sinking into his chest.

Jinger knelt beside Ommi. "He is a foolish man, isn't he?"

His mother laughed. Laughed. At him. He felt like snarling but stiffened his spine. "We must leave soon. I will gather what we need." He jabbed a finger at Jinger.

"You will rest until then. We foolishly expended your energy when you should have rested."

Her shy grin eased his concern but when she spoke it was to the firefox. "Yes, I understand there was no reason to tell him about sex magic until me. I don't know much about it either. You'll teach us both? Oh, I see." She glanced up at him from under her lashes. "Yes, we'll work on that."

Ignoring what Jinger's expression did to his reality, and his body, Taj focused on his mother. "She can hear you now?" Then he turned to Jinger. "You can hear Mother's words in your head?"

The pair nodded together. Jinger added, "When I first arrived and she tried to communicate with me, all I got were jumbled pictures and odd bits and pieces of things I thought I should understand. I tried, but attempting to figure them out made my brain tired. I know she was frustrated, too."

Then she turned her grin to Ommi. "Yeah, that's true. I barely believed I was trapped in another world. There was too much to think about and understand all at once."

Confusion drifted through Taj's mind. The changes in his world in just a few days were powerful and certainly needed time to assimilate. For each of them. "But now?"

A vivid picture of Jinger and him entwined on his bed burst into his mind just as Jinger rested her palm against the beat of his heart and replied, "It has to do with our... connection."

The soulfire danced around her hand. He covered her fingers with his and pressed her hand firmer against him. Yes, this connection, the powerful longing and completeness had changed him. Perhaps, there *was* a stairway to nowhere and everywhere. Belief nestled in his chest.

His mother rubbed against his calf and he bent to gather the firefox in his arms, completing the triad of love and magic. Together they could do much—but he dared not imagine defeating his father. Ib had gained unusual power. Taj had felt the vibrations in the stone of the castle when rescuing Jinger. For a moment he contemplated if he'd have felt and understood more of that power with his newly acknowledged magic.

He blinked away the thoughts. Ommi and Jinger waited for him. He gave a single sharp nod. "We'll leave after breaking our fast. Is that acceptable?"

The rust and white flag of Ommi's bushy tail lead Jinger and Taj along an overly winding and mostly overgrown path. Jinger curled her wings close to her body. Her control over the appendages had improved. She wasn't sure if it was because she'd become accustomed to their weight and balance and her fairy heritage had kicked in. Or if it had something to do with the man following her.

She suspected the soulfire had changed both of them, or perhaps it simply was a combination of everything she'd experienced the past days.

Even with her family and their growing knowledge of so many worlds, she had difficulty with the concept that days had passed for her in Ib's palace while Taj had experienced only hours. No, wait. Her uncle Bard and Gowthaman had been held captive for what they thought only a day or two, while in Faerie three months had passed. So, there was a precedence.

Not that there was any help for her in the knowledge.

When she got home, she'd record her experiences for Gowthaman and the library. He'd want Taj's statement as well. Concentrating on firmly seating those memories in her mind, she took a misstep and lurched to the side.

Taj was there in an instant, taking her arm and waiting until she regained her balance. He kissed her cheek and whispered, "Careful, *jannia*. I don't know this path."

She turned to peer at him. "But the trail started not that far from your glade."

Ommi yipped, command evident in the sound. Jinger chuckled. "Doesn't matter, does it? The trail is here now and we're supposed to be following Ommi." Because the path had finally widened, and if they remained close, they could walk together, she took Taj's hand.

"I believe Mother has many such pathways across the land," he said. "Come, she's impatient."

"Do you have any idea where she's leading us?"

He shook his head and remained silent, his attention focused on the forest around them. The sense of being watched settled over her shoulders. The skin between her wings tingled, but she was unable to determine if the feeling meant danger or curiosity.

The feeling remained until Ommi stopped in the center of a tiny, oval clearing. A structure, no taller than Jinger's knees, sat to one side beneath the low-hanging tree branches. Woven of thin, living twigs, the building was covered with a layer of bright yellow-green leaves. A single arching entry encompassed a third of one side.

Curiosity drew Jinger forward a step, but Taj's strong grip on her hand held her back. "Wait."

Ommi pointed her nose to the sky then crouched and rested her muzzle on her front paws. Taj tugged on Jinger's hand. "We need to sit."

"I know, she told me, too." The odd communication with Taj's mother still surprised Jinger each time pictures or the soft, faintly accented female voice invaded her mind. The feeling wasn't unpleasant, just odd. She felt Ommi's laughter.

Long minutes passed as they sat in silence waiting for the tiny house's owner. Jinger wondered if that creature had been what watched them along the path. She studied the dwelling, then noticed a tiny patch of disturbed earth to one side. Straight lines of a short grass with fat grain heads swayed in the gentle breeze. This was a peaceful homestead. It reminded her a bit of fairy farmers in her own land.

Were there fairies here? She didn't think so. Taj had been surprised at her wings. At her.

She glanced at him. He was just as curious, peering around the clearing. His shoulders were relaxed so Jinger released the tiny bit of concern she'd been harboring and rested her head against his shoulder. One of her wings curved over him. He lifted his free hand and stroked the darker edge. A delightfully sensual shockwave coursed through her. Here was another thing to explore more completely.

Taj grinned at her reaction. When she looked into his face, he arched one brow, looking more than willing to continue right then and there. Then his mouth flattened, he squeezed her fingers and nodded toward the far corner of the tiny building.

A small, golden-brown and furry face peeked around the building. When it noticed Jinger—and her wings— its black eyes grew wide. Jinger held back a chuckle. The animal reminded her of an animated cat who used his soulful, wide eyes to get whatever he wanted.

She didn't believe this animal wanted anything from them, though. Because they had stopped and waited until it made an appearance, they needed its help. Finally the tiny creature moved on two feet to a spot just beyond Ommi's pointed nose. It touched its forehead with a six fingered paw and bowed.

"I've not seen the querd since I was a small child," Taj whispered. "She assisted Mother with my care."

The creature moved closer to Ommi and chittered. The firefox replied with soft whoofs and growls. Their communication fascinated Jinger. "What is she?"

"I don't know what her true form may be, only that she was once drawn to this land, just as you were. Like you and Mother, Ib tried to use her to create his perfect son."

The bitterness in his voice no longer surprised Jinger. She realized no one in this land had ever experienced a love or joy even remotely similar to the accepting love of her family. Sadness welled in her chest. No, she couldn't imagine having such a lack in her life. She was so lucky to have been born into the clan. She couldn't wait to see each and every one of them.

Both transfigured animals turned their attention to her. She shifted under the intensity of the matching, dark gazes. Taj blinked and tilted his head in the manner he always had when his mother communicated with him. Ommi's smooth voice entered her thoughts.

Listen well. You both must do as I say, when I say. The

timing of the stairs and gateway is delicate. My son, I have not brought you here before. Even had you realized the strength of magic within you, alone, it would not be enough. Now, the bond you share with Jinger multiplies your abilities.

Jinger, your magic has grown in strength as well. Both from the bond with my son and from the agonies you suffered at Ib's hands.

Pain, at times, is a necessary evil. I would have kept it from each of you had I been able.

Now, with our friends' assistance, we may be able to gather the power needed to climb the stairway and escape this prison. For prison this truly is. It is not and should never have held any being but the sorcerer. This is Ib's prison. One he has occupied for millennia, forced and contained here by a fire spirit who cared not for Ib's repeated challenges.

At the mention of a powerful fire spirit, Jinger clutched Taj's hand. His expression darkened. "What's wrong?"

Jinger directed her question to Ommi. "A fire spirit? An elemental?"

The firefox nodded.

Tears burned Jinger's eyes and she swiped angrily at one lone droplet that escaped. "My family has had dealings with a fire elemental. The day I was on the beach, the day I was brought here, I was mourning my cousin. The elemental murdered him in the World Between Worlds. Actually..." She sniffed. "Actually Chance killed him, too. If Ib has power like that..."

He does not. Yet he is dangerously powerful.

Jinger sensed her laughter.

I have set stumbling blocks in his way, though I fear the delay will be barely enough for us to reach the stairs. Others here and along the path will delay him further and offer you what power they can spare.

"Mother, tell us more of this stairway. What are we looking for? How has it remained hidden?"

You have many questions, my son. We have little time for answers. I have kept the existence of the stairway from you, so Ib would not see the truth in your mind. The stairway goes nowhere. And everywhere. You need only know the key. If you are rested, we must hurry.

Urgency coursed down Jinger's spine. She closed her eyes and reached out her with senses as the Alastriona had taught her. The world around them was calm, yet vibrant with waiting. In the distance a bright spot of power pulsed. Long, thin tendrils of light squirmed around the pulsing, stretching out then retreating. "He's looking for us."

Yes. But night comes and his power wanes until the sun once again lights the tallest tower.

Taj flowed to his feet and tugged Jinger up next to him. "Then we go."

When he stepped forward, she pulled back. "What about the querd? We can't leave her here now."

The firefox's laughter danced through her mind. A second voice, smaller, weaker, blended with hers. *Do not allow your eyes show you the truth of others, Jinger. Look beyond appearance. Look beyond expectations. Though Ib murdered many of us, some he could not destroy. We have become strong and defiant. He had no notion what we were capable of then, and surely in his arrogance, he knows even less now.*

The tiny, mouse-like creature bent nearly double then straightened. The innocence disappeared from its eyes, replaced by cold, hard anger. Although the animal remained tiny, the outline of an enraged beast pulsed, growing ever larger with each breath. It was like a coloring book design gone mad. Jinger took a step back as the animal filled the clearing and grew to tower over them. A rapid chittering drew her attention to where the querd stood, arms outstretched. A grin bared needle sharp teeth. *Fear not, winged lady. He will be delayed as long as I and others who come are able. Go now.*

TWENTY-SIX

I b stomped through the seldom raised castle portcullis and stood spread-legged glaring at the forest. Intending to use the huge beast to travel quickly after the woman and his son, he'd commanded the unicorn to appear. The animal defied him.

His prey was on the move, fleeing in a direction seldom traveled. The forest held a different magic there, one he had ignored for too long. He took a few steps toward the overgrown path down the cliff toward the forest. The undergrowth parted and the unicorn appeared.

"You were commanded to be here at first light."

The animal flared its nostrils and stamped one huge hoof.

"You defy me? You risk the life of your young?"

Sparkling laughter filled Ib's head and the unicorn stepped to one side. The young one pranced forward, rose to its hind legs and pawed the air. Together the unicorns turned and galloped down the path, disappearing under the trees.

Anger burned through Ib, wasting energy. He struggled to call back the power finally pressing his hands together against his chest. If he must waste his abilities in a chase, he would choose the most rapid transportation he could create. The end result would be the same, he would have Jinger and his son would be no more.

Returning to the castle, he stormed into his workroom, snatched the ingredients he needed from his orderly shelves then stomped into the great hall. He glared for a long moment at the tapestry before ripping it from the wall and tossing it into a heap in the center of the room. Without his usual precision, he tossed the spell components into a small bowl, and spoke the incantation.

The tapestry twisted and rippled, lifting a few inches from the floor. Ib's voice rang through the hall with the second spell. The tapestry flattened and he stepped onto the weaving. He sat and touched the middle finger of both hands to the fabric, rising higher into the air. Narrowing his gaze, he flew the length of the hall.

Perfect. Much better than an uncooperative unicorn and searching for hidden paths. With his flying tapestry, he would avoid the shadows and continue to gain power. Sending an arc of fire toward the window, he blasted a large enough opening in the stone for the tapestry to fly through. Destroying the wall brought him a measure of satisfaction. He wouldn't be coming back to this prison.

The knowledge startled him. He'd planned to return with the woman. Now he realized the woman was leading him to the opening gateway. He sensed the growing concentration of power, knew if he peered into the distance he would discover the pale, wavering oval. He didn't need her to bear him a sacrifice.

She would be the sacrifice. Along with his worthless son and the bitch firefox.

Before this day ended, he would be free.

A moment of concern held him in place. His library. He couldn't leave the vast wealth of knowledge behind. While there were new powers and abilities for him to discover once free, he needed also to maintain what he'd already accumulated. He might need to construct a new crystal tower. Or cast a glamour. The vials and bottles he could leave behind, but not the scrolls and ancient tomes.

He'd concentrated too much on what he would gain and had forgotten what he'd already learned. Lowering the tapestry to the floor, he considered options. The smallest container wouldn't impede his escape.

Ib left the hall and descended to his library. This would be more quickly done had he still had the servant. No matter. Standing in the doorway, he spread his arms wide. Fiery currents arced between his hands then spread across the dark room. He curled his fingers, gathering the shrinking contents of the room into a small ball.

He blew on the ball, cooling the fire. His library now fit in the palm of his hand. Stuffing the cold, solid ball into a deep pocket in his robe, he returned to the hall. He settled on the tapestry and commanded it to rise.

Cool air flowed around him as he flew low over the forest. He kept his gaze on the opening gateway and smiled. This day belonged to him.

A huge dark figure rose above the treetops, a long arm extended toward him. Ib stopped the tapestry and hovered just beyond the creature's reach. He didn't recognize the creature nor remember one so large within the forest. Faint laughter tickled his brain.

Ah, he'd never forgotten that laughter. One of the first females who had failed him and earned transfiguration. What had she called herself. A querd? He wrinkled his brow. Hadn't she become a tiny animal? Increased size or not, it would not matter. "You will not stop me."

The querd bared sharp teeth and reached slender claws toward him. Ib prepared a spell but before he could cast the words on the wind, the querd pinched the tapestry between its claws and flipped him into the air. He landed in the highest branches of a tree. The tapestry fluttered to the ground.

Ib laughed. The instance the querd touched the tapestry, Ib knew the size was a projection, though how it managed to take physical action puzzled him. The touch must have expended most of the creature's energy because her form shrank and disappeared.

The tapestry had landed nearby, so he would soon be flying again. He knew his target. A nearly invisible winding stairway and the three who had already climbed halfway to the gateway.

He scrambled from the tree, retrieved his tapestry and renewed the flying spell.

His triumph was at hand.

Taj glanced back down the narrow staircase. It felt as though he'd been climbing for days.

Land, and the moss covered cairn that opened onto the stairway, were far below him. the height above the sea didn't frighten him, although how the stairs had narrowed the higher they traveled caused concern. He attempted to gauge the distance they'd come and how far remained to determine if the stairs would reach the now open and shimmering gateway.

His mother pranced through the air, circling and encouraging. Jinger had tired of climbing and now flew a few steps above him. He worried for her. Her wings had only been healed a day, yet she seemed more at ease with them than she had before. Drawing a deep breath, he willed the burning muscles in his legs to function. How was climbing so different than simply walking?

"Look. There," Jinger called and pointed.

A dark spot in the clear air. Rising along the stairs.

Ommi poked her nose against his back. He turned and bolted up the stairs. Ib had found them. The sorcerer was coming. In order to attempt the plan they'd made while climbing, they needed to reach the gateway first.

With a sharp yip, Ommi turned and landed on the step behind him.

"Mother, no, you can't fight him alone." None of them could.

Jinger tugged on his shoulder. "She only wants to delay him. Give us time to get to the portal. Then she'll join us."

"It's not a good plan."

After pressing her lips to his cheek, Jinger whispered, "I know, but right now it's all we've got. Come on."

"But..."

Go. I will be with you at the gateway.

"Mother? Yes." Taj shook his head and, taking Jinger's hand, raced up the steps.

The stairs ended in a narrow platform double the height of a man distant from the gateway. The edges swirled with deep, cobalt blue framing a beach with black sand. Shadows moved just beyond the clarity of the gateway. There were others there.

"Look, Taj. I've never seen anyone on the beach before. I bet they're my family. Looking for me."

"Or a trick."

Her joy deflated. "That's true, isn't it. This could be an illusion from Ib. Like one of his dreams. Tempting us with what we want most."

"Did he give you dreams, *jannia*?"

A flush of pink tinted her cheeks. "He did. And before you ask, he promised me a way home."

Taj studied the distance and lowered his brows. The success of their plan seemed doubtful. "I can't jump that far. Will your wings bear my weight as well as yours?"

"I don't know. I've never tried carrying anyone before. It's not that far. As soon as your mother—"

Chased by a ball of flames, the firefox flew past them. Taj turned to face the sorcerer as she circled back and hovered behind him with her front paws on his shoulders.

Jinger squeezed his hand then rested her free hand over his heart. "We can do this, Taj. I know we can. You are my soulfire. I love you."

Soulfire. The thing that awakened his dormant abilities. If only there had been time to learn what he might be capable of. Ib was close. Too close. Taj felt the sorcerer's heat. Saw how his lips twisted to a confident sneer.

"And I love you, my sweet Jinger. I wish to prove your soul made a wise choice."

She chuckled. "It did. I did. Now concentrate like Ommi told us."

He gave a sharp nod, focused on Ib and accepted the unusual, uncomfortable sensations of increasing power. What he felt was his. He may have inherited abilities from his father, but not the evil and lust for power. If given the opportunity, Taj would willingly give up any magical abilities. As long as Jinger stayed at his side.

Ommi touched her muzzle to his cheek, her love flowing over him. "Is it time, Mother?"

The affirmation touched his mind. Jinger kissed his cheek. "Let's do this."

Motionless, the trio waited. Soon Ib's laughter reached them, then his taunts and jeers. Taj drew a deep breath to clear his mind of memories and the hopes of his childhood. Ib had never been a father to him. He owed the sorcerer nothing. Except, perhaps, a thank you for causing Jinger's entrance to this world.

The absurd thought of being grateful to Ib made Taj laugh. He was ready.

Jinger sensed a shift in Taj, the slow beat of his heart, his calm breathing. Just today his magic had been awakened and they'd planned a daring escape. Now he faced his father. A deadly battle. She glanced up at the portal. The figures had moved closer but were still shadowed. Please let them be her family. All she needed to do was get Taj through the portal.

The sorcerer was powerful in this world. Ommi had questioned how much of that power would follow him into other worlds. Jinger had many questions for Taj's mother and had a feeling the firefox might actually be as powerful as the sorcerer.

Sitting upon a flying carpet, Ib crossed his arms and attempted a friendly smile. He had a long way to go to master the expression. She, Taj and Ommi had discussed whether to make the first move, or to remain on the defensive and decided to wait for Ib's actions. His under-estimation of their abilities should work in their favor.

As long as she had time to get Taj to the portal.

Ib pointed at her. "You will come with me."

"I don't think so." Thank goodness her voice didn't waiver. She needed to at least appear confident.

"Do you wish the others to die?"

Any verbal back and forth got them nowhere. Waiting for Ib to act was a mistake. Jinger knew what she had to do. Hopefully the others would react without question. "We. Will. Not. Die. Taj, now."

Jinger pushed off Taj. He turned, crouched, leapt higher than she anticipated. She caught him around the waist and beat her wings furiously. Teeth bared, Ommi sped toward the sorcerer and latched onto his arm.

While the sorcerer was distracted, Jinger lifted Taj toward the portal. Slowly they rose. He wrapped his arms over her shoulders and shouted encouragement but she had no breath to answer. Her strength waned far more quickly than she'd hoped. Still facing the struggles between the sorcerer and the firefox, Jinger had no clue how high she'd flown. Were they close to the portal?

Taj tapped her shoulder. "Turn," he said.

She nodded and shifted to face the portal. Close enough to the center of the opening, she pushed them forward. A familiar tingle covered her skin as they passed from Taj's world to her beach. Exhausted, she dropped him and fell to her hands and knees on the black sand.

"Jinger," a familiar voice called.

The portal behind her ignited in flames. Taj scrabbled backward across the sand, dragging her with him. Ommi tumbled over their heads, falling into a heap of fire-colored fur next to the cliffs.

A straight edge of thick fabric pierced the center of the portal, but advanced no further. Heat flowed over her. Laughing, Ib stepped onto the beach.

"Halt." Jinger knew the command in that voice. Nightshade. The tall, slender man holding a long fighting staff moved between her and the sorcerer. "You will not come closer."

Nightshade glanced at her for a split second before focusing again on Ib. "Welcome home. You okay, honey?"

Taj sat and asked, "Your family?"

"Yes," she said answering both Taj and Nightshade.

Two of the Alastriona joined Nightshade. Her cousin Bree, sword drawn, knelt at her side. "We were worried about you." Bree studied Taj then glanced toward Ommi. "Looks like you've got a good story to tell. Let's get rid of this character and go home."

"He's very dangerous."

"We sensed that. We can—"

With a cackle of laughter, Ib launched fireball after fireball at the warriors. Bree stood in front of Jinger and motioned with one hand. "Get back."

Taj rose. "We will assist."

Bree shook her head. "You protect Jinger."

"Agreed." He ducked to avoid a fiery attack.

"Hey, I can take care of myself."

Watching Ib, he bent to whisper, "I know you can, *jannia.* I only wish to care for my soulfire."

Knowing Bree heard the statement, Jinger glanced at the other woman, who, despite studying the sorcerer's movements, wore a huge grin. With a huff, Jinger allowed Taj to help her to her feet and they backed toward the cliff.

At Ommi's soft whimper, Taj knelt next to his mother. She nudged a cloth wrapped sphere toward him. Ignoring the ball, he touched her head. "You're hurt. Your leg is broken? Jinger, are there healers in your family?"

"Ommi, I'm so sorry. Yes, in fact Bree over there, she's one of the best."

The firefox yipped and nudged the ball. Jinger picked it up and cradled it in her hands.

The sounds of battle rang around them. Nightshade held the sorcerer in place with his staff, while the Alastriona deflected the fireballs. Ib lifted both hands into the air. "It is my right to claim this world. This and any other I choose. You cannot defeat my power. You will bow to me, or I shall destroy this world."

Nightshade chuckled glanced back at them and winked. "We've heard that before, honey. You and what army?"

"I need no army. I carry fire, the gift of the sun. In my hands is ultimate power. None shall stand before me."

The beach fell silent, even the waves made no sound. A gray haze formed next to the portal. A figure stepped through. "You are not to enter this, or any world. The Watchers set the decree."

Ib faced the young, blond man and made a sound of dismissal. Ib jabbed his finger toward him. "Who are you to deny me. Who are these Watchers?"

The young man lifted his sword. "I said you will not."

The blade cut through the air three times. Eyes wide, Ib stared at his bloodied wrists then down where his hands lay pale against the dark sand. He sputtered, disbelief in his jumbled words.

The young warrior retrieved Ib's hands, placed them in a pouch at his hip and turned to his gray portal.

"Wait," Nightshade said.

He paused then looked back, confusion filling his expression.

Jinger covered her open mouth with her hands. No, how could it be? "Chance?" she called. "Chance, wait. Bree, stop him. It's Chance."

Jinger lurched to her feet and stumbled across the beach but was too late. Before anyone else could react, the man stepped through his portal and the gray disappeared. She stopped and held her hands out toward where the portal had been. "Chance, come back."

A howl of anger jerked her attention back to Ib. He held both stumps tight against his stomach, his blood staining the dark fabric. He glared at her. "This is your doing. You will die."

His face set in pain and anger, he stumbled toward her.

Taj shot past her and lowered his shoulder. He ran into Ib, shoving him back. Pushing until the sorcerer teetered on the edge of his gateway. Then Taj straightened and planted one palm against Ib's chest. "You will not harm her. Nor my mother. Go back to your prison."

With one hard shove, Taj pushed his father through the gateway. In his follow through motion, he tugged the tapestry completely into Jinger's world. The gateway closed, disappearing with a snap.

Torn between where her cousin had disappeared and where Taj had returned Ib to his prison, Jinger remained rooted in the sand. Seeming in identical states of shock, no one else moved.

Until a low, feminine voice Jinger knew she should recognize called for Taj.

"Mother?" He rushed toward the cliff and gathered a beautiful woman in his arms. "Ommi, is it you?"

"Of course I am me, silly boy. Ib is dead."

"How do you know?"

Nightshade dragged the tapestry to them and wrapped the fabric around Ommi. "Not the finest of silks, m'lady, but should do until we can clothe you more fashionably."

"Thank you. You are the Nightshade?"

He chuckled. "*The* Nighshade? I suppose I am. And you are?"

"Ommi. Taj is my son. Now that I am no longer trans-figured, you wish to know what I am. I am... we are djinn."

Nightshade's brows arched. "Djinn? Don't think we've had any of those in the clan before. Welcome."

Jinger stood at Nightshade's side. Taj was a djinn. Like a genie? And he came from a bottle? She couldn't stop her laugh. "Does this mean we get three wishes?"

Taj look confused, but Ommi merely gave her a half smile. "That is legend only. Djinn choose who to honor with the gift of a wish. We are free beings."

"I'm sorry. I don't mean to be rude." The last thing she needed to do was alienate Taj's mother.

"You were not, child." She winced. "I fear this time I am unable to heal myself. My leg is badly broken."

"Breanna?" Nightshade called. "We need your talents."

When she joined them Bree faced Nightshade. "Could that have really been my brother? Why are you so damn calm?"

Nightshade shrugged. "Could be, honey. There's nothing we can do now if it was. Right now we need to take care of Ommi."

While Breanna healed Taj's mother, Jinger walked with him a short distance down the beach. She twisted the strange ball she still carried. "I... so much has happened. We're here safe. Ib is dead. My cousin might be alive. It's too much. When I was alone in your forest and even when I was just with you, all I wanted was my family. Now we're here and they're here and... And all I want is you."

"You have me, sweet Jinger. For the life of my soul. You're my soulfire."

"And you are mine. I can deal with everything, as long as you're by my side."

"We'll face our future together, *jannia.*" He stopped her manipulation of the sphere. "Mother says she took this from Ib before he... hurt her. It contains his library of spells."

"A library? Bree's husband will love this. Oh, we can give it to him to study, can't we? Or would that be dangerous?"

"As long as this husband does not wish to increase his power, or control others."

Jinger sighed. "He would not. He's been a victim of those who did though. He'll know how to contain any wayward spells. And how to keep this knowledge protected."

"Then he shall have it. Look, it appears Mother has been healed, at least enough to be taken from the beach."

A portal formed close to the cliff. Breanna waved to them as Nightshade carried Ommi through. Jinger acknowledged the signal. "We're going to have a lot of questions thrown at us. Everyone's going to want to know everything. My family can be overwhelming on a good day."

"Is this a good day?"

She loved when he smiled at her like that, eyes sparkling, his mouth oh so kissable. So, she did.

He broke the kiss much too soon. "Jinger, love, they're waiting for us."

"Are you ready to meet my family?"

"No, love. I am ready to meet *our* family."

TWENTY-SEVEN

Seated in one of the smaller chambers of the faerie castle, Jinger finished yet another telling of her experiences within the bottle. This time, thank goodness, scribes from three worlds captured her words. She was tired of repeating herself. Really all she wanted was to spend a whole lot of alone time with her soulfire.

Taj took her hand. "As always, you told your story well."

"Our story. I'm glad they wrote down what you and Ommi said as well. That makes the story more complete. Hopefully it will help if something like this ever happens again."

Members of many of the fey races represented by the council, with Ommi's assistance, had already begun working on magics to counteract that possibility.

When Jinger waved at him, Nightshade rose and crossed the room to her. "I've answered your questions over and over. Will you answer some of mine now?"

"Sure, honey," Nightshade said. "What do you need to know?"

"How did you happen to be on the beach?"

"When you didn't come back to the family gathering, Bree asked me to check on you. You've always gone to that beach. For being your father's daughter, you've become predictable, honey."

She stuck her tongue out at him.

Nightshade laughed. "See? When I got there, I sensed an odd electricity in the air and called for the Alastriona. They discovered the bottle and determined it was the source of the strange vibrations. And that your personal signature was all over the bottle."

Taj took her hand and kissed her knuckles. He was becoming adept at sensing her moods and when she needed support. She smiled her gratitude.

Nightshade continued, "We left the bottle on the beach and set a guard. For a few days nothing happened. Early on the day you returned, the bottle began throwing off energy. Bree, a few extra Alastriona, and I got to the beach moments before the portal opened. You know what happened next, dearheart."

"So what's going to happen to the bottle now?"

"The Alastriona will continue to guard it. You know they have a chamber created to contain magic."

"That's real?"

"Of course it is, honey. Before you ask, Gowthaman will be allowed to study it, see if he can find a connection to the fire elemental or any clue why we believe we saw Chance."

The wave of sorrow she usually experienced when anyone mentioned Chance wasn't as powerful. She knew Chance had appeared and saved them from Ib. Deep in her soul, she knew it for a fact.

"That's good to know, but not what I was going to ask."

She grinned at Nightshade's arched, perfectly groomed eyebrows. Her smile faded. "What will happen to the other creatures in the bottle? Like the unicorn and the querd? They aren't native to that world. They'd been transported there by the portal. By the sorcerer. If the bottle is locked away, how will they return to their worlds?"

Nightshade remained silent for so long Jinger feared she would only hear a negative answer. He turned his attention to Taj. "Your mother has abilities far beyond those of any of our known worlds. Magic we don't understand. Thankfully, she is willing to share her knowledge and use her talents for the benefit of others."

He grinned at Jinger and moved one hand in a loose-wristed wave. "Honey, the Alastriona and Ommi have that all figured out and have already begun assisting those who wish to leave the bottle world. If their world of origin can't be found, they are offered a place here in Faerie, or any of our known worlds."

"Thank you. I was so worried. I wonder where the unicorns are from. I'd love to see them again. Thank them."

Nightshade tapped his cheek with one finger. "Unicorns? Hmm. Oh yes, I do believe they have accepted a home here. Seems you made quite an impression on them."

Jinger burst from her chair to hug Nightshade tightly. "Thank you. Oh, thank you."

He patted her back then rested his hands on her shoulders and pushed her gently away. Whispering, he jerked his head twice toward one side of the chamber.

"You'd better get out of here, honey. One of the scribes is headed our way. You can answer his questions later. You and Taj go. Have some fun."

After she pressed a kiss to Nightshade's cheek, Jinger motioned to Taj. "Let's go. I want to show you something. My special place here in Faerie."

She led Taj through the door opposite the advancing scribe and into a courtyard where she created a portal. "I'm so happy I can do this again."

She knew Taj was hesitant to pass through portals, so she took both of his hands and walked backward, easing him through. Then she stepped to the side to allow him to look around the small glen.

Hie eyes widened as he studied the rocky outcropping and sparkling pond. "This is very much like the spring where we first encountered each other."

"Oh my gosh. It does look really similar. No wonder that place felt marginally safer than the rest of the forest. Except for your lodge, of course."

He gathered her in his arms. "I believe I fell in love with you in that glen. Perhaps it was the moment you laughed at me for biting into a rotten fruit."

"So, I'm like a rotten fruit?"

He took her lips in a slow, leisurely kiss. When she was breathless, he spoke against her cheek. "No, you are the sweetest of fruits. I will never taste my fill of you."

"Good. Are you... hungry now?"

"For you? Always, *jannia.*" He stroked her back, dancing thrills over her skin. "I do miss your wings."

"You only need ask, love." She stepped back, spoke her charm softly and watched his face. Without the magical strictures of the bottle, her shirt opened in back and her wings emerged painlessly. His eyes filled with desire.

Jinger returned to Taj's embrace and her wings wrapped around them, containing the explosion of teal sparkles.

"I love you, my soulfire," she whispered before his kiss made speaking unnecessary.

EPILOGUE

The rising sun streaked pale red orange across the sky. Sparkles of light danced on the dark water then were absorbed by the even darker fine sand. Near the edge of the frothy waves, a spot of pale light drew Ashir's interest.

Ashir had come to this empty world, lured by the pull of power. Scenting the air, he drew in the taint of battle and smiled. Not a battle between the common lives found in too many worlds, but the gathering of many magics. The combination was ambrosia and he flicked his tongue to capture more. That was why he had come. That more.

The pale thing on the sand—contained an ancient magic fueled by heat. The joyous burn of acid filled his throat yet he restrained the urge to spit fire and sank further into the shadows of the rocky monoliths.

He wasn't the only observer on the beach.

At the place where the cold, murky river met the clear, warm sea, Brona rested in the shallows. Born of the river but sent in disgrace to the open waters of the sea, she long ago lost the desire to be with her kind, to dance upon the flowers at the turning of the year. So long ago she no longer remembered even why she'd thrown herself into the merciless river.

The seas had been kind to her. Taught her. Encouraged. Showed her power and what could be done with desire and control. Created in her the need for more. Always more.

And there was that more on the beach. A pallid finger sliced from a hand contained more power than she'd imagined possible. She clasped her hands at her breasts and basked in the remnants of the heat and possibilities. Sighing, she visualized one of those possibilities—the young warrior who had so easily cleaved the hands from the magic wielder.

She pressed her palms against the sand and rose. That one had taken those hands and disappeared. She wanted those hands. Wanted him. She would use the finger to draw him again to this place and she would have both.

Her legs wobbled and she frowned. Remaining in the water for so long had given her the strength and ability to glide easily through the waves, but standing on land was difficult. Finding balance took precious moments before she curled her toes in the sand and stepped forward with eager anticipation.

A shir arched one scaled eyebrow. A woman, clothed only in her skin and long, tangled hair the color of pearls stumbled across the sand toward his prize. With a snort, he willed the change, mourned the shrinking of his bones, the tightening of his skin, the loss of his powerful wings. With a new magic he'd learned in the elf king's palace, he clothed himself in simple trews and tunic. He grimaced at the plain clothing then shrugged. It would do.

Unlike most of his kind, the makers hadn't granted him a tall, muscular human body, creating him instead slender and fine-boned. He'd learned to use this to his advantage, for his appearance generally failed to provoke fear. A benefit he'd perfected. He moved from behind the towering stones and strolled toward the dismembered finger.

He ducked his head and grinned when she noticed him and increased her pace. Timing his own steps in the loose sand, they reached the finger at the same time.

"This is mine," she stated.

He shrugged and said nothing.

"I will take it."

Another shrug.

Eyes narrowed, she glared at him.

He offered her a soft smile. "It appears, sweet lady, we desire the same thing."

"I hardly think so. Step aside."

The odd, harsh accent of her words delighted him. As did the essence of magic rising with her anger. He longed to taste that essence, then make it his. The longer he remained silent, simply studying her, the more agitated her breathing. She crossed her arms under her breasts, plumping the fullness. That, too, he would taste. And take.

He spread his hands. "Great magic lies at our feet. Immense power in a single, abandoned finger. You wish this power?"

The solid blue of her eyes darkened. Even without pupils, her eyes expressed much he could exploit.

"As do I. But I do not want to fight you, sweet lady." He lowered his voice to a sultry whisper. "I wish also for...other things."

"The finger is mine." Her words were not as determined and she glanced to one side, to the place where the warrior had disappeared.

So, that one had captured her interest, but her hopes lay in other directions. An eternity of lives had provided Ashir with the skills to read the desires and emotions of others. She wore her wanting like a thin cloak. One he could easily rip away with the barest effort. For now he would allow her to have her hopes. Just as he would have the prize.

"Come then, sweet lady, can you not feel the magic? There is enough to share. Enough..." He paused and let his gaze travel the length of her body, lingering on her breasts before rising to capture her gaze. "Enough for two."

He knew the moment she capitulated, and when her thoughts turned to possibilities and ultimately deception against him. He would have been disappointed with any other reaction and looked forward to the challenge of deceiving the deceiver. He would be the one to begin the dance.

Bowing low, he held out a small leather bag. "If you would place the finger here, m'lady, we shall begin to learn of its magic and power." He glanced at her from under his eyelashes, adding the softest touch of compulsion to his words. "And of each other."

After a moment, she snatched the bag from his fingers, scooped up the finger along with a handful of the surrounding black sand, and poured them into the bag. Watching him, she tightened the drawstring and weighed the bag in her palm.

He tensed, tightening his muscles for pursuit should she attempt to run. She would return to the sea so he angled minutely toward the water.

A sly grin stretched her lips before she returned the bag to him.

Acknowledging her challenge, he nodded once. "Well, then, m'lady? Shall we begin? I am called Ashir."

DEAR READER

T hank you for reading this tale. Bringing stories to life is one of my greatest delights and I hope you enjoyed your time in one of my worlds. Readers like you spark the energy needed to tell these tales. Again, thank you.

With today's world of vast reading choices, word of mouth is the best advertising. So please let others know about this book. Tell your friends, relatives, acquaintances, the dog next door (hey, you never know...). And please consider leaving a review at your favorite retailer or review site.

To keep up with new releases, sign up for *Starr Words*. Yes, it's a newsletter, but will appear in your email only occasionally. Your email is safe with me, will never be shared, and you can, of course, unsubscribe at any time. You can find the link on my website www. lizziestarr.com

Next, there's a bit about each of my books. Enjoy the love and discovery! Happy reading!

THE *STARR LIBRARY

THE KELTIC MULTIVERSE

By Keltic Design: *Double Keltic Triad 1*
  It ain't easy to be fey when you don't believe in fairy tales.

Fires of a Keltic Moon: *Double Keltic Triad 2*
  Can love find a way through time?

Keltic Flight: *Double Keltic Triad 3*
  What does she need to believe in love?

Wild Keltic Carouselle: *Double Keltic Triad 4*
  Falling in love is easy, the possibilities endless.

Keltic Dreams: *Double Keltic Triad 5*
  Passion blazes hotter than the desert sun

(Author's note: The action of the book Prince of Dark Ness takes place between Triad books 5 and 6. While it's not necessary to read Prince of Dark Ness here, it does give background into Lucidea's life prior to meeting Jaysson.)

A Faire Keltic Renaissance: *Double Keltic Triad 6*
It ain't easy being fey... and the subject of prophecy

Prince of Dark Ness: *Keltic Mulitverse*
A romantic fantasy
An ill-prepared Alfar-Sindhu prince struggles to protect two worlds from an ancient fire elemental.

(Author's note: This story takes place between books 5 and 6 of the Double Keltic Triad and introduces the heroine of book 6.)

Blue Keltic Moon: *Children of the Triad 1*
Love and redemption? Only under the blue Keltic moon.

Just My Imagination: *Children of the Triad 2*
Crossover with the Aspen Gold Series
Can his magic save her reality?

Jinger and the Djinn: *Children of the Triad 3*
It's only a bottle washed up on a beach...isn't it?

Candy Guy and the Chocolate Brownie: *A Keltic Multiverse Short*

Who better to assist a struggling chocolatier than a Brownie?

Sosa's Fate *A Keltic Multiverse Short*

By LizAnne Axtel

THE ASPEN GOLD SERIES

The Aspen Gold Series is a multi-author series set in the small, but affluent tourist town of Spenser, Colorado. I'm delighted to join with these six fantastic authors to bring you these tales. Find out more about the entire series at http://www.aspengoldseries.com/.

These are *lizzie's contributions to the series... so far.

Ryder's Heart: *Aspen Gold Series Book 3*

Ryder discovers an intriguing woman in his bed...

For Keeps: *Aspen Gold Series Book 4*

Hiding the truth is like denying the sun.

(Author's note: Barbara Gwen was one of the original authors who created the Aspen Gold Series. When I joined the group and planned my own story, we discovered our heroes were best friends. When Barb left this world much too soon, how could I not finish the book of her heart? For Keeps is by her and for her.)

Speechless: *Aspen Gold Series Book 8*
How many peonies does it take to get married?

Fortunate Cookie: *Aspen Gold Series Book 11*
This woman. Wearing Frosting. And nothing else...

Yesterday's Promise: *Aspen Gold Series Book 16*
Some Days are Diamonds: a short story

Just My Imagination: *Aspen Gold Series Book 18*
Crossover with the Keltic Multiverse: Children of the Triad
Can his magic save her reality?

Christmas Promises: *Aspen Gold Series Book 21*
The Perfect Snow Globe Christmas: a short story

FANTASY ROMANCE

Double Moon Destiny
On the night of the Double Moon a child is born, and the destinies of an acolyte and a rebel are changed forever.

Written in Stone: *'Structs in the City 1*
Will working with the sexy agent to keep the city safe be too dangerous for her heart?

Dead Lily Blooms: *At Death's Gates 1*
Someone wants vampyre Lily dead

Death and the Dryad: *At Death's Gates 2*
For ages uncounted, Master Death has assisted souls in transition. But what happens when love gets in the way?

CONTEMPORARY ROMANCE

Birds Do It!
A search for truth, switched babies, and a threat from the past

*lizzie also enjoys creating journals and guided workbooks for authors and other creatives. Look for them on her website.

COMING SOON FROM *LIZZIE STARR

Anything For Love: *Aspen Gold Series*

Niallan: *Stars of Jirvanta 1...SciFi Romance*

Rocc: *Stars of Jirvanta 2...SciFi Romance*

THE OTHER WRITERLY ME~~LIZANNE AXTEL

LizAnne specializes in sparkling hot short stories with happy endings!

TURQUOISE CREEK RANCH

Find the fortune of your heart's desire at Turquoise Creek Ranch

Makin' History : *Turquoise Creek Ranch 1*
   A chance meeting with a sexy biker turns into a night of passion hotter than the summer sun. Will they make their own history... together?

Makin' Amends: *Turquoise Creek Ranch 2*
   How can he make amends when he doesn't know what he did wrong?

Makin' Merry: *Turquoise Creek Ranch 3*
   A very cold, snow covered, grouchy Santa knocks on her door. Maybe Christmas won't be so bad after all.

Makin' Music: *Turquoise Creek Ranch 4*
   Coming April 2023

COMING SOON FROM LIZANNE AXTEL

Makin' A Splash: *Turquoise Creek Ranch 5*

Makin' Whoopie: *Turquoise Creek Ranch 6*

His Curvy Vinter; *A Hillview Resort Short*

MEET *LIZZIE STARR

*lizzie always made up games and stories to keep her company. So, a cunning witch lived in Grampa's weather research station and was only held at bay by waving a certain weed. An ancient road grader morphed into a boat carrying wild adventurers to islands filled with fierce lions and dangerous cannibals, which really looked a lot like sheep.

Now filled with fantasy, love, and romance with a sparkling twist, the stories of her imagination swirl their way into the mundane world.

*lizzie recently retired from her more routine life of being *the Lunch Lady* at a private school. According to the kids, she was 'the best cooker!' Yes, she misses the students and teachers, but is delighted now to start her days by telling stories rather than opening cases of chicken nuggets and counting milk cartons.

Her tag line of Author and lunch lady~~what a combination! no longer holds true (which makes her sad because she really liked that one).

Now you'll know *lizzie by her tales of...

~~Romance with a sparkling twist~~

Visit *lizzie's website at www.lizziestarr.com

facebook.com/authorlizziestarr

twitter.com/lizziestarr

instagram.com/authorlizziestarr

bookbub.com/profile/lizzie-starr

goodreads.com/lizziestarr